CAFFEINE NIGHTS PUBLISHING

BEFORE THEY DIE

David Barry

Fiction aimed at the heart
and the head...

Published by Caffeine Nights Publishing 2020

Published in Great Britain by
Caffeine Nights Publishing
4 Eton Close
Walderslade
Chatham
Kent
ME5 9AT

caffeinenights.com
caffeinenightsbooks.com
British Library Cataloguing in Publication Data.
A CIP catalogue record for this book is available from the British Library
Also available as an eBook

ISBN: 978-1-913200-02-2
Everything else by
Default, Luck and Accident

For Emma and Tain

Chapter 1

Sunday 19 February 2006

He was just another customer, a long way from a crime scene that would take place later that night, feeling confident no one would remember him. But the man he was about to meet was another matter. The scumbag stood out like a turd on a bowling green lawn. A sleazeball in track suit bottoms, loser written all over him. Still, the arsehole was perfect for what he had in mind.

However anonymous he looked and felt, Gormen was relieved to find the Manchester pub was reasonably crowded for a Sunday evening. Glancing at his watch he saw that it was a few minutes past five, just a half hour to go before he was due to meet the small-time thief. He took a tiny sip from his pint, looked around the seedy pub – the sort of smoky back-street boozer where an air extractor was rarely used, as if the customers enjoyed the stale reek of tobacco fumes and the occasional stench of urine whenever a toilet door opened – and congratulated himself on his rise from humble origins to a sophisticated and affluent lifestyle.

Making certain no one was watching, he fumbled in his anorak pocket for the Zippo-style lighter and handkerchief and kept his hands under the table while he wiped the lighter clean of prints. Then, holding a corner of the lighter with the hankie, he placed it on the table in front of him by the large metal ashtray brimming with stale dog-ends. Next, he took from his other pocket a packet of twenty Silk Cut, having previously removed some cigarettes from the pack to make it look as if he smoked, and quickly wiped the box, placing it open, next to the lighter.

A perfect set-up for the perfect crime. His egotism swelled in his breast as he thought about it, and he permitted himself a thin and subtle smile. In a little while the loser would be walking into his trap, a plan that was one hundred per cent fool proof.

He sipped his beer slowly while he waited for Terry Baldwin, the small-time housebreaker, to arrive. The man had been easy to recruit and easily tempted into this audacious scheme by the lure of easy money. Four days ago, Baldwin had been on trial at the Crown Court, but due to a technicality and a police cock-up he got off with a 'Not Proven'. The felon gave the arresting officers a triumphant smirk before swaggering from the court in his cheap charity shop gear, heading for the nearest boozer to celebrate his narrow escape, and living to steal another day.

Gormen had observed the no-hoper throughout the short trial and marvelled at how the arsehole hadn't even bothered to come suited and booted for his defence. Then he followed him to the pub, knowing he was the perfect candidate for the proposition.

Keen and smelling easy money in the offing, Baldwin turned up for their meeting fifteen minutes early. Gormen watched as he shuffled over to his table, shoulders hunched, like a method actor portraying a shifty demeanour. He wondered how old the burglar was, but it was difficult to guess his age. Because he was slight, and had a thin, craggy face, he could have been anywhere between late thirties and early fifties.

'Hello, Terry. I'm glad you could make it.'

Baldwin nodded, his eyes narrowing suspiciously and his mouth twitching.

'It struck me after our meeting on Friday, you got my name, but I never got yours, pal'

'Name's Peter.'

'And that's it? Just Peter?'

He could have told him his surname was Gormen without any complications. After all, Gormen was a false ID, with passport and driving licence in that name, but he wanted the dickhead to know as little about him as possible.

'Yeah, that's it, *pal*,' he replied, emphasising the pronoun. 'That's all you need to know. It's better that way.' He stood up. 'Before we get down to business, what are you drinking?'

'Seeing as you're buying, Peter, I'll have a pint of Stella.'

'OK. Take a seat and I'll get you a drink.'

As Baldwin flopped into a chair, and Gormen turned away, the housebreaker said, 'Mind if I have one of your ciggies?'

Gormen stopped and turned back, restraining a smile. 'Sure. Help yourself.' He allowed the smile to develop as he walked to the bar.

Hook, line and sinker.

It was so simple. All it took was a little thought and forward planning.

When he returned to the table, Baldwin, inhaling deeply on one of the cigarettes, looked up questioningly, and accepted the beer without so much as a 'cheers'. He downed half the pint, then leant forward across the table as Gormen sat down and spoke out of the side of his mouth recidivist style.

'So, what's this all about, pal? What you got in mind?'

'I want you to do a spot of burglary for me. I know exactly what I want you to steal, and I'll pay you for it.'

Gormen took an envelope from his inside pocket, holding it carefully by the edges, and slid it across the table. Baldwin grabbed it and checked the contents, his eyes widening.

'There's two hundred quid – just to show my serious intentions. And I'll give you two grand for the painting.'

'Painting?'

'That's right. I saw this painting on the *Antiques Roadshow*, found out who the owners are and where they live, and decided I'd like to own it. I'm a collector.'

The envelope disappeared into Baldwin's pocket before he spoke. 'What did they reckon the painting's worth?'

'Somewhere in the region of ten grand.'

Baldwin's lips twisted sideways, and he tugged at his nose with thumb and forefinger. 'And you're asking me to take the risk for only twenty per cent of the painting's value?'

Gormen sighed like he was dealing with a child. 'That's an estimated value.'

'Even so, I take all the risk.'

'There's very little risk. The house is a large cottage, and there's no burglar alarm. The occupants will be leaving at eleven forty-five tonight…'

'Tonight!' Baldwin exclaimed loudly, followed by a head twitch from side to side like a small rodent on the lookout for predators.

'It has to be tonight, Terry. Tonight, I know for sure the house is empty. It'll be easy pickings, believe me.'

Baldwin frowned deeply and peered at Gormen through narrowing eyes. 'So how come you know what time they're going out? And who the fuck goes out that late?'

'Burglars do,' Gormen said with a laugh. When Baldwin didn't respond he added, 'Look, I've done some research, haven't I? Amazing what info you can pick up in a local pub. The owners of the cottage must be at Manchester airport well before two a.m. I heard tell that a cab's picking them up at eleven forty-five. After half midnight, you'll be able to help yourself to the painting. And you're welcome to take anything else of value you might find.'

'Oh, thanks a bundle, Pete,' Baldwin sneered. 'Supposing there's nothing else worth having? Eh?' He leant back like he was a big tough gangster, instead of the runt of a dysfunctional family, crossed one leg over the other and knocked back the remaining half pint. The effect was ruined by a wave of lager missing his mouth and trickling down the side of his chin. 'Shit!'

Gormen leant back in his seat, locked his fingers together, stretched his arms out and smiled confidently. He could afford to be generous, because this creepy little loser was not going to get anything but a nasty surprise. On the other hand, he didn't want to show he was being too generous in case the arsehole smelt a rat. He may have had loser practically stamped on his forehead in day-glow, but Gormen could tell the man was imbued with cunning and self-preservation, as witness his recent escape from prosecution.

Taking his time, Gormen took a swig of bitter before he spoke. 'Like I said – I'm a collector, so I don't want to sell the painting. But I'd be happy to be generous and go to three grand.'

Baldwin jabbed a forefinger in Gormen's direction. 'Make it four and we have a deal.'

He pretended an inward struggle before relenting. 'I really want this painting, so...less than the two-hundred I've just given you. OK?'

Baldwin smiled and banged his pint on to the table. 'Deal!'

Gormen leant forward to shake the burglar's proffered hand, which was limp and moist.

'So where is this cottage I'm turning over?'

'Other side of Manchester. Whaley Bridge. On the way to Buxton. I've got you an address and a map.'

He took another envelope out of his inside pocket, holding the ends carefully between his palms, so as not to get a complete print on it. He hoped the burglar would believe the unusual way of the way of holding the envelope was nothing more than an art lover demonstrating the way a small paining is held. He smiled reassuringly as he placed the envelope on the table and watched as Baldwin pulled out a sheet from inside – the sheet he had printed from the computer and used latex gloves to fold it before placing it in the envelope. Even if his prints were all over it, it was doubtful it could be traced to him; but he always eliminated all the risks, just in case, because he was a pro. It was how he had survived all these years without so much as a ticket for speeding.

Baldwin studied the map then looked up. 'This sounds too easy. What's the catch?'

Gormen saw the way the burglar's lips went thin and taut, suspicious tension in the man's face, so he shrugged nonchalantly and smiled. 'There's no catch, Terry. I just want this painting. It means a great deal to me.' He leant forward and forced breathy passion into his voice, playing the role of art junkie. 'This artist is one of the finest nineteenth century British artists, and he's been seriously underrated up until recent years. His technique was way ahead of its time, and the way he mixed the pigment like the old masters of the seventeenth century…'

'So, it's a fucking painting worth ten grand,' the burglar interrupted with a sneer. 'No need to give me a fucking lecture.'

Gormen suppressed a smile. 'Sorry, Terry. I get carried away when I talk about art. I suppose we've all got interests we feel passionate about.'

Baldwin, whose only interests were booze, horses and dogs, usually in that order, asked, 'If I nick this painting, when do I get the money for it?'

'I'll meet you here tomorrow night. I'll have the cash then.'

He saw the greedy glint in the burglar's eyes. It was probably more money for a theft than the petty thief had ever obtained. And now that his victim was well and truly hooked, Gormen couldn't resist adding, 'Meant to ask you: most people when they appear in court, dress up a bit. You know, suit and tie, that sort of thing. But you turn up in track suit bottoms, with a polo shirt under your anorak. Any reason for that?'

Baldwin shrugged. 'Nah. Hate those wankers – magistrates, judges, social workers. They're all the same. Judge you on appearances.'

He ground out his cigarette in the ashtray and Gormen made a careful note of its position in relation to the other dog-ends.

'But wouldn't you make life easier for yourself by playing along?'

'I've got my own methods for dealing with them. Let them think I 'aven't got two pennies to rub together. That's why I've only ever had probation 'stead of custodial.'

Gormen frowned thoughtfully. This bloke was such a loser he might jeopardise the plan. It needed to look like a burglary gone bad, nothing else. Sensing the slump in atmosphere, the burglar asked him if there was anything wrong.

'Yeah, I'm worried about the sort of transport you're using for the job. You were in court on Thursday, if you've got a vehicle on the police radar—'

Baldwin waved it aside. 'Don't worry about it. I've got a mate who has a breaker's yard, and he looks after me whenever I need a motor. Proper paperwork and everything's hunky-dory. So, about the painting – just in case there's a few of them on the walls – how will I recognize your one?'

Before he could stop himself, Gormen told him it was a woman in a blue smock reading a letter by a window. He realized, as there was no painting anyway, that he could so easily have described something vague, like a seascape, instead of a Vermeer. He had taken a risk in pandering to his superiority over this lowlife in case he underestimated the man, and the description of the Vermeer triggered something in the man's subconscious. But Baldwin merely nodded thoughtfully and finished his beer.

'Another?' Gormen offered.

'Yeah, don't mind if I do.'

Gormen took out his wallet and handed Baldwin a ten-pound note, saying, 'I just need to send someone a text on my mobile. D'you mind getting them in?' He nodded at the remaining beer in his glass. 'This bitter's not going down too well. Would you get me a small Bell's?'

While Baldwin was getting the drinks, Gormen took out his BlackBerry and wrote a short text for his contact. It read:

'Tonight. Problem sorted.'

He sent the message and switched the phone off just as Baldwin returned with the drinks. Plonking the glass of scotch onto the table, the scrawny burglar remained standing while he knocked back half a pint of his Stella, then said he needed the khazi. Gormen watched him go, making certain he was out the door before taking two small brown paper bags and the hankie out of his pocket. He held the cigarette lighter by the corners, dropped it into one of the bags, then reached into the ashtray and lifted out the stub of Baldwin's cigarette and dropped it into the other bag. He quickly consigned both bags to a pocket inside his anorak and knocked back his scotch. As soon as Baldwin returned from the toilet, Gormen stood up.

'You off?' the burglar asked.

He nodded. 'Yeah but take your time. Finish your drink. And try to remain sober for tonight.'

'No problem. See you here at six tomorrow then?'

'I look forward to it.'

Without a glance at the table, and the packet of Silk Cut he was leaving behind, Gormen patted the burglar on the shoulder and headed for the exit. He turned when he got to the door and saw Baldwin light another cigarette, then shove the packet into his pocket.

As he stepped out into the cold and dreary street, he smiled, warmed by the hand of power that touched him.

It was all going according to plan.

Chapter 2

John Keneally leant back on the sofa when he got to the end of the report, his tired eyes straining as he squinted at the screen. His laptop stood on the coffee table and he stared at its screen thoughtfully, feeling exhausted now he had ploughed his way through all one hundred and ten files of the entire document. He picked up his wine glass and drained the last drop of smooth claret, savouring the final mellow taste of the expensive vintage. He was tempted to open another bottle, then thought better of it. He had to drive to London, leaving no later than ten for the three-p.m. meeting at *The Times*. It was a big day, and he knew the shit was really going to hit the fan. And even if the newspaper held back on the story, he had made up his mind to speak in the Commons, using parliamentary privilege to keep him legally safe. He was on a mission, a drive to expose….

A noise startled him, coming from the back of the house. He thought it may have been the cat flap, then remembered that Parsley died six weeks ago and was now buried near the apple tree at the end of the garden.

He sat up, carefully placed his wine glass on the table and concentrated on listening for alien noises. There was nothing. Just a curious buzzing in his ears, a reaction from the late-night silence and his exhaustion. Getting paranoid now the file was ready to be delivered, his overworked brain started to imagine all kinds of crazy scenarios. The flickering of the muted television screen didn't help, giving the living room a ghostly and surreal feeling of abandonment, as if he was trapped in a lonely film set instead of his home. If Sheila had been with him, he'd have felt better, and there would have been a roaring fire in the grate, with the comforting crackle of burning logs.

There it was again. A creaking noise. Like someone getting closer, walking stealthily towards the living room. If only he'd thought to set the burglar alarm. But who does that when they're at home? Panicking, he got up, reached over to the fireplace and grabbed the poker. For a fleeting moment, wondering if he was overreacting, he froze, poker in hand, straining to hear every sound in the house. Silence. All he could hear was his own shallow breathing. He wanted to go and check the hall, dining room and kitchen, just to make certain there was no one there. But he knew for certain that all the doors were locked. If someone broke in wouldn't he hear loud noises like glass breaking? How could anyone break in without creating a terrific din? He sighed tremulously, easing the extreme fear out of his body. Convincing himself that his reaction to what he thought was an intruder was disproportionate, and probably nothing more than his overactive imagination coupled with the peculiar noises all houses make late at night, he thought he might go and check the other rooms downstairs, just to make sure. But keeping a tight grip on the poker.

He crossed the room, treading quietly on the thick pile carpet, and stood before the living room door. He was right-handed, and to open the door he would need to transfer the poker into his left hand, putting him at a disadvantage. But he told himself, he was being ridiculous, and this was nothing more than his own paranoia tormenting him. Switching the poker to his left hand, he reached for the cold china doorknob with his right and began to turn it slowly clockwise. It squeaked slightly, and he winced, holding his breath. He waited, summoning up the courage to pull the door open wide. He took a lungful of air, hoping and praying the noises he heard were nothing more than his imagination, and hoped to confront no more than an empty hallway, and then could laugh at his ridiculous behaviour. In his head he counted to three. *One. Two. Three.*

As he flung open the door and saw the dark figure framed in the doorway, his breath surged from his stomach to his throat, and a nightmare scream in his brain froze him for an instant. But this was no nightmare. This was reality. Then the adrenaline kicked in and he raised the poker in his left hand, knowing he had no time to transfer it to his right. Instinctively, he took a step back, needing space to swing the poker. But there was no strength in his left hand, and before he knew it the intruder raised a bent leg, and then it shot out like a battering ram and kicked him in the knee. The pain was unbelievably intense as his leg was forced backwards. The poker flew out of his hand and he heard glass smashing as it spun into the tray of drinks decanters. The intruder moved closer. Needles of pain shot through his leg as he started to collapse, his leg buckling under him. Then a gloved fist caught him in the face, and he felt a terrific bump as his head hit the floor. Head swimming, only half conscious now, he was vaguely aware of hands gripping his shoulders and rolling him over. Then choking and fighting for breath as his pounding head was forced into the carpet and his arms were pulled backwards. More pain as rope cut tightly into his wrists. Hands grabbing him again, turning him onto his back. He tried to focus, blinking his eyes rapidly, trying to see what was happening. But all he could see was a glare of jagged light across the ceiling, as if he was in a hospital theatre being operated on but semi-conscious. Hands grabbed his legs, pressing them together and more rope bound them tightly. As his head started to clear a bit, he became aware of how helpless he was. So helpless he wanted to cry.

***

Now his victim was bound, with a strip of gaffer tape over his mouth to stop him screaming for help, Gormen decided to ransack upstairs first. Not that the MP could be heard crying for help in this detached house, but you couldn't be too careful, just in case a neighbour decided to call around. Though it was highly unlikely on a Sunday night gone eleven.

There were three rooms upstairs, one of them used as an office. First, he ransacked the two bedrooms, pulling open drawers, scattering the contents across the floor. He found a large suitcase in the built-in wardrobe of the master bedroom, grabbed a handful of Keneally's wife's jewellery and shoved it hurriedly into the case. Next, he raided the office, pulling more drawers open, ransacking them and then letting them fall onto the floor. He found a mobile phone on charge, tugged it out of the wall socket and put it in the suitcase, along with a few other items: a travel alarm, an electronic dictionary and encyclopaedia, an expensive-looking fountain pen and a portable radio. He also found a leather-bound desk diary with Keneally's name inside the front cover. Perfect. He snapped the suitcase shut, hurried downstairs and checked the dining room, where he put a Waterford crystal vase in the suitcase before returning to the living room.

Before going upstairs, Gormen had sat Keneally in one of the easy chairs facing the sofa and coffee table. As he entered the living room, the MP stared at him, his eyes watery and fearful. Gormen ignored him and lay the suitcase on the floor, opened the lid, then added more items to the load, including an antique carriage clock which he took from the mantelpiece, several silver-framed family photographs, and a small landscape oil painting in a gilt frame hanging on one of the walls. He closed the case, walked over to Keneally and ripped the gaffer tape off his mouth. The MP gasped and panted as he tried to suck in air, his shallow breathing causing his chest to heave as if he was having a panic attack. Gormen wondered if the fear might bring on a heart attack.

He stood over him and said soothingly, 'It's OK. I'm not going to hurt you.' He waited for the man's shallow breathing to subside, until it eased to a steadier rate, then demanded in a flat tone devoid of any sympathy, 'Where's the file? The complete dossier.'

'File? What file are you talking about? I don't understand,' Keneally replied in a voice as coarse as sandpaper.

'Don't fuck me with me. I want the copy of the file James Gaskell gave Leonard Albion. You don't think I've gone to all the trouble of breaking in for…' He gestured to the suitcase. 'For that pile of shit, do you?

Keneally blinked several times before speaking, and looked up at the intruder, aware that this man was no ordinary burglar. He looked towards the coffee table and nodded. 'The file is on the laptop. It's all there. I just finished reading it.'

'And would you happen to have another copy? On a memory stick, for instance?'

The MP shook his head. The response had been quick, Gormen noted. Too quick.

'Where is it?' he demanded.

'Where's what?

'I haven't got time to fuck about. I want the memory stick with the copy you intend giving the journalist tomorrow.'

'I don't know what you're talking about.'

'No? We'll see about that.'

Gormen picked the poker up from between shards of broken glass on the carpet, soaked and smelling of alcohol. He stood in front of the MP, the gloved fist of his right hand gripping the poker tightly, his jaw clenched tight.

'I'll ask you once more: where's the memory stick?'

Keneally shrank back into the chair, his eyes wide and pleading. 'Please,' he begged. 'I don't know…'

Before he could complete his denial, the poker swung in an arc over the intruder's head and it came crashing down on his knees. The agony was unbelievably shocking and intense. For a moment he was stunned, and then the unbearable pain coursed through his nervous system and he opened his mouth to scream.

Gormen clamped his left hand over the MP's mouth, muffling his anguished cries. He pressed hard on the man's mouth, smothering the groans of agony, waiting for the pain to ebb, as tears trickled onto his black leather gloves.

Eventually he eased his hand away from Keneally's mouth and warned him, 'Don't make a sound. Suffer in silence, or you'll get another one like that – twice as hard next time. Do I make myself clear?'

Keneally nodded.

'So, where's the memory stick with the files? I won't ask you again.'

'In the car,' Keneally croaked. 'There's a briefcase in the boot. It's in there.'

'And where are the car keys?'

'On the coffee table next to my laptop.'

Gormen walked over to the sofa, and sure enough the keys were tucked tight against the laptop. He placed the poker on the sofa, took the keys and walked towards the door, calling over his shoulder to Keneally as he went, 'And don't try calling for help when I'm gone, otherwise I'll fucking kill you.'

The car, a black BMW, was parked half inside the open door of the garage, facing inwards. Opening the boot, he found a brown leather executive case and flicked it open. Sure enough there was a yellow flash drive, some papers, notebooks and pens. He stuck the flash drive in the inside pocket of his anorak, closed the case then slammed the boot shut.

When he returned to the living room he went straight to the laptop, dropped the car keys back on the table, moved the poker aside, sat on the sofa and took the glove off his right hand. Then he moved the cursor so that the laptop screen lit up again. He saw that Keneally had reached the last page of the dossier he was reading, so he held the cursor, highlighting the document from the bottom of the page and scrolled upwards.

'What are you doing?' Keneally asked.

'Deleting the files. And don't worry, I'll be taking the laptop with me, so I can destroy the hard drive.'

Reaching the top of the document, he pressed the delete button and the entire report disappeared. He gave Keneally a cocky grin. 'And there it was gone.' He patted his side where the pocket containing the memory stick was. 'Presumably I now have the extant document. Oh, how stupid of me. I almost forgot. Lord Albion had the original, but that was decades ago. I expect he'll have made certain it's gone the way of all incriminating evidence since then. Ashes to ashes.'

Tears rolled down Keneally's cheeks. 'So now what happens?' he sniffed.

'You may well ask.'

Finding the flickering television irritating, he reached for the remote and clicked it off. Then he took his BlackBerry out of his pocket, pressed one of the buttons and waited. It was answered after only one ring, as if the person was waiting for the call.

'Hello, Peter. How's it going? I hope you've got good news for me?'

The voice was soft and smooth, a little above a whisper, talking to Gormen as a hypnotist might, using a relaxation technique.

'I'm at Keneally's now. And I have the only existing document on a USB flash drive. When I get back you want me to destroy it along with his laptop?'

'Yes, of course. And how will you do that?'

'Don't worry. I'll smash it to shreds with a hammer and dispose of it. No one will ever be able to read this document again.' But as he said it, a tiny smile twitched at the corners of his mouth. He had other plans, intending to keep the flash drive in a safe place. It would be his insurance policy in case he ever found himself in a tricky situation. And, face it, there was no one he could really trust. It was dog eat dog in this world.

'Just make sure you do that,' the smooth voice told him. A slight edge had crept into it, almost as if the man could read his mind. 'Oh, and one other thing.'

'What's that?'

'Presumably Keneally has studied the document thoroughly and knows the contents backwards and can recall names, dates everything.'

'I suspect that's the case.'

'So, you know what you must do, Peter.'

Gormen focused on the MP, who was listening intently, trying to guess what was being said at the other end of the call. His eyes seemed to have shrunk inside his skull and he suddenly looked like a man in his late seventies instead of the robust, portly fifty-six-year-old Member of Parliament who was one of the few idealists left.

'I'll see to it,' Gormen said, careful not to call his associate by name, even though it made little difference now. He cut the call, then switched the laptop off and closed the lid.

Another glance in the MP's direction told him the man could instinctively guess what the outcome of this situation might be. He was intelligent enough to understand that his intruder hadn't bothered to wear a mask, knowing his assailant had no intention of leaving a witness behind.

'Listen,' he said. 'That document contains a hundred and ten files. I could hardly remember any details, let alone recall names of those involved. And, in any case, there's no proof.'

'This is very true,' Gormen replied pleasantly as he stood and slipped the glove back on his right hand. 'So, what are you trying to say?'

'I'm just trying to explain that now you've destroyed all the evidence…' His voice was so hoarse now he could barely be understood. 'There's no point in … continuing … and I have money.'

As Gormen picked up the poker, Keneally cringed back into his chair. 'Please! Please!' he begged.

Gormen raised a reassuring hand and smiled. 'Don't worry. I'm just going outside to break a window to make it look like a genuine burglary. I'll be right back.'

He walked past the MP's chair, who had now begun to shake violently. As he reached the living room door, knowing Keneally could no longer see him, Gormen turned, raised the poker and brought it down with full force on the man's head. It made a sickening crack and he saw the skull split open. He thought the first blow would have killed him, but just to make certain, he raised the poker high then struck him forcibly again, this time splitting the skull wide open. He averted his eyes from the disgusting mess of the man's head and let the poker fall onto the carpet. Hurriedly now, he got the cigarette lighter from the bag in his pocket and shoved it under the sofa, and then threw the burglar's cigarette butt onto the tiles in front of the fireplace. Finally, he grabbed the laptop and glanced around the room, just in case he'd missed anything. Satisfied he had thought of everything, he picked up the suitcase and left the house, leaving the front door ajar. All he had to do now was plant the suitcase in the other house and soon the police would have all the evidence they needed to put Terry Baldwin away for life.

Chapter 3

Friday 28 February 2014

He was startled by the sudden noise coming from the hall downstairs. At first, because he was watching and listening to Metallica on his computer, he wondered what it was. And then, when he heard the rattling of the letter box becoming more frantic, he guessed it was her. And he guessed at the state she was in, otherwise she'd have rung the doorbell. He considered ignoring it and wondered if she'd go away. But a glance at his watch told him it was dangerously close to his mother getting home from work, so he needed to deal with the situation as quickly as possible.

Sighing, he switched the computer into sleep mode and hurried from his bedroom. As he dashed downstairs, he shouted, 'Shut it, Eva. I'm on my way.'

Marmite, his mother's treasured black cat, ran from the hall as he leapt the last few steps and lunged at the front door. He flung it open wide and there she was, hair dishevelled, dark brown eyes like glass marbles and a lopsided grin on her face that told him she was high, even if she wasn't entirely wasted.

She pushed passed him into the hall and leant back against the wall, pleased with the way her entrance had disturbed the calm of her boyfriend's home.

'Mum'll be home any minute now,' he protested.

'So what, Justin? So what? You're not scared of your mother, are you?' She pointed at him teasingly, circling her index finger and laughing. 'I've been on the ganja, bro. Some top-class gear, man.'

For some reason, even if she was of a mixed-race parentage, he was always slightly embarrassed by her use of street jargon, and always felt uncomfortable and unnatural using it himself.

He shut the front door hurriedly and glanced at his watch again. 'It's not that I'm scared of Mum – no. It's just things are awkward, what with me not having any work. And if she thinks we're spending the money I sponged off of Nanny and Grandpa on booze and that –'

His girlfriend smiled knowingly, waved it aside, and threw her arms around him. 'Remember the ice we had last week? Well, your naughty little Eva's got some more.'

He remembered that crystal meth high all right. And he'd been wanting a repeat performance ever since. Craving it like mad. And the sex was unbelievable.

As if she knew what he was thinking, she said, 'So how about it, Justin? You up for it.'

'Listen,' he said urgently. 'Mum'll be home any minute now. As soon as she's had her tea and packed a few things, she'll be off for the weekend. She's going to that Animal

Rights demonstration up in Lincolnshire. But if she finds you here, she'll… Why don't you pop out to the local boozer for an hour? I'll come and get you after Mum's gone, then we've got the whole weekend ahead of us.'

'OK,' she agreed, with another crooked smile. 'But no more than an hour.' As she sashayed towards the front door, he stopped her with a hand on her arm.

'Just before you go, Eva – why don't you let me have the stuff?'

She screwed up her face quizzically. 'Stuff?'

'The crystal meth.'

Her eyes narrowed with suspicion. 'What d'you want with my crystal meth?'

'To put it in a safe place until Mum's gone. If some cops stop and search you, we're fucked. Better let me keep it here until I come to get you.'

She thought about it for a moment before rummaging in her shoulder bag. She handed him a small, black plastic bag, the sort dog walkers use to scoop up dog-mess, then kissed him on the cheek. 'Don't be long, Justin. I want us to have some fun tonight, man.'

'Yeah. Me too.'

She opened the front door and he shut it hurriedly behind her, leaning back to collect himself for a moment. Then he strode towards the stairs and took them two at a time. He knew his mother suspected him of taking drugs. He had once convinced her it was nothing more than marijuana, just the occasional puff, nothing regular. But he still didn't trust her not to go searching his room, as she had when she found his stash of weed that time.

He glanced around his bedroom. Where could he hide the ice? If his mother found it, she was street smart enough to know what it was, so he couldn't risk it. He needed a really secure hiding place.

His eyes alighted on a corner of the room, just behind the door, the place where Marmite sniffed and scratched away at, as if searching for mice. He knelt down and tugged at the carpet. It came away without too much effort, just a couple of crooked tacks dangling from the seam. He pulled it right back and tapped the floorboard which rattled loosely. He pressed one end and the other rose up, then slid his hand under and lifted it. He was about to drop the bag of crystal meth into the space when a bright yellow object caught his eye. He stuck his hand in and lifted it out. It was a USB flash drive. He frowned deeply, wondering how it could have got beneath the floorboard in his bedroom.

'What the fuck!' he said aloud.

Chapter 4

Wednesday 12 March 2014

Mike Halliday watched his stepdaughter as she hurriedly shovelled muesli into her mouth. Even though 14-year-old Natalie was now old enough to walk the half mile to school, he had offered to drive her because it was raining yet again. The *Today* programme on Radio 4 played softly in the background; listening to it had become a habit, like buying Sunday newspapers.

Mike checked the time on his watch and sighed as he looked out of the window at the dreary day, rivulets of rain streaming sadly down the kitchen windows. All he could see outside were the vague shapes and shadows of his neighbours' semi-detached houses in this west London enclave, and he felt a sudden longing for his old life. As a Met detective inspector in Counter Terrorism Command, he'd had his work cut out. It was tiring and stressful but never dull. Then, two years ago he made the momentous decision to leave the force. He wanted to spend more time with Marianne and Natalie and be a proper parent. So, becoming a private investigator, working as a franchisee for a large company who offered him the west London territory in which to operate, tempted him as an acceptable solution. Now Marianne seemed to be the main breadwinner, and his investigations were becoming part time, mainly serving writs to debtors and the age-old story of spouses wanting to know if their partners were cheating on them.

'Why are you sighing, Dad?' Natalie demanded, irritated by his disquiet.

'Oh, nothing, sweetheart. It's just that it's such a dreary day.'

'And you've got no work on, have you?'

Mike shrugged and smiled reassuringly. 'You never know. I've got an appointment to see a publisher at eleven-thirty.'

Natalie got up and put her cereal bowl and spoon in the dishwasher. 'What do you think they want?'

'Until I meet them, I've no idea.'

'Maybe it's to find out if a book someone submitted has been plagiarised?'

'That could be quite interesting I suppose,' Mike said as he stood up.

Natalie pulled a face before going out into the hall. 'Yeah,' she called out. 'Like paint drying.'

He laughed dutifully and was about to follow her out when something caught his attention on the radio. The story was about a document containing more than a hundred files which had been handed to Lord Albion in the late 1980s when he was Minister of Information and Home Affairs, a document with details about paedophiles in high government offices and subsequent cover-ups. Leonard Albion, who at first denied receiving the document, later claimed he couldn't remember being given them, and had probably passed them on to his private secretary to deal with. The MP James Gaskell, who delivered the documents to Albion, died of a heart attack in 1990. Now a Labour MP, Malcolm Reeves for Lewisham South, was calling for an investigation.

Frowning as he switched the radio off, Mike wondered about the coincidence in hearing about an MP named Reeves, and his appointment to meet Joanna Reeves, the CEO of the publishing company. He dismissed it as a fairly common name and followed Natalie out into the hall.

His car, an automatic Volvo, was parked in the street, enabling Marianne to get hers out of the small garage when she left for work just after eight. They both turned their collars up as they came out of the front door and made a dash for the car, neither wearing overcoats. He wanted to admonish her for not wearing a raincoat and knew it would be hypocritical as he rarely did so himself, and preferred to occasionally carry a collapsible umbrella, which he invariably left somewhere, in taxis or trains. He had lost two in the past month, so now he was all out of umbrellas.

As they set off the short distance to Natalie's school, the windscreen wipers began squeaking, and he realized the rain had stopped.

'I knew we wouldn't need raincoats,' he chuckled. 'So, how's school going these days?'

Natalie sighed. Whenever he gave her a lift to school, it was always the same question. 'It's fine, Dad,' she replied, then changed the subject. 'How easy is it to trace missing people?'

He didn't answer right away and used the sudden braking at a T-junction as a brief moment to reflect on her question – the one he'd been dreading over the years as Natalie grew up. As he took a left turn, out of the corner of his eye he could feel her studying his face as she waited for an answer.

'That all depends,' he said. 'Why?'

'I'm not asking because I want to trace my real father, you know.'

'I just thought you might be curious. It happens as children grow up. They feel a need to know their proper parents.'

'Well I don't, that's for sure. Mum asked me once, and I'm like – no thanks. Bastard left us. Never got in touch again. So why would I want to see a wanker like that?'

'Language!'

'Oh, come on, Dad. You've heard worse.'

'So why did you ask me about tracing people?'

'One of my mates at school was asking. She's adopted and wants to trace her real parents.'

'Well, there are many ways of doing it. But it can sometimes be fraught, and sometimes it's better not to know. Bloke in America traced his father and he turns out to be a prolific serial killer.'

'Oh, cool!'

In spite of feeling slightly shocked by her attitude, he realized it was a typical teenage response, and shook his head with a tolerant smile. 'I know that might seem attractive, Natalie. And kids always dream about their parents being something exciting instead of routine and dull. But think about it seriously. Would you really want to learn that your father mutilated or tortured innocent people?'

She was silent for a moment before answering, and then she said, 'Might make a good plot for a movie that. An adopted detective traces his own father who turns out to be the murderer he's looking for.'

'Doesn't sound like there'd be a lot of laughs in the story.'

Mike squinted as he as he got to within two-hundred yards of the school gates and, seeing brake lights glowing in the gloom, he knew he was following a long stream of cars with parents who had decided to give their offspring lifts because of the inclement weather.

'It's OK, Dad. No need to drop me right outside. Here's fine.'

He found a space near the kerb and pulled in. She leant over and kissed his cheek.

'So, what are you going to tell your friend – about searching for her parents?'

Natalie shrugged and pouted. 'No idea. I said I'd ask you.'

'Any reason for that?'

'Well, she knows you're a private detective.' Seeing Mike frown, she added hastily, 'We all know what our fathers do. We talked about it. And they think private detective's really awesome.'

'So that's why… what's your friend's name?'

'Maxine.'

'So that's why Maxine asked you to find out how to trace her parents. What are you going to tell her?

'What you said.' She opened the car door and started to get out. 'That her father might be a serial killer.'

'Yes, but, Natalie…' he began, but she had already slammed the door shut and walked away with a wave of her hand. And then he laughed as he recalled his own youth, filled with strange ideas and heated fantasies, all of which seemed important before evaporating as time put constraints on the imagination.

As he drove back home, he wondered what his meeting with the publisher was about. Although the CEO's secretary had made the appointment, she had been circumspect in keeping the reason under wraps until the meeting.

He wondered if Natalie was right. Perhaps it was a case of plagiarism. Not exactly riveting, but anything was better than serving writs or obtaining proof of an adulterous partner.

Chapter 5

As the rain had stopped, Mike walked to Ealing Broadway station and caught a Central Line train to Notting Hill Gate, and from there took a black cab to an address just off High Street Kensington, where the publishing company was located. The building was a double-fronted Victorian building of about three storeys, with a gleaming blue Georgian-style door, and a brass plaque on the side with the engraved name FORUM BOOKS on it.

Mike had looked them up online and discovered they published mostly non-fiction books, histories, political autobiographies and biographies, and were one of the major companies in that field.

As he paid for the taxi, rain lashed down signalling the start of another heavy downpour, and he raised the collar of his suit jacket, tugging it from beneath the strap of his expensive leather man-bag, a joint present from Marianne and Natalie from last Christmas. Shaking his head from the wet, he dashed up to the door and pressed the bell. It buzzed automatically as if they were expecting him, and he pushed open the solid door. Wiping his face and forehead with a hankie, he walked into the reception area, a large airy and light room, displaying framed posters of some of their most successful publications.

The receptionist, a young red-haired woman, greeted him with a grin. 'No raincoat or umbrella?'

He returned her smile. 'I like to live dangerously. And I thought it had stopped for the day. I'm here to see Joanna Reeves.'

The receptionist looked down at her notepad and said, 'Mr Halliday? She's expecting you. If you'd like to take a seat and I'll buzz her.'

He eased himself into a comfortable sofa by an enormous coffee table awash with magazines and newspapers and waited while the receptionist spoke on the internal phone, telling either Joanna Reeves or her secretary that there was a Michael Halliday waiting in reception. When she put the phone down, she looked across at him and smiled in an over-familiar way.

'I know you're a wee bit early, but she'll see you right away. It's on the first floor, and it's the door at the end. You can't miss it. It's got Joanna's name on it.'

He rose, thanked her and left the reception area. As he climbed the stairs, noticing the luxury thick pile of the stair carpet, he wondered what a successful publisher could possibly want with a private detective. By the time he reached her door his interest was fired up to such a degree that he only hoped it wouldn't turn out to be an anti-climax and something as dull as Natalie had suggested.

As soon as he tapped on the door it was opened by an overweight middle-aged woman. 'Good morning,' she said. 'I'm Delia – Mrs Reeves's PA. If you'd like to follow me, Mr Halliday.' She crossed the small office, opened the door and ushered him into the CEO's presence.

From behind a large desk cluttered with paperwork, Joanna Reeves rose to greet him, stretched across the desk and offered him her hand. 'Good to meet you, Michael,' she said.

He shook her hand briefly and told her he preferred the less formal 'Mike'. She smiled, gestured for him to take a seat, and told him she also preferred to be called 'Jo'. She offered him coffee, which he declined, and then she asked her secretary to tell anyone phoning she was in a meeting for at least the next hour. The door swished quietly on the carpet as her PA exited, and there was a brief pause while the two strangers sized each other up.

When the CEO made the appointment to meet the private detective, she imagined someone a bit tough and unkempt looking, like an ex-commando. Instead, she was surprised to find Mike Halliday was slim and neat, dressed in an expensive-looking three-piece suit, with trendy closely shaved dark hair, with tiny flecks of grey on the sides. His face was surprisingly young and untroubled, although the wrinkles around his eyes and neck suggested he might be in his late forties or early fifties. And then there was the man-bag. Not exactly in keeping with a tough private eye.

Seeing her staring at the bag, he ducked his head, raised the strap over, put it on the floor and removed an A4 pad and pen from it, ready to take notes.

'First of all,' she said, with an almost imperceptible and preparatory clearing of her throat, 'I want to insist that what is said in our meeting, stays in this meeting. This is highly confidential, and it should not get into the media. That is of vital importance.'

Mike nodded seriously. 'Absolutely. Any job I take on for any client is in the strictest confidence. And even if I decide not to take the job – which has been known on odd occasions – it remains confidential, and whatever was said in the meeting is wiped out and forgotten about.'

Her eyes glinted as she smiled. She had a rounded attractive face, full lips and shoulder-length brown hair with blonde streaks. Her figure was curvaceous, and she wore a black dress with an abstract silver necklace, like a German expressionist streak of lightning, and matching earrings. Mike guessed she was somewhere in her mid-fifties.

'That's good to know, Mike. Because Forum Books have come by some information of a highly incendiary nature. And this will need to be thoroughly and secretly checked out. We don't want to leave ourselves open to a large lawsuit.'

'This information,' Mike began, frowning, 'is it in a book you've been sent?'

'How did you know?'

'I'm just guessing. You're a publisher. Presumably this is how you come by most information.'

'Yes, I'm sorry. I didn't mean to underestimate you. Perhaps I'd better start right at the beginning. My husband's a Labour MP, and he has been calling for an investigation into files about the cover-up of paedophiles, some of whom are high-ranking officials in the government; and the document containing all the files, which was allegedly handed to Lord Albion back in the late-eighties, conveniently disappeared.'

'Your husband,' Mike said, raising a questioning eyebrow, 'would he happen to be Malcolm Reeves for Lewisham South?'

Smiling, Jo Reeves replied, 'I shan't underestimate you again, Mike. Presumably you've seen or heard it on the news.'

'Actually, I only became aware of it this morning on the *Today* programme.'

'Well, I don't have to tell you how terrible a crime child abuse is. My husband would like to see them all in jail, whoever they are. We have two sons, one still at university, and we really love family life. But when it comes down to these evil men taking advantage of underprivileged children…' She broke off, and her eyes became misty. 'Do you have any children, Mike?'

'We have one fourteen-year-old daughter. She can sometimes be a handful, but we love her very much. I would kill anyone who laid a finger on her.'

He meant it as well. The fact that she wasn't his flesh and blood had nothing to do with it. Her blood father had abandoned his family when she was somewhere between two and three, and Mike had met her mother a year later. He had bonded with Natalie and had been a responsible father to her ever since. What did it matter that they didn't share the same DNA? And, after bringing her up as his own child for almost ten years, why go to the trouble to explain she was his stepdaughter?

Jo Reeves shifted in her seat awkwardly and Mike thought it was probably because of his remark about killing an abuser. He suspected that as a liberal-minded, socially aware citizen she might suppress any emotional desire to seek revenge and choose the proper legal routes without resorting to revenge and vigilante behaviour. He stared at her almost defiantly, waiting for the protest about his attitude. But she surprised him by nodding and smiling, as if she approved of his sentiment. Then she looked down at a layer of A4 paper on her desk, tapping it with her index finger.

'These pages are a synopsis for a book which looks as if it is based on the missing document that was handed to Lord Albion towards the end of the eighties. It's badly written, and it would need to be ghosted to reach a reasonably high standard. But what we've been sent anonymously has named a few names and gives details of certain well-known paedophiles who died before they were prosecuted – suggesting they may have been protected, and the exposure came conveniently after their demise.'

'Presumably you're talking about the likes of Cyril Smith and Jimmy Savile?'

Reeves nodded. 'And there are many others named, many of whom are still very much alive. Notwithstanding the corruption of some of the high-ranking police forces who may have been complicit. My husband has been trying to suggest an amnesty for some of those officers, so they won't be afraid to come forward and give evidence. But he seems to have hit a brick wall where that's concerned.'

'That's not surprising,' Mike observed, rubbing his chin thoughtfully. 'A lot of serving officers won't want to rock the boat for fear of losing their pensions. But how can you be sure that this suggested book is taken from the missing files?'

'Because of what my husband does. Obviously, rumours fly around parliament and, like a lot of gossip, is easily dismissed without foundation. So much in this synopsis suggests that the anonymous sender must have access to the original file. But it needs to be checked out. We couldn't possibly risk publishing anything about this without knowing for certain if it comes from the original dossier or not.'

'Wouldn't that be a bit tricky without knowing what was in the original dossier?'

'Exactly. Which is perhaps where you come in. Presumably you are experienced in surveillance, and your staff and colleagues know how to conduct themselves when confidentiality is required.'

This was the moment Mike dreaded, when he needed to explain about his one-man operation, and how he occasionally used a virtual, serviced office if he needed to interview anyone. He coughed lightly before speaking.

'I'm a one-man band. I don't employ any staff.'

She raised her eyebrows, but it looked as if she was deliberately feigning surprise and already knew what the answers would be.

'I sort of work as a franchisee for a large company who sometimes put work my way if it happens to be on my patch. But I mainly work for myself. It's better that way, because I can keep costs down for my clients, especially when investigations run on for any length of time.'

'But how can you possibly keep someone under scrutiny for any length of time if you've got no back-up, no support?'

'Presumably you contacted me from my website.' She nodded. 'So, you'll know I worked for the Metropolitan police for many years, and for the last five of them I was a detective inspector in counter terrorism. So, I know all there is to know about electronic surveillance and tracking. Go back forty years and keeping someone under twenty-four-hour surveillance would take a team of at least twelve operatives. Minimum. Now someone can be observed remotely from a laptop in real time.' He pointed his finger at the thin manuscript on her desk. 'I can keep anyone named in that book under close scrutiny for however long it takes and know exactly where they go and what they get up to.'

'And what would it take to find the person who sent us the book idea anonymously, and who may have a copy of the original document?'

Mike pursed his lips and looked sceptical. 'Well, unless it was sent to you by recorded delivery or…' He broke off as she shook her head emphatically.

'I'm sorry, Mike, but Delia opens my mail and deals with it. She thinks it was sent ordinary first-class post, and she hasn't a clue where it came from. The envelope has been thrown out.'

'So presumably your PA read it before you saw it?'

'Yes, but Delia's been with me for donkey's years. She's discreet and trustworthy.'

'So, someone sent you this extract anonymously, with fragments of the actual document to prove it's the genuine article. What d'you think he or she hopes to get out of it?'

'A big fat advance. Once we've agreed and decided to go ahead with the book, he – or she – will come out of the woodwork and let us have the document.' She handed Mike a sheet of A4 paper to look at. 'That's what came with the book synopsis and extracts, with no name or address. It looks as if it was written on a computer and printed out.'

He read it, but it didn't tell him anything different from what she had just told him, other than the fact that the person planned to telephone in just over a week's time to find out if she was interested, otherwise he or she would have to try another publisher.

'At this stage there's no way of finding out who this is,' Mike said, waving the paper before placing it back on the desk. 'Not that it matters. What's important is the fact that everyone leaves a trail of some sort, going back to the start. The original document that was handed to Lord Albion – presumably the MP who handed it to him had the copy, which has somehow passed down a line over the years. So, what I will need to do is start with the MP who gave the original to Albion.'

'He died of a heart attack in 1990.'

'So I believe. Was he married?'

'Yes, but not long after he died, James Gaskell's wife emigrated to Canada.'

'Well then…' Mike began, but Jo Reeves interrupted him.

'My husband looked into it. His wife died out there nine years ago. They had a son, but we didn't think he would have known about the file, as he was only eight-years-old when his father died.'

'If his father had a copy of the original file, you never know. He might have some information he can give me. Any idea where in Canada he and his mother settled?'

'No, but he shouldn't be too difficult to trace with a name like his.' She paused for dramatic emphasis. 'His name's Tarquin.'

Mike snorted. 'Tarquin Gaskell. You're kidding.'

'I know,' Jo Reeves said, stifling a giggle. 'Wonder if he hates his parents for it? Still, it might make tracing him easier. Though I doubt he'll know very much. If you can trace the whereabouts of this anonymous and spectacularly untalented author, all well and good. But that wasn't really what I had in mind.'

She pushed the thin manuscript, which consisted of no more than a dozen pages, towards Mike.

'What I had intended, what I'd like you to do is keep a couple of the people mentioned in here under observation for a while. See what they get up to. I suggest you start with Sir Geoffrey Scranton. He was an MP but is now a financial consultant to the Treasury. And Malcolm's heard rumours about him for years. He'd be in his mid-sixties now, and probably still up to his disgusting old tricks, which James Gaskell wanted investigating back in the late eighties.'

'I take it you're happy to engage my services for this investigation.'

'Absolutely. You've obviously got a good track record from your time in the Metropolitan Police. And you clearly have little time for child abusers.'

'That's a massive understatement, believe me.'

'Now let's get down to the subject of fees and costs.'

For the first time in months Mike felt optimistic. This was something he could get his teeth into, as well as the prospect of earning money while exposing people he considered to be the scourge of society. And as long as he was able to keep his temper in check and not jeopardise the investigation by resorting to vigilante methods, then he would be performing a service to society.

Chapter 6

As soon as he returned home, Mike made a coffee and took it into his study. His workplace, which would have been the third upstairs bedroom had it not become his office, was on the small side but adequate for how he conducted his business, using electronic gadgets, cameras, with much time spent searching the internet. Although the room was impersonal, clearly a space used solely as a place of labour, he liked the fact that it was impersonal, enabling him to concentrate entirely on work. The only strip of personality showing in the room was a bookshelf on which stood around two dozen books, mainly reference works and no longer of much use since the internet was often a faster provider of information, although Mike occasionally used London maps and guides if he was about to dash out and didn't want to boot up the computer. But there was one book, that looked to be in pristine condition and was rarely opened. The spine on the book indicated that it was a dictionary, but when removed from the shelf it opened to disclose that it was a secret box containing many business cards for whenever he needed to masquerade as a salesman, company director or employee of bogus companies. That, he knew, was sometimes the only way of getting people to talk to him now he no longer had the benefit of using a warrant card.

Not that he had forsaken his warrant card entirely. It lay at the bottom of the secret dictionary, and about a year ago it had led to a massive row with Marianne. They didn't keep any secrets from each other. Although her work as manager of a family planning clinic was rarely of sufficient interest for her to conceal anything of a confidential nature; he, on the other hand, did have to retain a certain amount of client confidentiality. But he trusted his wife implicitly and knew that anything he told her would never go outside the walls of their home. Though he was often circumspect about what he said in front of Natalie, knowing what teenagers are like when they want to impress their friends.

But the argument happened when Marianne was in their bedroom and needed to look up a word in the dictionary. Before he could stop her, she had dashed into his office and discovered the book-safe and his old warrant card. That was when he had to confess to her that eighteen months before he planned to leave the Met, he had deliberately lost his warrant card, reporting it as possibly stolen when he might have had his pocket picked on an Underground train. She accused him of deviousness and questioned him about his methods during his years in the police, about whether he had ever falsified or planted evidence. He swore to her he hadn't, which was true; but because of the theft (there was no other word for it) of the warrant card, he lost some of her respect. He promised he would never use the warrant card, telling her it was purely a safety net, in case something of vital importance cropped up one day. She made him agree it would have to be a life and death situation, and he promised to abide by her proposal, a suggestion made with extreme reluctance on her part.

As he sat at his desk sipping coffee, he opened LinkedIn on the computer. He subscribed to the premium rate, as it was a way of reaching people directly by email, although he didn't think it had provided him with much in the way of value for money so far. On the search engine he typed in Tarquin Gaskell's name. There were many Gaskells, only three of them located in Canada. There may well have been dozens more, but none who were LinkedIn subscribers. The last one on the list caught his eye. A James T Gaskell, located in Edmonton, described as a Project Manager for a construction company. There was no photograph, just an outline of a male head and shoulders where a picture should have been. He wondered, because of Jo Reeves's comment earlier on that Tarquin Gaskell might have found his first name an embarrassment, that maybe he changed it, perhaps using his father's name as a mark of respect and elbowing the embarrassing first name into second place. Or perhaps his second name was James and he just reversed them.

Mike decided to send James T Gaskell an email mentioning the missing files Gaskell's father investigated in the eighties. He took a chance on the name and asked the recipient to get in touch urgently. If it wasn't the same man, it didn't really matter. Either there would be no response, or he would get an email telling him he had the wrong person. As he was about to press Send to James T Gaskell, he couldn't help smiling. James T was the first name and initial of Captain Kirk of the Starship Enterprise.

Once the email had been sent, he looked at his watch. It was almost one p.m.

Because of the time difference, if it was the same person, he would expect a response later that evening. He then did a Google search on Sir Geoffrey Scranton to see what he looked like. He found several press photographs, the most recent showing a man with a large bear-like face, jowly with several chins, a thick neck and bulging stomach. It was a distinctive face, and Mike thought it unnecessary to print out a copy for recognition purposes. He opened one of the drawers in his workstation, grabbed an electronic tracker, closed the computer, then went downstairs and made himself a quick ham sandwich.

***

Scranton lived in a large detached house set back from the road on Highgate West Hill, the steep hill leading to Highgate Village in north London. Jo Reeves had given him Scranton's address, which she obtained from her husband, and Mike drove up the hill past the ex-MP's house, turned the car around near the top of the hill, then parked about fifty yards from the house on the opposite side of the road, facing down the hill. He put a CD of The Best of David Bowie 1969/1974 in the player and prepared for a long wait. This was the worst part of surveillance, the initial wait for the target. Once he managed to secretly attach the tracker, he could relax and do the tailing by using his tablet, smart phone or laptop.

He was on a single yellow line but if he kept his eyes peeled for wardens, he didn't think it mattered. On the seat next to him lay his camera with its telephoto lens at the ready. Not that he needed it at this stage. After studying Scranton's photograph on the internet, he knew the ex-MP would be easy to recognize.

Sighing, he glanced at his watch. It was two-fifteen. Maybe, he thought, Scranton was out for the day, or even out of the country. Which would mean a long and tedious wait, and all for nothing. The only thing that gave him faint hope that Scranton was at home was because when he had driven slowly up the hill and looked in through the gates, parked in the driveway in front of the house was a silver BMW, which he had been told by Jo Reeves was Scranton's car.

The CD got as far as track 12, "Diamond Dogs", when Mike's attention was drawn to the nose of the BMW easing carefully out of the drive at Scranton's house. He switched the CD off and switched the ignition on, hoping Scranton would turn right and go down the hill towards central London, which he was counting on. If he went up the hill, it would mean turning the car around in the busy, narrow road, and he might lose him.

He was in luck. The BMW turned right and shot down the hill at speed. Mike pulled out from his parking space and followed about a hundred yards behind. There were no other cars between his and Scranton's, so he had no worries about losing his target. But a sudden thought hit him. What if it wasn't Scranton who was driving, but his wife? Not that it mattered. If she had borrowed the car to go shopping or to meet a friend, he could still attach the tracker beneath its rear bumper at some stage, ready to observe the ex-MP's routines and habits from a distance.

As they neared Kentish Town Tube station, a small yellow Fiat shot out of a side road and got between his Volvo and the BMW. He concentrated on keeping the BMW in his sights, in case other cars got between them. But when traffic lights at Camden Town changed to amber, he saw the BMW shoot forward across the junction; then, as the light switched to red, the Fiat braked sharply in front of him. Mike cursed loudly, saw there was a gap on the offside of the Fiat, put his foot down and overtook it. He shot across the junction just as traffic from the other roads began to shoot across. He heard a sharp squeal of brakes, followed by cacophonous and angry tooting from several vehicles as he made it across the junction, not far behind the BMW, whose brake lights kept wavering as it slowed down. It looked as if Scranton was looking for an address or somewhere to park. Nearing Euston station, Mike saw the BMW stopping at a parking meter, so he braked and pulled in by the kerb on double yellow lines near a Chinese takeaway. He was less than twenty yards behind the BMW. If it was Scranton who was driving, he hoped and prayed his tail had gone unnoticed. After all, the man was probably a serial child abuser, always looking guiltily over his shoulder; or was the man too wealthy and powerful to worry his bloated little head about exposure of his indecent activities?

Dropping his chin onto his chest, to give the impression he was reading a map or looking for an address, Mike peered cautiously through the bottom of the windscreen. He saw it was Scranton all right, as the overweight ex-MP waddled to the meter and fed it with a handful of coins, before strolling a few yards and entering a building. Because of the angle, Mike couldn't see what the building was, so he got out of the Volvo, made sure there was nothing coming and stepped out into the road to get a better view of the building.

It was a massage parlour. And he didn't think it was one that employed genuine masseurs.

He got back in the car, waited a few minutes, giving Scranton time to get booked in, then got the small black electronic tracker out of the glove compartment. At the far end of the road, near Oakley Square, he could see a male traffic warden ambling along, ticketing cars. Mike headed towards Scranton's BMW, knowing he had to hurry if he didn't want to get a parking ticket. As people were walking along on both sides of the street, he pretended he was the BMW's driver. First, he approached the driver's side and reached for the handle. Then, as if remembering something, he went to the back of the vehicle, rubbing his hand along the bumper, as if he was looking for a scratch or dent. He smoothed his hand along the bodywork lovingly, giving an impression he cared a great deal about his car; and as soon as no one was watching, he leant over and clamped the tracker by its strong magnet to the underside of the bumper. He dashed back to his own car and saw the traffic warden, a young Asian man, was now only yards away. As he turned the Volvo's ignition, he saw in his rear view mirror the looming warden approach and laughed as he pulled away from the kerb.

'Better luck next time,' he said.

He would have liked to get a photo of Scranton leaving the massage parlour. Not that it really mattered. Consenting adults, and all that. At least he had the tracker in place now and it had been comparatively easy. Now he could head for home, relax and wait and see if there was a response from his email to James T Gaskell.

Chapter 7

At nine-thirty that night, Natalie retired to her room. Sitting close to Marianne on the sofa in their living room, Mike waited for her to quiz him again about the investigation. He had mentioned as much of it as he could over dinner but toned down the extent of Establishment child sex abuse because of Natalie's presence. He told them he was looking to obtain evidence incriminating a retired MP for having sex with a child back in the 1980s, but hadn't offered much more than that scant information, choosing instead to dwell on details about the publisher and her MP husband. He also told them he needed to speak to a man in Canada, who was a possible connection to the case.

Marianne held out her empty wine glass to Mike, saying, 'Now Natalie's gone up, you can tell me – were you holding anything back?'

He picked up the bottle of Chianti from the coffee table, refilled their glasses, then leant across and kissed Marianne's cheek as he handed her the wine. Even after their ten-year relationship he still found her incredibly attractive. She was six years younger than him, with auburn hair, and if he had been asked to describe his wife, he would have said petite and French-looking. Her pale skin and small upturned nose reminded him of a pre-Raphaelite painting he remembered seeing at the National Gallery.

'Well?' she prompted him.

'It's not just about Geoffrey Scranton and child sex abuse. It's about a file which was supposed to be handed to Leonard Albion in the eighties, a document revealing half the bloody cabinet was at it, probably. And now the file has turned up and I'm going to try to trace it, starting with this man in Canada.'

'That's if it's the right man.'

Mike looked at his watch and sighed. 'I think Edmonton's about seven hours behind us.'

'Which means it's gone three o'clock out there.'

'Thanks. I think I could have worked that out.'

Marianne pouted and shrugged. 'I wouldn't get too hung up on him ringing, if I were you. Gaskell must be a common name. And even if it is him, he might not want to speak to you – in which case, he'll ignore your email. And if this file is so important, and can damage a lot of powerful people, he may well want nothing to do with it.'

'But that's not right,' Mike protested. 'This should come out in the open. That's why his father wanted justice for all those victims of abuse.'

'Yes, I agree with you, Mike. However powerful or important people are – or think they are – they should be prosecuted for those ghastly crimes against children. But that still doesn't alter the fact that you might have reached a dead end where this Gaskell's son is concerned.'

He nodded solemnly and was about to sigh his dissatisfaction when he heard the phone ringing from upstairs. The breath caught in his chest and he stopped for a moment to listen. It was his office landline, a line which he used for business purposes and kept separate from the family landline. 'That might be him!' he said, and leapt up, plonking his wine glass on the coffee table. 'I can't see who else would be my ringing my office now.'

Marianne shook her head dubiously. 'You never know. Don't get your hopes up.'

'I think the word might be serendipitous,' he called as he dashed upstairs, having counted six rings already. As he reached the door of his office, which was next to Natalie's room, she shouted that his phone was ringing. 'I know,' he called back breathlessly. 'I'm getting it.' He shut the door behind him, so that Natalie wouldn't hear the conversation, and snatched the phone from his desk.

'Hello?'

'Am I speaking with Michael Halliday?'

The voice was clear and authoritative, with a trace of an American accent. Mike found it hard to make a distinction between Canadian and US accents, so he assumed he was hearing Gaskell's Canadian accent.

'Yes, this is Mike Halliday,' he replied.

'I got your email. First of all, I'd like to ask why you want to talk to me about the file my father gave Leonard Albion in 1989?'

Mike felt a buzz of satisfaction, knowing he had hit on the right person. 'Because I'm investigating the case against him,' he said, 'and other cabinet ministers suspected of crimes against children.'

'You're a private investigator, is that right?' Mike was about to reply but Gaskell continued, 'I checked you out online. Would you mind telling me who you're working for?'

'I'm working for an MP named Malcolm Reeves. He's a Labour MP for Lewisham South.' Mike held back from giving Gaskell details about the mysterious book synopsis sent to Forum Books, thinking it would complicate the issue at this stage. 'He wants to reopen this case and start an investigation as to why the original file given to Leonard Albion disappeared.'

'Good. It's about time someone did something about this horrendous case.'

'Your father, I believe, before he suffered his heart attack, was pursuing the matter. And he gave the original file to Albion, didn't he?'

'Yes, and years later, after my mother died in 2003, I discovered she had a copy of the file on a floppy disk.' Gaskell must have sensed Mike's excited intake of breath, because he added, 'But don't get your hopes up. It has since then vanished.'

Mike wished he'd sipped water with his wine, because his throat suddenly felt parched. 'How d'you mean vanished?'

There was a slight pause before Gaskell began to explain, 'After my mother died, I found the disk and converted it to a flash drive. Unfortunately, I have since then disposed of the floppy.'

'What happened to the flash drive?'

'Let me finish. Because of my work commitments at home here, I couldn't devote much time to this issue, but I felt that something should be done about it. I vaguely remembered a friend or colleague of my father's – I was only seven or eight at the time, but after a little research I discovered it was John Keneally MP. I came to the UK and visited him at his home in 2005. And after talking to him it became clear to me that he could be trusted to pursue the child abuse case, so I gave him the USB drive containing the document.'

'What happened to it?'

'I have no idea, because John Keneally was murdered in 2006. His house was burgled, and the intruder killed him.'

'So presumably this intruder took the flash drive?'

'Well, no. It's not that simple. A case was discovered with items stolen from Keneally's house, but there was no flash drive in it.'

'What did the police think happened to it?'

'No one knows. Keneally's wife also said that her husband's laptop had disappeared.'

'What happened to the intruder?'

'He was sentenced to life, with a recommendation that he serve a minimum of twenty-five years.'

'Could he have had an accomplice, maybe, who stole the flash drive and computer?'

'It's possible, I suppose. But that's as much as I know. I was devastated when I found out about Keneally's murder, especially as that sensitive document had vanished. So that's it, I fear. A dead end, so to speak. I don't know where you go from there.' There was a subdued pause before Gaskell added, 'I just don't know.'

Mike's mind was racing now. Far from being a dead end as Gaskell's dark pun suggested, someone had the file. There was a definite trail now leading to the person who had surfaced and approached the publisher.

'All I can do,' Mike said to break the gloomy silence, 'is to see if I can find out if someone worked with the burglar.'

'Well, if the police couldn't all those years ago, I don't see—'

Mike interrupted him. 'One last question, if you don't mind.'

'Go ahead.'

'Do you happen to know the burglar's name?'

'I think it's…let me see…Baldwin. Yes, I'm certain it was Baldwin. But there should be a record of it somewhere. His trial would have been around the spring or summer of 2006 I dare say.'

'Yes, the trial details shouldn't be too difficult to find. And I'll see how it goes from there. Thank you for responding to my email, James.'

'You're welcome, Mike. I just wish I could have been more help. If you do find anything out – though it's doubtful – and if your MP chap manages to ruffle a few feathers, would you let me know?'

'Sure. Let me have your number.'

Mike scribbled the number on a notepad, thanked Gaskell once more and hung up. When he went back downstairs to the living room, Marianne looked up at him expectantly.

'Do I take it by that grin on your face that it was the man from Canada.'

Mike nodded, his grin widening. 'Yes, he thought he couldn't be much help. Little did he know just how helpful he was.'

Marianne threw him a quizzical frown, so he sat down to relate to her the phone conversation in detail.

Chapter 8

Thursday 13 March 2014

Marianne was at work, Natalie had just left for school, and the house was quiet, which was how Mike liked it. No radio, no television, no music playing. Just silence with nothing to interrupt his thinking as he sat at his desk and sipped from a mug of fresh coffee. The first thing he did was use his laptop to check the tracker on Scranton's car, but the screen indicated the BMW was stationary at the house in Highgate. Then he researched Terry Baldwin on the internet. By typing in his name and cross referencing it to John Keneally, it didn't take him long to discover the burglar was in a Manchester high security prison, having spent eight years there and still protesting his innocence. His mother and his sister campaigned diligently for his case to be reopened, but the Home Secretary had on countless occasions rejected their pleas because there was insufficient new evidence to warrant further investigation.

Mike read the newspaper reports of the case thoroughly but didn't learn anything more than what Gaskell's son had told him – that there was a reason to suspect that either Baldwin was telling the truth about being set-up or he had an accomplice who took Keneally's laptop and the missing USB flash drive. There was only one way of finding out and that was to speak to Baldwin himself, which would involve a trip to Manchester. Perhaps if Baldwin's mother was due a prison visit, he might be able to persuade her that it might be in her son's best interest to be interviewed by someone who could throw new light on the case.

He was just about to start searching the internet for details of how he might contact Baldwin's mother when his landline rang. It was Jo Reeves, wanting to know how he was getting on with the tail on Scranton. He told her the tracker was now in place and described the ex-MP's visit to the massage parlour.

'I don't care if he's paying for sex, so long as it's with adults,' she said. 'It's children I'm concerned about. And there was something I forgot to tell you during our meeting yesterday, which might make your job easier. We know he has regular meetings in the city, and he parks his car near the Barbican. This will save you having to investigate when this happens, as you would be wasting your time. These will be genuine financial meetings, with nothing untoward happening.'

Mike winced as he sipped his coffee which was now stone cold. 'Incidentally,' he said, 'I've got some information about the file, part of which found its way to your organisation. Gaskell's mother had a copy of it, and in 2006 young James Tarquin passed it on to John Keneally MP who was murdered, and there is some mystery about what happened to his laptop and the file which he had on a memory stick. His alleged murderer is a lifer in a Manchester prison who claims he was innocent and stitched up for the crime. If I can get to speak with him, I might get further along the trail in finding out what happened to this file.'

'So, apart from keeping an eye on Geoffrey Scranton, what's the next move in finding out who might have the file?'

'I think I need to interview the prisoner – find out if he had an accomplice, or whether he's telling the truth about being stitched up. It'll involve a trip to Manchester.'

'Or couldn't we just wait until the person who sent us the book gets in touch? He or she will have to reveal themselves if they want payment and will have to produce the rest of the file.'

Mike could see she had a point, but he doubted it would be that simple. The person could use an intermediary and might want payment anonymously in cash.

'I don't think,' he began reflectively, 'this person's going to come out of the woodwork so openly. If it were that simple, you could just do nothing and see what transpires. But from what I've learnt about John Keneally's murder, and a burglar being convicted for the crime, and then the laptop and file vanishing into thin air, it starts to look...well, I hate to say this, but it starts to look like some sort of conspiracy. And there's got to be a link leading to whoever sent you the synopsis and the first few chapters of the book.'

'I think you could be right, Mike. Go ahead and interview this burglar if you think it's important. When are you planning on doing this?'

'I'll need to get his permission first. And prisoners are only allowed so many visits in a month. Fingers crossed he might not have used up his quota. Then maybe I could get to see him early next week.'

'Good. Incidentally, have you found time to read the book extract?'

'Yes. And you're right. I don't think it'll make the Pulitzer Prize. Whoever wrote it either should have gone to

Specsavers or never went to school. But, as you say, it is specific about certain names and places. It reads as if it's based on the genuine article. Of course, I haven't read the genuine article, only the first few pages of the file, so I'm only guessing. But it does seem as if it was written as part of an investigation that took place nearly thirty years ago, and we now know what happened with some of the named sex predators such as Jimmy Savile.'

She coughed several times, as if her throat had gone dry, and he thought he heard her gulping a drink afterwards.

'Excuse me. That's better. Now there is one other thing, Mike. Malcolm and I would like you and your wife to join us for dinner as soon as possible. I don't know if you're free tomorrow night. I know it's short notice, but I think it would be invaluable to speak with Malcolm about this.'

'I think we might be free. I'll have a word with Marianne at lunchtime. I've got your number and I'll text you. I'm ninety per cent sure it'll be OK. Whereabouts d'you live?'

'Wimbledon. I'll email you the address. And there's someone else we'd like you to meet.'

'Oh?'

'Yes. A man called Dennis Lorcan. He's a billionaire banker and financier – a real mover and shaker. He's also on the board at countless high-flying businesses and organisations. And, unusually for a banker in this day and age, he's a philanthropist, and he's just set up a charity, not only for the protection of children, but mainly to help the victims of abuse. I'll invite Dennis and his wife to join us, if you can make it.'

Mike thanked her, promised to text her later, and hung up. He thought about this sudden dinner party invitation and smiled as he pictured Marianne's dilemma of wondering what to wear.

Then the laptop screen drew his attention. Scranton's car was on the move. Mike watched the screen closely to see if it headed south down the hill towards Camden Town, then across to Islington and the City. But the car went up the hill to Highgate Village.

Mike stood up, picked his car keys up from the desk, and got ready to depart and head after Scranton's car. Then, knowing London as well as he did from all his years in the police, he realized the best way to get to the City from there would be along Holloway Road to Islington, then down past the Angel and Old Street to Barbican. It was the most direct route. He picked up the laptop and his coffee mug, went downstairs to the kitchen, reheated his coffee in the microwave for forty seconds, then sipped it slowly as he observed the laptop screen open on the kitchen table. By now Scranton's BMW had reached Seven Sisters and would be heading straight on for Highbury and Islington. But his car changed direction at Seven Sisters. Instead of heading for the City, he was now heading north.

Mike downed his coffee, turned his laptop off, dashed upstairs to fetch his camera, then left the house hurriedly.

***

It took him just over an hour to drive to Scranton's location, a rambling Victorian house in Barnet, with a board out front which stated baldly: Gwent Guest House. As he drove slowly past the house, a forbidding Gothic monstrosity with triangular gables over the second-storey windows, he glanced through the open gates to steps leading up to a porch and a stained-glass front door. He caught a glimpse of a large printed notice attached to the side of the porch which read NO VACANCIES. The downstairs windows were obscured from the road by tall hedges on either side of the entrance gate, but he spotted several vehicles on the drive, in front of the house, including Scranton's BMW and a minibus. He tried to read the writing on the minibus, but he didn't dare loiter as he drove past in case someone happened to be looking out of one of the windows and spotted him. He drove to the end of the road, which was a cul-de-sac, turned around and drove back towards the guest house, pulling into the kerb and parking behind a row of cars about fifty yards from the house and on the opposite side. From where he sat and waited, he could just about see the front door and the minibus in front of it.

He picked up his camera from the passenger seat, made certain there was no one about, and stared through the viewfinder, focusing the telephoto lens on the minibus. As the zoom on the lens sharpened, he was able read the writing on the side of the bus clearly. It read: 'Drummond Children's Home.'

He clicked the camera, taking a shot of the minibus. Then, as he lowered the camera and thought about the occupants of the vehicle who might be visiting the guest house, and the reason for their visit, he shivered, and felt helpless needles of tears pricking his eyes. He wiped his eyes with thumb and forefinger, feeling nauseous now. An almost uncontrollable anger swept over him, so that he wanted to run out of the car, tear over to that house, and force his way in. But deep down he knew it would be a foolish way of conducting this investigation. What if the only minibus visitor to the guest house was the driver, and he went barging in and found nothing of importance? No, the only way, he told himself, was to collect as much evidence as possible. The pictures would be time and date stamped and would at least provide proof of Scranton's visit to the guest house, along with the suspect minibus from the children's home parked outside.

According to the GPS tracking device, Scranton had arrived at least forty-five minutes before him, so he settled down to wait, wondering how long it would take. As it was now coming up to twelve-thirty, he thought it was a good time to call Marianne about the dinner invitation for tomorrow night. He dialled her direct line and she answered almost immediately.

'Hi, it's me,' he said. 'How d'you fancy dinner with the publisher and her MP husband tomorrow night? And please don't tell me you've got nothing to wear. You've got a wardrobe full of nothing to wear.'

'Hah-hah!' she enunciated. 'I've never heard that one before. So, where do they live?'

'Wimbledon. Which isn't too bad a journey.'

'And who's driving?'

'I'll drive,' he offered reluctantly.

'Great. Maybe we could invite Natalie's friend Megan for a sleepover, and I'll make them something they can heat up.'

'Is that wise?'

'D'you mean my cooking or inviting Megan for a sleepover?'

Just then Mike saw the front door of the guest house opening. It was Scranton, who called something over his shoulder before exiting, pulling the door closed.

'I've got to go,' he told Marianne hurriedly. 'I'll see you later.'

He clicked the phone off and grabbed the camera. He aimed it at Scranton, letting it whir and click as he took a stream of pictures of the ex-MP leaving the house and getting into his car. The BMW shot out of the gate and Mike kept the camera whirring and clicking as Scranton's car headed back towards the main road. He didn't think following him was necessary now, as he could track his movements from any location. More importantly he wanted to know who would be getting into the minibus. Especially as what he had read from the anonymously sent extract from the book and file had hinted that there was a guest house in north London where members of the Establishment and powerful celebrities sexually abused young children. It said that the file would go on to name some of the well-known people who had visited the house over many years, which was rumoured to have been happening since the 1980s and needed thoroughly investigating.

Ten minutes later, a man and a woman appeared, the man holding a young boy of about ten by the wrist, and the woman holding the hand of girl of about the same age. Mike could tell by the children's demeanour that these kids were ill-treated, broken and had retreated into themselves, their lives a living nightmare.

Once more he restrained the impulse to dash across the road and rescue them. Instead he clicked away, taking dozens of pictures, and thought he would be better armed if he had concrete evidence of what went on at that house, especially it was strongly rumoured in the missing file.

He thought about Scranton's visit and shuddered

Whatever happens, I'll get you, Scranton.

Far as I'm concerned, no rules. No need to go by the book now.

The book goes out the window.

And however long it takes, I'll have you.

And that's a promise.

The minibus drove out of the gate and headed off in the same direction as Scranton's car. Mike kept clicking until it reached the main road and turned left. As he lowered the camera, he realized how tense he was. His hands shook, and he felt sick, knowing he had done nothing to help those children. He wanted to alleviate their suffering, and almost wept at how impotent and useless he felt. He felt dirty and ashamed. He had done nothing, just taken a number of photographs.

Clenching his jaw tightly, his shoulders tense and aching, he vowed his investigation would soon uncover anyone and everyone, whoever they might be, involved in the sexual abuse of innocents.

Chapter 9

Friday 14 March 2014

As they arrived outside the house in Wimbledon Village, Mike whistled softly. 'Must be worth a couple of million, I should think.'

'A conservative estimate,' Marianne replied

A reasonably large 1920s house, the Reeves' home didn't appear overly ostentatious and looked like a cosy family home that just happened to be in a hugely desirable area. It was detached, with a small gravel drive in the front but no garage. There was a second storey, under an overlapping roof, and to one side of the building jutted a small tower with a circular window like a large porthole. It was an unusual property, unconventional and architecturally fascinating.

Three cars were parked in the drive: A Saab, a Fiat and a Jaguar. Mike guessed the gleaming Jaguar would belong to the banker, and rather than squeeze in close behind it, he parked the Volvo in the street on a single yellow line. As it was gone seven-thirty it wouldn't matter.

Marianne shivered in her flimsy dress as they scrunched across the gravel drive, and Mike slid a comforting arm around her shoulder as they walked up to the front door. Feeling as if he was being watched, Mike glanced back at the Jaguar and noticed a dark figure sitting behind the wheel, staring at them both. Marianne also looked back. When she saw the man, she felt a momentary stab of alarm. She leant closer to Mike.

'Who d'you think that is?' she whispered.

'Probably the banker's chauffeur.'

'And they just leave the poor sod sitting outside while they enjoy dinner?'

'That's the price he pays working for a wealthy man.'

A moment after Mike rang the doorbell, they glimpsed through the stained glass of the front door Jo Reeves's shape as she emerged from the living room to greet them.

'Hi! You must be Marianne,' she said with a smile as she opened the door. 'I'm Jo.'

They shook hands and Mike offered her the bottle of Rioja he was clutching.

'Oh, thank you. You really shouldn't have bothered. I'm just glad you could make it. Come in and meet Malcolm and our other two guests.'

As they followed her along the hall, Marianne was taken aback by their hostess's attire. She was dressed casually in double-denim, jeans and a Levi shirt, and Marianne felt overdressed in her best Harvey Nichols cocktail dress and stiletto heels and was annoyed with herself for trying to impress. Clearly Jo Reeves liked to dress down for the weekend, even if they had guests. Marianne hoped the banker's wife had made a sartorial effort.

Before Jo Reeves ushered them into the living room, Mike noticed the hall's enormous polished oak staircase, and the shelves that ran from the bottom of the stairs to the top filled with hundreds of books. He couldn't help wondering if they had been read or were simply collected over the years and had become a form of decoration. He couldn't imagine anyone had found the time to plough their way through what amounted to a lifetime of reading.

From upstairs there came a heavy thud, the sound of a body hitting the floor. Jo Reeves paused with her hand on the door and said, 'That's our black Labrador Ellie.' She leaned close to Marianne and lowered her voice to explain, 'I've had to shut Ellie in one of the bedrooms because Dennis has an allergy. And I had to thoroughly vacuum all of downstairs.'

As they entered the large living room, with two enormous sofas in an L-shape in front of a marble fireplace, a man got up from one of the sofas ready to receive the introductions. He had blond thinning hair and looked as if he had once been a robust rugby player but had let age and over-indulgence do its worst. He wore a shirt and tie, with the sleeves of the shirt rolled up, and had removed his suit jacket which lay on the arm of the sofa. Jo Reeves introduced him as Dennis, and then introduced Jennifer, his wife, who remained seated. Marianne was glad to see the banker's wife also wore a cocktail dress and high heels, and she began to feel more at ease. Finally, the hostess introduced her husband, who stepped forward from a table behind one of the sofas where he was mixing gins and tonics. He contrasted sharply with Lorcan, and together they looked as if they could have worked as a comedy duo. Whereas the banker was short and dumpy, Reeves was tall and angular, measuring a good six feet four. He shook hands with Mike and Marianne and thanked them for coming at such short notice

Clearly, Mike noted, this was not so much a social occasion as a business discussion. He and Marianne sat down on one of the sofas to the right angle of the Lorcan couple and Malcolm Reeves offered them drinks. Marianne asked for a gin and tonic, but Mike said he would make do with just a tonic water as he was lumbered as the driver.

The banker sniggered at that and said, 'I thought you Met detectives have a bit of leeway if you're stopped by the rank and file.'

Mike shook his head. 'I'm no longer a detective.'

'He's gone private,' Jo Reeves said.

A log fire crackled and burned in the marble fireplace. Above the mantelpiece hung a silver-framed abstract painting of what looked like multi-coloured toothpaste being squeezed from a tube. Marianne studied it for a moment. It didn't seem to be in keeping with the rest of the room, which was conservatively chintzy and most of the furniture was comfortably expensive and antique.

'And Jo's company has engaged you to investigate this dreadful business of child abuse within the Establishment, is that right?' the banker added.

Mike nodded. 'I expect Jo has told you all about the mysterious book synopsis that arrived and is purported to contain material taken from the missing file from the eighties.'

'Most peculiar that,' Lorcan observed. 'Just turning up suddenly after all these years.'

'It was stolen from a murdered MP eight years ago.'

'Yes, Jo told me. John Keneally. I remember reading about it. Terrible business. But I thought he was robbed by a burglar who was sentenced to life in prison.'

Malcolm Reeves handed Marianne and Mike their drinks, they thanked him, and Mike turned to Lorcan, shaking his head. 'He has always claimed he was innocent.'

Lorcan snorted. 'Don't they all, though.'

'Yes but reading about the case has given me enough room for doubt – I think he could be telling the truth. He was caught burgling another house. An empty, unfurnished property that was on the market for renting. He had a suitcase taken from Keneally's house, filled with items stolen from the MP's home, but no laptop or memory stick. I think Keneally was murdered because he knew the contents of the file, and whoever murdered him, destroyed the laptop – probably because it contained the information – and the perpetrator also needed to destroy the flash drive.'

Everything was still in the living room as they all listened to what Mike had to say. After he finished speaking, apart from a car braking in the street, and the crackle of logs in the fireplace, everything was deathly still as they thought about the motive for Keneally's murder.

Jennifer Lorcan, frowning deeply, was the first to break the silence. 'If whoever murdered him wanted to destroy the document, why has it now resurfaced?'

Marianne glanced at the banker's wife, wondering if she was years younger than him. She was slim, and her face was free of wrinkles, but her age was hard to guess because of her smooth, stretched, Botox-injected skin.

'Perhaps,' Mike speculated, 'whoever took the flash drive intended to use it for blackmail. Anyone named in the document would probably want their name kept out of it, so a blackmailer—'

'That doesn't explain,' Malcolm Reeves interrupted, facing everyone as he leant against a corner of the fireplace, 'why this person, whoever it is, now wants to publish and make it public.'

Mike shook his head. 'No, I have to admit, that doesn't make much sense.'

Jo Reeves opened the living room door with a flourish to gain everyone's attention. 'Why don't we go next door? We can continue this discussion over dinner. I forgot to ask; I hope everyone likes sirloin steak.'

Everyone nodded and mumbled their appreciation.

'And Maria's an excellent cook. Now if you could tell me how you'd like your steak cooked –'

'Mike and I usually like it medium,' Marianne said.

Lorcan waved a finger between himself and his wife. 'Ditto us two.'

'That's easy then,' Jo Reeves smiled and left the room.

Her husband followed her to the door, holding it open. 'Shall we?' he said.

The four of them rose and shuffled out to the dining room next door. A large refectory table took up most of the room and was laden with antipasti, various cooked meats, and four bottles of wine, two white and two red already open. They all sat down, Marianne relieved to find herself sitting next to Mike instead of being ushered into a seat beside the banker, as was usual at dinner parties. She sat opposite his wife instead.

Jo Reeves returned from the kitchen, saying, 'I asked Maria to put the steaks on in forty-five minutes, when we can sit back and enjoy them, having had a thorough discussion.'

As Malcolm Reeves poured everyone wine, Mike kicked off by asking Lorcan about his involvement with the charity he ran for victims of child abuse. The banker slurped almost half a glass of wine before replying.

'After I heard about Malcolm heading an enquiry to reopen and investigate the case of Lord Albion and the missing files, I felt so disgusted by it all, I contacted him and offered to start the charity for victims of sexual abuse. So far my trust has invested five million into the charity.'

'Most of it. Dennis's own money,' his wife made a point of adding.

Mike helped himself to a portion of sun-dried tomatoes and Parma ham, and asked Lorcan, 'What sort of help does the charity offer the victims?'

'Counselling mainly. These people need a great deal of ongoing guidance and support. And sometimes we'll be able to offer financial help. Because of their unfortunate mistreatment and circumstances, they might be unable to cope with holding down jobs and integrating into society.'

'But wouldn't it be better,' Marianne said, 'if the charity existed to try to put an end to child abuse, rather than functioning to ease their suffering after the event?'

Lorcan stared at her a trifle coldly and she added quickly, 'Please don't think I'm criticizing you for doing everything you can to help these poor children, who may be traumatised in adult life. But I just wondered if some of the money could be better spent in stopping child sexual abuse.'

Lorcan sighed and shook his head, as if he had to struggle with these questions himself and found it difficult to come up with answers. 'I see where you're coming from, Marianne, but as we've seen in all walks of life – not just in this case of Establishment figures – that it's a problem that goes back years and years right across society. It's difficult to stamp it out. And –' He paused and looked at Mike. 'We happen to think that stopping child abuse rests with the police and the law.'

'Yes, Dennis is right,' Malcolm Reeves stated. 'Catching and punishing the culprits should be left to our police and legal system. But Dennis's charity is there to offer help to the poor victims, whether they be young working-class girls, orphans or children who have suffered at the hands of priests or youth leaders.'

Lorcan sniffed loudly. 'You wouldn't believe some of the horrendous stories I've heard during the day to day running of this charity. One of my charity workers told me –' He stopped as he stared into the distance, and his eyes clouded over. His knife and fork dropped with a clatter on to his plate and he covered his eyes with both hands. 'It's so hard to…to believe some of the things that go on,' he mumbled. 'I can't help being affected by it.'

There was a long and embarrassed hiatus before he eventually took his hands away and composed himself. 'I'm sorry. I shouldn't let it get to me.' His eyes glistened with tears.

His wife leaned close to him and squeezed his hand. 'It's all right, darling. You're with friends. They understand.'

'It's difficult trying to face these things,' Marianne said softly. 'Especially if you're family orientated. Do you and Dennis have a family, Jennifer?'

There was a short pause before Jennifer Lorcan answered. 'Dennis has two children from a previous marriage. But we haven't got any children.'

Rich man buys himself a younger model, Marianne thought unkindly, then swept the uncharitable thought from her mind. After all, however wealthy this man was, he was doing something to help people.

'So, tell me, Mike,' Lorcan said, recovering rapidly and adopting a business-like manner, 'how is the investigation going? I know you've only just started, but Malcolm tells me you're going after Geoffrey Scranton, yes?'

Mike nodded. 'Yesterday I tailed him to a guest house in Barnet. He spent just over an hour there and I took photographs of him leaving the premises. A minibus from a children's home was parked in the drive, and a bit later two children – a boy and a girl of about ten – were led out. They looked as if they had been traumatised by whatever had gone on there. Although I took photos, I wanted to rush over, break into that disgusting place and stop whatever was happening.'

'That's terrible,' Jo Reeves said. 'Maybe you should have done.'

Lorcan shook his head. 'No, I think Mike did the right thing. I believe there was mention of a north London guest house in the document –' He looked towards Jo Reeves who nodded her confirmation. 'So, it's evidence that is needed. And now Mike has the photographs.'

'That's right,' Mike agreed. 'I've already got evidence. And if Geoffrey Scranton returns to that guest house, there's no reason I can't go after him. Force my way into the house if necessary.'

'But how can you do that? I mean, an unwarranted intrusion would make any evidence inadmissible.'

'I'm a private citizen now. If I broke in and created havoc, the police would have to be called. And if I made such a disturbance, they wouldn't need a warrant to enter the premises. It's a way of bringing everything out into the open and putting an end to what goes on there.'

Lorcan pursed his lips while he mulled this over, then fed a large portion of smoked salmon into his mouth.

Malcolm Reeves, full of understanding and sympathy, nodded his head thoughtfully and said, 'I can see how you feel, Mike – and if I'd been there, I would be moved in the same way – but you may well end up being arrested and charged for breaking and entering. And, although Jo wanted you to go after Scranton, you need to focus on finding the person who has the document. Without it we can't reopen this investigation which goes back to the late eighties and….'

'And without it,' Marianne chipped in, looking at Jo Reeves, 'you haven't got a book deal.'

Mike noticed the way Jo Reeves's lips tightened at Marianne's sudden interruption. Then she composed herself, relaxed and smiled charmingly.

'I know it might seem as if we are in it purely for a book deal, but let me assure you, Marianne, that because of Malcolm's involvement in raising questions in the Commons about the way the file which was given to Lord Albion disappeared, and his pressure to reopen and investigate these allegations, means our intention is to make it as public as possible.'

Marianne flushed. 'No, I'm sorry. I didn't mean to imply –'

Jo Reeves waved it aside magnanimously. 'I'm sure you didn't. But as we've been sent what looks like an extract of the genuine document, we must run with it, and do as much as we can to make it public.'

'Why do you suppose,' Mike asked, 'this person selected you as a publisher? Would he or she have known you're married to Malcolm and picked you for that reason?'

'I think that's a distinct possibility. It looks like more than a coincidence. And it's something Malcolm and I have discussed. Perhaps it's not just the money that motivates this person.'

'You mean they might also want to destroy these Establishment figures?'

'Exactly.'

Lorcan leant forward in his chair and stared at Mike intently. 'Tell me, Mike, what's your next move? If this person has no intention of revealing himself, how do you propose to go about finding him?'

'Well, my next move will be to visit Terry Baldwin, the man who's serving time for Keneally's murder. I'm seeing his mother on Tuesday morning. She's due a visit to see her son that afternoon, and I'll be going in her place. He may be able to answer a few questions and give me some details about the man he claims stitched him up for the crime.'

'Such as?'

Mike shrugged. 'I'm not really sure until I question him. But there may be some details which were overlooked by his barrister during the trial. If he is innocent of the murder – and I suspect he is – the poor bastard didn't stand a cat in hell's chance. So, he might be able to tell me a few things the police and lawyers missed.'

'It's probably a better way to conduct this investigation,' Malcolm Reeves proposed. 'I'm not sure it's a good idea to force your way into that guest house. That could lead to all kinds of complications.'

Lorcan pointed his fork at Reeves. 'You don't really believe that, do you, Malcolm?'

'What do you mean?'

'Someone has to expose what goes on in that house, and Mike may have come up with the perfect solution. That's if Scranton returns to that house, of course.'

'I think he probably will,' Mike said. 'Maybe not right away, but if he's been getting away with it for more than twenty years, he'll consider himself immune from danger. But even if he doesn't return to that house soon, I think I might, to try and find out who's been managing it over the years. Someone must have been running things for the high and mighty, and I'll soon bring them back down to earth.'

Marianne grabbed Mike's hand and addressed the rest of the table. 'I'm not sure I like the idea of my husband resorting to strong-arm tactics. It's like something out of the movies. It could end badly.'

Jo Reeves nodded emphatically. 'I quite agree. But what I think we should all agree on is that we should allow Mike – and we might remember that until quite recently he was a senior Scotland Yard officer – we should allow him to conduct the investigation in his own way.'

She smiled at Mike.

Lorcan raised his glass in a toast. 'I agree. Let Mike deal with it in his own way. I'll drink to that.'

They all raised their glasses and stared at Mike, who smiled modestly.

'Thank you,' he said.

***

Marianne was silent for a long while as they set off for home; Mike could almost hear the wheels turning in her head and the cogs snapping into place as he waited for her to say what was on her mind. They travelled the length of Wimbledon Common before she spoke.

'I think what you're doing – this investigation – is worthy and important and could expose a great deal of nasty people and help young children in the future.'

She paused, and he prompted her.

'But?'

'I have grave doubts about one person tackling it alone. It's not like when you were in the police, and you had a large and effective organisation behind you. You have no one to back you up, and from what you've told me so far, these are powerful people in the government.'

'All the more reason to expose them and bring them to justice.'

Marianne snorted sceptically. 'But that's just it. You can't do that on your own. It worries me, Mike. This could be dangerous. You might be risking your life with this case.'

'It was sometimes risky in the counter terrorism squad.'

'But not like this. This is one man up against…against God knows who. This is all a bit scary.'

'Just a bit?'

'Don't split hairs. You know very well what I mean. And what about that MP who was murdered? It was probably to silence him because of what he knew. You can't do this all on your own.'

'It's not like I haven't got any back-up, sweetheart. I'm not working entirely alone.'

'I suppose you're going to tell me these people we had dinner with will be right behind you every step of the way.'

Mike chuckled to lighten the way the conversation was going. 'At least they're influential. Malcolm Reeves is in the shadow cabinet. And as for Dennis Lorcan – know what his bonus was at the Federal Western Banking Group last year? Six million. That was just his bonus, plus his salary and shares. And he ranks high on the *Sunday Times* rich list.'

'How d'you know all this?'

'You know me. I like to do a thorough research on every case I'm involved in, however big or small. And Lorcan I discovered is also on the Steering Committee of the Bilderberg Group.'

'Who?'

'The most powerful European and American organisation, with a membership consisting of heads of state, crown princes, chief executives of major investment banks, oil companies, arms manufacturers – in fact, every powerful global corporation you can think of. Their list of personnel reads like a Who's Who of the most robust men on earth. And they are mostly men. Everyone from Donald Rumsfeld to David Rockefeller. The most powerful people on the planet, shaping our lives and our destinies, and keeping the wealth and power for the select few. So, although you and I may not like them, approve of them, isn't it good to know that at least we've got one of them on our side?'

'Dennis Lorcan? But all he's done is give money to charity.'

'At least he's involved with Malcolm Reeves, who is attempting to expose these paedophiles.'

Marianne stroked Mike's leg affectionately. 'I know you think I'm fussing, but I worry about what you're getting into. At the same time, I feel…well, at least you're doing something important.'

'As opposed to what I usually do – snoop at keyholes to spy on adulterous couples.'

'I didn't say that.'

He laughed to show her he was joking. 'You didn't have to.'

'Just promise me one thing, darling.'

'What's that?'

'If things start to look risky, back off.'

'You mean just drop everything? Walk away as if nothing's happened.'

'Yes, that's precisely what I do mean. I don't want Natalie to lose a father.'

'Yes, to lose one father looks like an accident, to lose two…'

'She's only ever had one father,' Marianne interrupted. 'And that's you. So, promise me you won't do anything dangerous.'

'OK. If I think things are getting hairy, I'll get in touch with some old colleagues in the Met for some support. I promise. How's that?'

He braked sharply as they sped down the hill towards Putney. Marianne slammed her foot on an imaginary brake.

'What are you doing? Trying to wake me up?'

Mike laughed. 'I just remembered that speed camera on the way here. Good, we should be home by eleven thirty.'

'Why? Have you got something planned for tonight?'

'Yes. I intend to open a bottle of wine. I've got some catching up to do.'

Chapter 10

Monday 17 March 2014

The meetings were never in the same place twice Gormen observed as he got into one of the lifts at Waterstone's bookstore in Piccadilly. He checked the time on his Rolex. Thirty seconds to ten a.m. By the time he got out of the lift on the fifth floor and walked into the wine bar, he would be bang on time.

But there was something worrying about this meeting. He sensed there was something very wrong, and there was a finger of blame pointing at him. The call had been cursory. Short, sharp and charged with hostility, and he wondered what he had done wrong, if anything.

The lift bell pinged as the doors slid open, and the automated voice gave him the floor number and told him the doors were opening. He turned right and walked into the bar. Marshall was sitting in a far corner near the window with a view of the skyline. He had obviously chosen this location at this time knowing there would be hardly anyone here just yet, although there were two Japanese men sitting a few tables away, drinking large glasses of white wine, and in another corner a man with a rucksack by his feet sat at a table drinking coffee, reading a paperback book.

As he went to sit down, Marshall waved an index finger at the large coffee in front of him, then pointed to the bar. 'Go and get yourself a coffee, so we're not interrupted by the service. We need to talk.'

As he ordered a large cappuccino at the bar, Gormen watched his hand shaking slightly as he counted and sorted the coins in his hand to pay for it. He let the coins drop noisily onto the counter, calming himself by pushing each coin neatly to one side until he had the right amount. It was a way of calming his nerves. Although nothing much scared him, he always felt a deep unease whenever he met Marshall. He glanced over his shoulder to where his contact sat. The man was staring at him. Unblinking and unmoving. Like a lizard on a rock. That was how Gormen thought of him. Some sort of reptile. Cold blooded. His shaven head smooth and shiny, with sunken cheeks and indentations at the sides of his head as if he was imploding.

He turned away from the man's unnerving stare and picked up his coffee. Holding the saucer with one hand, and the cup in the other to stop it from shaking and rattling, he carried it over to Marshall's table.

'Is something wrong?' he asked as he sat down, knowing Marshall liked to get straight to the point.

Even when things ran smoothly, he still felt keyed up in the man's company. It would have helped if he knew his first name. It didn't feel right calling him by his surname, like an old public-school acquaintance, and there was no way he was going to call him *Mr* Marshall, so he never addressed him by any name.

'After you eradicated the problem in two-thousand and six,' Marshall began, accusation heavy in his tone, 'you killed the laptop and hard drive, yes?'

Gormen nodded, wondering where this was leading.

'What did you do with the memory stick?'

So that was it. What had gone wrong? Why did Marshall suspect him of hanging on to it? And how could he possibly know after all these years? Gormen had hidden it, concealed it where no one could find it. He hadn't intended using it. Unless he was cornered like an animal. But even if Marshall suspected him of hanging on to the document, there was no way he could possibly know for certain. And Gormen knew enough about the psychology of interrogation techniques, so he held Marshall's gaze with a steady look, never once letting his eyes flicker in another direction.

'I destroyed it. Why?'

'How did you destroy it?'

'I smashed it to smithereens with a hammer. There was no way that could be pieced together again. Even if the bits were dug up from a landfill site.' He chuckled to show how ridiculous it was.

Marshall stared at him coldly, like an interrogator waiting for a confession. 'And you're sure about this?'

'Of course, I am. I smashed it myself. As soon as I got back to London.'

He moved to pick up his cup, then stopped, knowing his hand would shake. Marshall smiled humourlessly, almost as if he knew the reason for Gormen's hesitation.

'Drink your coffee before it gets cold,' he said, his eyes narrowing slightly, waiting for Gormen's response.

Gormen nodded and raised the cup, holding it steady in both hands. He blew on it and took a sip, relieved the adrenaline rush gave him the confidence to display a calm exterior, even though inwardly he suffered convulsions of fear. He placed the coffee cup back on its saucer and gave Marshall a quizzical expression.

'So, what's this all about? I don't understand what's up.'

'Someone claims they have the document, the one you took from Keneally.'

'But that's not possible. There must have been another copy made of those files. It can't possibly be the one I got from Keneally.' Heart pounding but outwardly maintaining a calm appearance, Gormen added, 'So who is this person who claims they've got the document?'

'We don't know. Not yet, anyway.'

Gormen tried not to let his relief show.

'But it's definitely a copy of the original document. The person has approached a publisher, intending to publish it as a book.'

'Jesus! That's bad.'

'It gets worse. The publisher's husband is none other than Malcolm Reeves, the MP who has started asking questions in the Commons about what happened to the original document given to Lord Albion and wants to reopen the investigation.'

'But if they've got the files, won't they just go ahead and publish?'

'It's not that simple. Apparently, they've only been given an extract. But it's enough to prove it comes from the original document. And the person who has the complete document is demanding money for the rest of it and intends approaching them within a week. Which doesn't give us much time.'

'What do you want me to do about it?'

Marshall folded his hands in front of him, almost as if in prayer, and stared into Gormen's eyes. The look was intense and searching, and Gormen could almost read his mind, knowing the man didn't believe his story about destroying the flash drive.

'I want you to tell me the truth.'

Gormen felt his throat drying up.

'The truth? What the hell are you talking about?'

'You didn't destroy that flash drive, did you?'

Gormen let sudden anger escalate as he glared back at Marshall. 'I told you. I smashed the fucking thing with a hammer.' And for the performance to be convincing he had to believe he was an innocent man affronted by accusations of guilt. 'There must have been another copy. For Christ's fucking sake, anyone can copy a file. There could be fucking dozens of them for all we know.'

Marshall raised a hand and smiled. 'OK. I believe you. I just had to be sure.'

Staring at him warily, Gormen sighed and shook his head, saying, 'Of course you believe me, because it happens to be true. And you have to ask yourself: why would I kill the golden goose?'

'Yes, you do all right from us, don't you? Quite a good living. And it's not as if you've had to do very much for it in recent years.'

Gormen shrugged. 'Well, things have been running along smoothly. Just one or two minor issues to sort out.'

'Up until now. Until this mysterious copy of the document turns up. It's something we'll have to keep our eye on and sort out when the time is right. I'll let you know when I need your services. It'll probably be sooner than you think.'

Gormen felt a cold trickle of fear run down his spine. Since the Keneally elimination, it was true, he'd had a cushier time of it. Now he might be called upon to take risks. The ultimate risk which could end up with him serving a life sentence. And he worried about that flash drive which he hadn't destroyed; which was concealed under the floorboards in his son's bedroom.

'How's your family?' Marshall asked, almost as if he could read his mind.

Gormen hated it whenever the man enquired about his wife and son. He got the impression there was always a concealed threat behind the question, polite as it seemed.

'Oh, ugh, I think they're fine,' he replied.

'Think?'

'I haven't seen them for a while. But you've just reminded me: I'll have to get in touch soon.'

'Your cover still intact?'

Gormen nodded, feeling relieved now the meeting seemed to be coming to an end.

'It's never been blown. And there's no reason it will be in future. Providing everything remains cool.'

Marshall grinned at Gormen's choice of words. 'Things are only cool when there are no complications. You must realize that. But now, with the emergence of this toxic document, which mustn't be allowed to go public under any circumstances, things have altered. We'll be keeping a close eye on these publishers and endeavouring to discover who has this file. And when we do—' He gave Gormen the hint of a thin smile, but his eyes were grey and cold. 'We'll be in touch.'

The meeting was over. Gormen rose, wondering whether to say a few words in parting, but decided against it. He nodded at Marshall, turned and exited. He saw by the indicators that all three lifts were on the ground floor, so he took the stairs, holding the handrail for support. He felt shaky, as though he wanted to lie down to recover after strenuous exercise.

And he needed to go home as soon as possible – maybe tomorrow. They weren't expecting him back for a while yet, but he needed to know if his son had found the flash drive. Because if he had....

He didn't like to think about that, or the consequences. He wished now he had done as he'd been asked back in 2006 and destroyed the file. On the other hand, he told himself, perhaps it was another flash drive which someone had copied. Keneally's wife, maybe?

He knew he was desperately trying to convince himself, but there was an awful doubt pounding away in his head like a bailiff's knock. What if it was his son who had found the file and approached the publisher? The ramifications from such an action would unleash terrible events which he couldn't in his most nightmarish thoughts contemplate. If that was the case, his son would become his next target.

And there was no way he could let that happen.

Chapter 11

Wednesday 19 March 2014

Having been thoroughly searched twice, and handed over all his belongings for safe keeping, which would be returned after the visit was over, Mike sat in the visitors' room at the table he'd been allocated and waited along with all the other visitors for the inmates to arrive.

Presently, keys jangled, and several officers ushered prisoners into the hall. Many of the female visitors greeted their husbands or boyfriends with sympathetic smiles and kissed briefly, as though the meeting was nothing more than a homecoming.

Having seen the old newspaper reports of Baldwin's trial, along with the convict's photographs, Mike expected to meet an even thinner, weasel-faced felon, shrunken beyond recognition. But he was surprised to find himself looking up at a healthier-looking specimen than the creature who was sentenced to life almost eight years ago. Baldwin's face had filled out, and his shoulders were broader, suggesting regular exercise, and his stomach was rounded. It flashed through Mike's brain that perhaps Baldwin was one of the few who thrived on prison grub.

'Mr Halliday?' Baldwin enquired, even though he knew which table Mike would be seated at.

Mike gestured to the seat opposite and told him to call him by his first name.

As he sat heavily, Baldwin said tentatively, 'Good to meet you, Mike.' It came out sounding like a question, as if he was testing the ground. 'My Mum says you might be able to get me out of here.'

It was straight to the point. Knowing he was probably the man's last remaining hope, Mike felt sorry for him. This was not going to be easy, and he knew the chances of proving Baldwin's innocence were slim.

'That depends.'

'On what?'

'On finding the man who did commit the murder.'

Baldwin froze, and his eyes turned glassy. Then suddenly, giving in to despair, he banged his head hard with the heel of his hand.

'Jesus Christ! I thought you came here to help me. You talked to my mother and she said you might be able to prove my innocence. I never killed him; you know.'

'I know you didn't.'

'Then how—' He gestured helplessly with open palms. 'How you gonna find the man who done it? D'you think some geezer's gonna own up to it after all these years. Oh, I done it, guvnor. I killed that Member of Parliament an' I thought it was time I confessed.'

His voice rose as he imitated a chastened killer, and Mike saw one of the prison officers make a move.

'Calm down, Terry.' He leant forward and whispered, hoping Baldwin would drop his voice to the same level. 'Listen to me. This man who stitched you up for the crime did it to destroy information Keneally had. And this information in the shape of a flash drive has come to light. Which means it could probably lead us to the killer. But what I need from you is as much information as you can give me, starting from the beginning. You said at your trial you met this man in a pub.'

'That's right. The Hob and Kettle in Crumpsall.'

'And how did you arrange to meet there?'

'I was up in court on a burglary charge, which I got off of, and he must have followed me from the court.'

'And he wanted you to steal a painting from an empty house, is that right?'

'Yeah, except I never knew it was fucking empty. It was up for rent. But I did find the suitcase that was stolen from Keneally's house. And I hadn't been there more than five minutes when the law pulls up outside, flashing lights and all.'

'Were the police questioned in court?'

'Of course they was.'

'And did they say why they were alerted to this empty house you burgled?'

'They says it was a neighbour who phoned. I've had eight years to think about this. The cops couldn't tell who this neighbour was. Stands to reason it must've been the guy who topped Keneally.' Baldwin laughed bitterly. 'Yeah, I don't have to tell you how I was well and truly stitched up. Leaving a fucking fag lighter at the scene of the crime? Leave it out. It had my fucking prints on it cos that evil bastard left it lying on the table at the Hob and Kettle that night. He must've stuck it in a bag when I was out in the bog. I should've fucking realized.'

'Why would you? When you were held in custody after the neighbour telephoned the police, how soon after did they discover Keneally's house had been burgled and he'd been murdered?'

'Well, as the house I burgled was empty, they wanted to know where I'd got the stuff in the suitcase which was in the empty house. I couldn't tell them, cos I never had a clue. I told them the truth cos I never knew anyone had been murdered. I thought I was just up for a minor housebreaking charge, especially as the fucking house was empty.'

'So how did they discover Keneally's murder?'

'They found his diary with his name on it in the suitcase.'

'And they called around to investigate?'

'When I was arrested, it was in the early hours of Monday morning. Later on, after they searched the suitcase and found his diary, the cops went to his house. That's when they found him.'

Mike looked thoughtfully towards the ceiling as he tried to picture the scene.

'Just a minute, Terry: why would the police have broken in to Keneally's place without knowing there was anything wrong?'

'That's just it. Apparently, they found the door was open, so they let themselves in. That's when they found him. The police made out I panicked an' left hurriedly, leaving the door open.'

'And an hour later you go and burgle an empty house. Did no one ask what you did in the hour between killing the MP and burgling the empty house?'

'My defence mentioned it in court, but the prosecution suggested I was a cold bastard and sat in my van recovering before I committed the second burglary.'

'And didn't the defence mention the suitcase? Why would you take it with you into the empty house? You would have left it in the van.'

Baldwin shook his head rapidly. 'The defence never mentioned it. And the prosecution made out I was stupid as well as cold-blooded.'

'Think back to the meeting with this man in the pub, Terry. While you were there, you'd have got a good look at this man. Can you describe him to me?'

Baldwin bit his bottom lip as he tried to remember. 'I think he must've been over six feet, cos I'm only five-seven, and I noticed he was quite tall when he stood up. He had darkish hair – you know – dark brown, but it was hard to tell cos it was cropped short. Trouble was, his face was a bit ordinary, except—'

'Except?' Mike prompted.

'Although he was white and looked English, his features looked like he might have been related to a black geezer way back in the past. His nose was wide, and he had thick lips. But not so as you'd notice. Apart from that, he looked ordinary. I only remember his face looking like I just described it cos I've had years to think about it.'

'So d'you think you could identify him, if you saw him again?'

Baldwin chuckled. 'Is the Pope a Catholic?'

Mike saw Baldwin was more relaxed now, now that he was remembering, getting it off his chest, and most importantly talking to someone who was trying to help him.

'Could you guess this man's age?'

'Somewhere in his late thirties, I reckon. Or he could've been in his forties.'

'So, he'd be late forties or early fifties now. If I managed to get a photo of this man—'

'Yeah, I think I'd recognize him. People don't change that much.'

From the way Mike looked at him, Baldwin could guess what he was thinking, and added, 'I know I've changed, put on a bit of weight, but you still recognized me right away.'

It was true. Although the runt in the newspaper photographs was scrawny and looked to be in ill-health, Mike had to admit the man sitting opposite him was easily identifiable, in spite of his improved appearance.

'Yes, people don't change that much. I think maybe I could recognize someone I was at school with. But there's something I need to know, Terry.'

Mike paused, wondering how the burglar would take it.

'Go on.'

'I know you didn't kill John Keneally. And you claimed the man who set you up wanted you to steal a picture for him. When you broke into that empty house, did you have an accomplice?'

Clenching his fists to keep his anger in check, Baldwin breathed in noisily through his nostrils and gave Mike a venomous look.

'I thought you was here to try and help me.'

'I am.'

'Yeah? Well, if you knew about the painting, you must have read about it in the papers. You know fucking well I never had no accomplice.'

'What happened to Keneally's laptop?'

'Oh, for fuck's sake! Do I need to spell it out? The guy who topped him took it. You're just like the rest of them – making up a story about an accomplice. It looks to me as if there's people who wanted whoever murdered him to get away with it.'

'What gives you that impression?'

'Everything about it stinks. What was on that laptop that was so important? His wife mentioned it during the trial, and that's when they accused me of having an accomplice and giving him the laptop. And then it was all forgotten, like. No one gives it another thought. And I'm accused of murdering an MP for a few poxy household goods.'

'Yes,' Mike agreed. 'They wanted it to look like a senseless crime.'

'They?'

'It's starting to look as if this is part of a larger conspiracy.'

'Well, hallelujah and thank fuck for that. But are you the only one who's managed to work it out?'

Mike shook his head. 'I have a client who has employed me to find out what happened, Terry. It may take a few more weeks, but I'm hoping to ID the man who murdered Keneally. As soon as I find him, I'll get back up here with his picture and you'll be able to confirm it for me. That should get the wheels rolling, and then, as there'll be fresh evidence, we can make a new application for your release'

Suddenly, without warning, tears sprang into Baldwin's eyes and streamed freely down his cheeks. He made no effort to stem them or wipe his face, as if the tears soothed him.

'Thank you, Mike. I appreciate what you're doing. Thank you.'

Chapter 12

Knowing his wife was at the doctor's surgery until at least five, where she had worked as a receptionist since the early nineties, Gormen decided the best time to check and see if the memory stick was still in place was mid-afternoon. She and Justin thought he was on the other side of the world, so returning home now would require some explanation. Not that it was so difficult to lie and pretend. His whole life was a deception, a brilliantly cunning masquerade, which always gave him a buzz. Even his marriage was a sham. After Pauline became pregnant in 1995, they married. But what gave him the biggest buzz of all was the fact that she became his legal spouse in his false identity, a name stolen from a child who died in the 1980s. Her marriage certificate, and Justin's birth certificate, were in his false name, and he often wondered about the legality of such a contract.

As he turned into the street where they lived, not far from Wood Green Tube station, and saw the rows of squat terraced houses in this drab multi-cultural street, he smiled. This was the other side of his dual identity coin. Returning from his smart Docklands flat to this very ordinary existence. For years he had enjoyed living a double life, and it gave him the ultimate satisfaction, adapting to each separate life, knowing he could step out of one world and into another with hardly anyone knowing. Even close friends remained unaware of his two lives. But there were some who knew about his dual identity. Those for whom he worked. Those who owned him was nearer the truth, especially now he was in so deep. But he was intelligent enough to accept that he had to serve someone in a higher authority, even though it remained a mystery who his true masters were. Still, at least it afforded him two contrasting lifestyles, which was how he liked to operate.

He parked his Citroën no more than fifty yards from his house, the one purchased in Mr and Mrs Gormen's name, with a joint mortgage, all of which he paid for, leaving Pauline to deal with the household bills. A fair arrangement, he thought.

He cut the engine and remained seated in the car for a minute, staring at the front door. The fact that he considered this to be his true home he never for a moment thought strange. He smiled, almost chuckled indulgently at the ordinariness of the house, and the care his wife took over its appearance. The hanging basket on one side of the small porch, and the highly polished brass letter box, were symbols of his solicitous personality as parent and husband. He felt he had arrived home at last. This was a genuine family residence, even though he could step out of it whenever he chose and satisfy his bachelor life in Docklands. And here, having returned to his real home, he felt deep loyalty towards Pauline and Justin, loved them, and would never let anyone harm them. They were his cushion, and just one of the reasons for his existence in at least half his life.

But there was now the added worry of the document surfacing, which either his son had discovered and approached a publisher, or there was another copy of the dossier. He hoped and prayed it was the latter and convinced himself Keneally may have given another copy to someone. All it took was another memory stick loaded in a computer and the transfer could happen in a second. First of all, though, he decided he would see if the memory stick was still intact in its hiding place. If it was, then there would be no need to confront Justin, as there was probably another copy on the loose.

Before going indoors, he got the small suitcase out of the boot. Although he had clothes and personal belongings here at his home in Wood Green, he still had to keep up the pretence that he had been away for a while on a long journey, so he had filled it with gear from his Docklands flat.

As soon as he unlocked the front door and stepped inside, and put his suitcase down, Justin appeared at the top of the stairs.

'Dad! What are you doing home?'

'Things got a bit tricky out there with the government, so here I am.'

He spread his hands out in a welcoming gesture, frowning at his son's spindly frame as he came downstairs, and worried if he was eating enough, as any normal parent would. Justin's black jeans fading to dark grey were baggy and he wore a sweatshirt with an American Ivy League college logo on the front.

'Good to be home, Justin,' he said as his son stepped off the bottom stair. He hugged him briefly and took a step back to look at him. 'You eating enough? You look a bit – well, a bit undernourished. Mum not looking after you?'

Justin shrugged and pursed his lips. 'Yeah. But she's out all day. And some weekends she goes away on these Animal Rights demos.'

Gormen felt irritation rising to the surface, although he tried to keep it at bay, knowing how being away from home for long periods of time must affect his son. He controlled himself and said quietly, 'You're eighteen now, Justin. You're quite capable of looking after yourself. Your mother works to pay the bills.'

'I know. And I've looked for work but—'

A petulant shrug again, which Gormen dismissed as typical teen attitude. He wanted to suggest work along similar lines to his own – well, his work in the past when he started out. But that would mean blowing his cover, so that was out of the question. And then he remembered why he was here. To check out the concealed memory stick.

Smiling, he reached into his back pocket, drew out his wallet, and gave his son two twenty-pound notes.

'What's that for, Dad?'

'You had lunch yet?'

Justin shook his head and chuckled. 'I've not had breakfast yet. I got straight onto the computer and forgot the time?'

Gormen sighed and shook his head. 'Go and get us a takeaway, and beer to wash it down.'

'Beer?'

'Why not? You're eighteen now. You need ID?'

'No, they know me at the off-licence. Shall I get pizzas?'

'Whatever you like.'

'Thanks, Dad.'

Gormen watched as his son grabbed a parka from the hall coat peg, and hurried out of the front door, slamming it. Gormen stood, deliberately controlling his breath to calm himself. He was scared at finding the flash drive missing, which would mean a terrible confrontation with his son, and then the possibility that his cover might be blown after all these years. But the worst fear of all was what would happen if Marshall found out.

Just in case Justin forgot anything and returned suddenly, he followed him out of the front door, pretending he might have left something in the car. But as soon as he saw his son turning the corner onto the main road, he went back indoors and hurried upstairs to Justin's room.

He knelt down behind the door, took a penknife out of his pocket, slid a blade out and eased a corner of the carpet up. He took his time, careful not to tear the edges of the carpet, then carefully slid out a couple of tacks that had been used to nail it down. As he pushed the floorboard, then raised it, his eyes straining into the dark hole, a voice in his head begged for the memory stick to be there.

He looked down into the cavity, and there it was, the yellow plastic USB drive, the one he had killed John Keneally for, lying just where he had left it. He blew his breath out, relieved this flash drive was not the culprit. There was obviously another copy out there. There could well be several in someone's possession. He felt relieved his own immediate worries were over. He was off the hook. His son was innocent. Perhaps he should now destroy the stick. But if another one had surfaced, then there wasn't much point. And he might still need this one as a guarantee of his safety.

And then he stared at the yellow plastic stick. Had he placed it in that position? He couldn't be one hundred per cent certain, but he could swear he had placed the stick with the cover protecting the USB plug pointing towards the door. Now it was facing the other way. No, he couldn't be sure. His mind must be playing tricks. He was becoming paranoid. Scared of what would happen if they found out he had kept Keneally's file.

On an impulse, he decided the best course would be to take the memory stick – he could decide what to do with it later – and either destroy it or find somewhere else to conceal it. Not at his Docklands flat, that was for sure. If they suspected him of keeping the file, they might turn the flat over at some stage to hunt for it.

He grabbed the memory stick and shoved it into the zippered pocket inside his anorak, then put the floorboard back into place, shut the penknife, and used the side of it to bang the tacks back in place.

Frowning deeply, he stood up and looked at his son's computer. If Justin had found the USB drive, he might have read it and copied it on his computer. Gormen thought it would take a while for his son to order pizzas and buy the beer, so he went to the desk and saw the computer was in sleep mode. He clicked the start button, but it required a password to open it.

He thought about it for a moment. Justin loved their cat Marmite. He typed it in and got the message telling him it was wrong. What else could it be? He knew Justin had a girlfriend. What the hell was her name? And then he remembered. Eva. That was it. Just three letters. A little short for a password. Could Eva be the diminutive of a longer name. Evangeline or Evangelina, maybe. He typed them in, one at a time, but neither gave him access. He racked his brains for anything his son might use, staring at the screen for ages, immobilized, his mind blank as he waited for an inspired guess to light up in his brain. Nothing. It was then he realized how little he knew about Justin, having spent so little time with him. He'd been away for months at a time – once for a stretch of nearly six months. No wonder he knew so little about his son.

He snapped out of his reverie as the front door slammed, and then his son called out from the bottom of the stairs:

'Dad? Where are you?'

He froze guiltily. Although it was his home as much as Justin's, and he was perfectly entitled to be in his son's room, he suddenly felt vulnerable. He always had to be the one in control. Now for the first time in years he was conscious of how his world might disintegrate unless he restored order to his unscrupulous occupation.

Hearing Justin walking along the hall and going into the kitchen, he clicked the computer back into sleep mode, then walked stealthily out of the bedroom, climbed the four steps on the landing, tiptoed into the bathroom and flushed the toilet cistern.

After washing his hands, he came downstairs, whistling happily, and calmly entered the kitchen, did what he always did whenever he found himself in a tight spot – behaved as if he hadn't a care in the world.

Chapter 13

On the train back from Manchester, Mike thought about his meeting with Baldwin, hopelessly aware he hadn't got information of any real value. But at least he didn't have to rely entirely on newspaper reports of the trial and speaking to the burglar in person convinced him the man was innocent of Keneally's murder. The only useful bit of information was the missing hour between the murder and the burglary of the empty house, which meant Baldwin was still driving through Manchester as the murder took place. Why hadn't the police checked this out? Why hadn't they looked at CCTV around the time Baldwin claimed he set off for Whaley Bridge? And now, with a gap of eight years, there was no likelihood of digging this up as evidence.

Although Jo Reeves was his client, having met the forlorn, overweight burglar's mother Tracey, whose fading-hope eyes clung to the desperate dream that one day her son might be exonerated and released, he felt a deep compassion for her. That her son was once an unregenerate thief was not in any doubt, but the eight years inside may have changed him, and he didn't deserve a life sentence for a murder he didn't commit. And so, he had offered Baldwin's mother the slim hope that he would do all he could to help secure her son's release. Mike knew it was an uphill battle, because he was only too aware from his time in the Met that most crimes are solved quickly, not after a gap of eight years, unless new forensic evidence comes to light.

He sighed and stifled a yawn. It had been a long and weary day, first the train journey in the crowded Standard Class compartment, then the meeting with Baldwin's mother late morning, followed by the visit to the Manchester prison shortly afterwards, and now the return journey back to Euston. At least the return journey was not so busy, and he managed to find a seat at a table with no one sitting next to him. As the train sped south, he searched the internet on his tablet, attempting to discover the whereabouts of the Keneally family, his wife or children. He drew a blank as far as the MP's wife Elizabeth Keneally was concerned, but discovered he had two children, one of each sex. He trolled the social media but found nothing for the son whose name was Sean Keneally – at least, there was no one of that name who had a connection with the murdered MP. Which didn't surprise him, as there were still thousands of people who never touched the social media, and either regarded it with suspicion or couldn't be bothered with it. But he had more luck where the daughter was concerned because Julia Keneally never married, and was a general practitioner living in St Albans. It wasn't difficult to find her medical practice and an email address, so he sent her a short email, saying he was looking into Terry Baldwin's case, and there may have been a miscarriage of justice, gave his mobile number, and asked her to ring him as soon as possible.

As the train left Stafford station, he looked at his watch. Nearly 5.15. He looked St Albans up on the map and saw it was less than ten miles from Watford; even catching a cab from there wouldn't be out of the question. What he really wanted to do was talk to Keneally's wife, but he knew the only possible way of finding her was through the daughter, and she might be reluctant to give her mother's contact details to a complete stranger on the phone. Experience had taught him it was easier to get information out of people face to face. That was if she responded to his email. But just coming up to six, and only five minutes from Watford, he debated whether or not to get off the train, hoping Dr Julia Keneally might contact him. Guessing most GPs' surgeries ended about six, he made a snap decision and left the train at Watford.

He went into the station buffet, bought a can of lager, sat at a table and sent Keneally's daughter another email, telling her he was at Watford station, would like to meet her to discuss the terrible events of eight years ago, and could be in St Albans in less than half an hour. Less than five minutes after the email was sent, his mobile rang. An unknown number. He pressed the receive symbol.

'Hello? Mike Halliday,' he said, feeling that slight surge of excitement which, he got whenever there was a response to his enquiries.

'It's Julia Keneally here.'

'Thank you for responding to my emails Dr Keneally. I appreciate it.'

'Though I really can't see how I can help. I appreciate you are doing all you can to help Mr Baldwin – and none of the family ever thought he was guilty – but unfortunately none of us know anything which might help his case.'

'What about your mother?'

There was a slight pause before Julia Keneally answered.

'Even if Mum did know something – which I very much doubt – I'm afraid she wouldn't be able to provide you with any information now. Mum's in a home, and she has Alzheimer's. Unfortunately, it's at a quite advanced stage, so she doesn't recall much that happened in recent years, just confused events and people she may have known forty years ago.'

Mike stifled a sigh. 'Oh, I'm sorry to hear that. But you don't know whether or not she may have had a copy of the files that were missing, presumed stolen, from your father, do you? Maybe on another memory stick, or even a hard copy, which she could have passed on to someone else.'

'No, I'm sorry. I don't ever recall her mentioning copies of the files. I'm sure she would have done in view of the information that came out during the trial. And, of course, she knew what Dad was working on.'

'What about your brother? Would he have any information?'

'Richard's knowledge of anything bordering on politics is zilch.' She gave an ironic chuckle. 'He's an artist and he's lived in Brittany since the late nineties. He refuses to have anything to do with politics. It was always a source of discontentment in our family when he was growing up. I'm afraid, that's that. Sorry I couldn't be of any help.'

Mike took this as his cue to end the call. 'Well, thank you for your time and taking the trouble to call me, Dr Keneally.'

'Well, good luck with your investigations. I hope you find the man who really killed our father. I'd like to see him brought to justice.'

'I'll see what I can do.'

He ended the call and checked her number. It was a blocked call. He couldn't blame her, contacting a total stranger to talk about her father's murder. If he needed to get in touch with her, he would have to email, though he doubted there would be any reason to contact her again.

He finished his beer and went out onto the platform and checked the indicator. There was a London train in ten minutes. Relieved he hadn't made a wasted journey to St Albans, and would be home by about half-seven, he also felt frustrated by the sheer lack of information for all his efforts. Although, during his years in the police, he knew how important elimination is in an investigation, and he had at least eliminated any further copies of the document leaking from Keneally's family.

But the frustration he felt, as he waited for the next London train, almost amounted to a deep anger. Perhaps it was the end result of a long day spent chasing ghosts, or maybe it was because he felt the need to fast track his investigation, especially as his mounting anger wanted to put an end to the child abuse taking place at that guest house in north London.

He resolved he would speed things up tomorrow and pay the guest house a visit. It was time to ignore advice about doing things by the book.

Time to use robust methods.

Chapter 14

Having been away from his home in Wood Green for more than two weeks – and before that he was away for almost six months – Gormen became displeased, as he often did, with just how cramped and untidy the dining room at the back of the house was, especially when he compared it to his spacious Docklands apartment, where he lived his contrasting life in ultra-modern minimalist surroundings.

Making a comparison, he guessed the square footage of his Docklands apartment was greater than his Wood Green house, which was an Edwardian two-up, two-down, and the small kitchen at the back of the dining room was an extension, built in the late 1940s, along with the upstairs bathroom above it. Prior to that there had been no bathroom, simply an outside WC, and the occupants of the early twentieth century used a tin bath in front of the fire. Because Gormen paid the mortgage on the house, every month his wife diligently saved a quarter of her salary and gradually modernised each room. Even though space was at a premium, at least it looked comfortable and homely in a rather trendy middle-class way, the doors stripped back to their natural wood, the doorknobs made of white china with flowery designs.

Gormen and his son sat at the antique stripped-pine table, a table which was far too big for the room, and had become a convenient dumping ground for all manner of objects: Pauline's make up box and a mirror, where she made last minute adjustments to her appearance before dashing off to work; National Geographic magazines, appropriated from the surgery where she worked; envelopes containing invoices and bills; an Oxford Concise English Dictionary; a small wind-up torch; three scented candles on blue and white china saucers; a box of sticky paper notes; and several paperback books on planet-saving subjects. And to add to the untidiness of the table there was now a large Domino pizza box, two dinner plates scattered with the skeletons of pizza crusts, and four empty Carlsberg cans.

For the last hour Gormen had struggled to keep the conversation going with his son and both had lapsed into an awkward silence. When they first sat down to eat, Justin asked his father why he hadn't gone to Indonesia as planned, and the desultory reply gave him grounds for suspicion. For years he believed his father was a committed Greenpeace warrior travelling to different parts of the globe to deal with situations where governments or corporations were ruining the environment or destroying the natural habitat of vulnerable wildlife. And when his father mumbled a perfunctory excuse about Greenpeace not needing him for a while, he began wondering about the stories his father told them whenever he came home from a world-saving expedition. The exploits weren't exactly fanciful, but Justin had taken to searching online for the events and comparing them to what his father said. Sometimes they were accurate, but Justin realized that anyone doing a little research could come up with the same stories. And then there was the memory stick he had found under the floorboard. How had it got there and who had put it there? When he read it, he realized it may have had something to do with his father, and his mind whirled with a torrent of questions concerning his father's identity. How had he and his mother never noticed that whenever the Greenpeace warrior returned from some exploit in a tropical clime he was as pale as the day he left? He remembered his mother mentioning it once – a long time ago, when he was still at school – and his father went into a long and involved account of time spent concealing his identity by wearing balaclavas whenever action was called for. For years he believed it, but not now he had found the file and read it. He surmised his father was mixed up in something dodgy, and he suspected it had nothing to do with saving the planet. Then, feeling guilty about distrusting his father, whose exploits in saving the planet he admired, in spite of the long absences he and his mother suffered, he told himself he was being unnecessarily suspicious. After all, the document was clearly compiled some time in the eighties, before he was born, so it could have been hidden many years ago.

When he sat down at his computer and read the file, at first, he felt overwhelming disgust and wanted to contact the press and bring those bastards in government down, the whole corrupt lot of them. It was Eva who stopped him, suggesting they could still do it and make money out of it. He hadn't taken much persuading, especially as he'd heard of celebrities and politicians selling their memoirs for six figure sums. And English was the one subject he'd been good at in school. Neither he nor Eva at that stage thought it was anything to do with his father, and it was simply a rogue file that had somehow been placed there before his parents bought the house. Neither of them worked out that during the eighties a document would have been stored on a floppy disk.

Justin knocked back the remaining beer in the can and crushed it. He was fed up with the stifling silence and tricky conversation and wanted to get his headphones and listen to music. And that was when something clicked in his brain. Thinking about music downloads instead of CDs, the link took him to discs. Of course! Back in the eighties data was stored on a floppy disk, and he knew enough about computing to realize memory sticks weren't around back then and he was mistaken in thinking the USB flash drive was hidden before his parents bought the house.

To break the monotony of their silence, Gormen rose, trying not to sigh. 'Another beer?' he offered.

'Yeah, why not?' Justin replied.

While his father went to the fridge to get the beer, Justin picked up the pizza box and empty beer cans. 'I'll just take these out front and stick them in the bin.'

He carried them out of the front door and dropped them in the wheelie bin in their tiny paved area at the front of the house. As he returned along the hall and glanced up the stairs, he thought about the memory stick lying there in its hiding place. He looked at his watch. It was gone six. His mother would be home any minute now.

As he sat at the kitchen table again, his father handed him another beer, then remained standing.

'You not having another?' Justin asked.

Gormen shook his head and stuck his hands in his trouser pockets. 'Might have one a bit later.' He felt restless and was worried about Marshall and the resurfacing of the documents.

Justin sensed there was something wrong and looked up at his father, his eyes narrowing. 'If Indonesia was cancelled, where were you for the past week?'

'Paris.'

'Why Paris?'

'That was where the planning meetings took place. All highly secretive, of course.'

'Of course.'

Something in his son's tone put Gormen on his guard. Had he imagined it – was there suspicion in that simple statement? And the way his son now avoided eye contact with him. He thought of embellishing the lie, providing details about Paris. He knew the city well, making regular visits there with one of his girlfriends. And he knew the importance of details when it came to lying.

'The reason for choosing Paris is because the French members…' he began, then was relieved to hear Pauline's key in the front door.

'Hello? Peter?' she called out.

'In here,' he replied.

She entered the dining room excitedly and a trifle breathlessly. 'I thought I spotted your car,' Dumping her handbag on the kitchen table, she threw her arms around Gormen and kissed him. When she drew back, she looked him in the eye questioningly. 'But you're supposed to be in Indonesia to stop that deforestation. What's happened?'

'We had a meeting about it in Paris, and it was cancelled. So – I came home.'

Pauline didn't question the fact that he'd been in Paris, but from the corner of his eye he could feel Justin staring intently at him. He avoided looking in his direction, choosing instead to gaze into his wife's eyes. Then he smiled and held her at arm's length, taking pleasure in her appearance as if he had been away a lot longer than a few weeks. She was still attractive in a cute and cuddly way, her jet-black hair like a fine curtain, and her pale delicate face which highlighted the green in her eyes. He never found it difficult to show his love for her, however much he lied, because every time he was with her, he was able to convince himself that she was the one. His one true love. His home was his bolthole, the setting to which he could escape from the black reality of his occupation.

'I'm glad to see you home, Peter,' she said. 'I really am. But those thousands of trees that are being sacrificed for palm oil—'

'Don't worry,' he assured her. 'I'll be going out there very soon. At the moment it's too dangerous.'

'You must tell me all about the talks in Paris. First, I'll make us something to eat.'

'Sorry, Pauline, but Justin and I have already eaten.' He gestured to the dinner plates.

Pauline stared at the crusts and shook her head. 'Not pizza again, Justin. What sort of topping did you have? The meat they use in those places is probably factory farmed.'

Justin avoided looking at his father, guessing he might back him up and deny the pepperoni topping. 'It's OK, Mum. We had the seafood one – anchovies and tuna.'

His father nodded, colluding in the lie.

Sighing, his mother said, 'I don't know, Justin – you'll turn into a pizza one of these days. And I see you're on the beer.'

'Nothing wrong with that, is there?'

'I'm just going to put the kettle on. I don't suppose you want any tea?'

'No thanks. I'll take this beer up to my room, there's a couple of things I wanna research online.'

His mother's eyes lit up. 'Anything to do with the potential job you hinted at?'

'Maybe.'

'I don't know why you're being so secretive about it.'

Justin picked up his can of beer and stood up. 'Yeah, well – I'll leave you to it.'

As he left the room, Gormen gave his wife a quizzical stare. 'What's this about a job?'

'He won't say. But a few days ago I was on about him hanging around the house and not looking for work and he said he had a big project coming up. Something really big, he said. But he won't tell me what it is.'

Gormen frowned deeply.

'What's wrong?'

'Nothing. I just worry about him, that's all.'

Pauline slid her hand down Gormen's arm and smiled. 'At least he's got something in mind. I only hope it works out for him. Now, I'll make some tea, shall I? Then you can tell me all about why the Indonesia protest has been cancelled.'

He knew his wife would probably check out the Greenpeace website later, and she would discover the protest and talks were still going ahead, so he had to think of an excuse as to why he wouldn't be participating in the exercise.

***

As soon as Justin shut the bedroom door, he leant back against it, leaving it for a moment before checking the hiding place under the floorboard, just in case his father or mother decided to come up to his room for some reason. He heard the muffled sounds of them talking in the room below and thought it was safe to check the cavity.

He knelt down hurriedly and tugged the carpet, noticing how much more frayed the edges were becoming, then raised the floorboard and stared into the empty hole. There was nothing there. The memory stick was gone. And it didn't take a lot of working out to guess when it happened. No wonder his father had been so considerate in sending him out for beer and pizzas.

After replacing the floorboard and carpet, he sat on the edge of his bed thinking it through. His father had obviously taken the flash drive, but Justin had no idea what he planned to do with it. Blackmail, perhaps? And what was his old man doing with it in the first place?

He chewed his bottom lip as he thought about it. He was confused. For years he had admired his father, thinking he was an activist, involved in Green issues. But now he guessed his father was involved in something dirty and despicable; something to do with child abuse. Why else would he have hidden the stick containing the files in the first place? And why had he now removed it? A thought struck him. Perhaps his father intended making the document public, which would mean he and Eva would miss out not only on a massive payment, but all the glory attached to setting the ball rolling to expose those evil bastards.

Now was the time to make his move and contact the publishers again. No later than tomorrow. Especially as his father had the memory stick containing the document. Not that it mattered now because Eva had insisted they make another copy. He was glad he had listened to her.

And soon it would be payday.

Chapter 15

While Marianne prepared dinner, and Natalie was in her room supposedly doing her homework, Mike sat at the workstation in his study and searched the internet for any information about the named and shamed paedophiles – mainly Cyril Smith and Jimmy Savile. It incensed him to think how convenient it was for those two grossly indecent offenders to die before justice could be served, and he suspected there were many other public figures from the seventies and eighties who might conveniently pass away peacefully before being exposed as child abusers and given hefty jail sentences.

Mike's disgust grew as he searched the web for newspaper articles and websites devoted to disclosing the unpalatable truth about Savile and Smith, and he felt sickened as he delved deeper and deeper into this nightmare world of paedophiles. Repelled by every word he read on the subject, his revulsion swelled like a malignant growth as he read about Savile denying he ever went to Haut de la Garenne, a children's home in Jersey, where it was rumoured that children had been abused then murdered. But there was a photograph of Savile surrounded by children at the home, smiling like an evil predator. Nauseated, he clicked away from the site and found another site with photographs of the celebrity's funeral. There were a few well-known figures Mike recognized, but he was aware that many celebrities were genuinely fooled by Savile's diabolical manipulations. But the thing that struck him the most was the number of Freemasons there were in attendance, dressed in the regalia of their arcane fellowship. And then he spotted a Freemason in the background, a long way from the coffin, clearly apprehensive at being too visible.

Mike peered closely at the photograph. The face looked familiar. But where from? He clicked the mouse to enlarge the photograph, but it became too grainy for him to identify the man. He returned to the clearer picture, took a magnifying glass out of his desk drawer, and studied the man's face carefully. There was no way he could put a name to the face, but suddenly he remembered who he was and when they had met.

It was about four years ago, when he worked in counter terrorism. He remembered his boss, Detective Chief Superintendent Nash, ordering him to be interviewed in a secure environment by a total stranger, a man who had to remain anonymous for reasons of state security. Mike guessed this man was either MI5 or MI6 and wanted information about a group of suspected terrorists in north London.

He squinted and stared at the photo for a long time. He was certain this was the same man. A secret service agent, dressed in Freemason regalia, and attending Savile's funeral.

Just then, Marianne called out that dinner was ready, so he came out of the site and closed the computer.

***

After Natalie had gone to bed, they sat for a while watching *Newsnight*, which happened to have an item about paedophiles, with a psychologist explaining there was a difference between child abusers and paedophiles. Mike reached for the remote and switched it off in disgust.

'Is it getting to you?' Marianne asked.

Mike sounded angry when he spoke, as if Marianne had said something to upset him.

'How dare that psychologist claim there is a difference between abusers and paedophiles. Don't paedophiles abuse children? Their victims are probably traumatised and must live with the damage for the rest of their lives. Psychological damage can be just as bad as physical pain.'

'You didn't give her a chance. She may have got around to saying that.'

Mike gave a disgruntled mumble and raised himself from the sofa. 'Well, it leaves a nasty taste. So, I think a brandy nightcap will clean the palate. You going to join me?'

Marianne looked up, frowning concern. 'If you can't beat them, may as well.'

Mike went out to the kitchen and came back moments later with two liberal measures of cognac. He handed Marianne a glass, then sank heavily onto the sofa close to her. He sipped his brandy in brooding silence until Marianne asked him what was wrong.

'What do you think?' he said. 'The more I learn about this case, the worse it becomes. I find this whole network of Westminster paedophiles hard to comprehend. Greed and corruption for money I can understand. And even terror for ideological reasons. But it's beyond me this wanting to have sex with small children. Why for Christ's sake? Why? Some of these people are so influential they could snap their fingers and get loads of women or young men into their beds. Surely they can't be that inadequate they feel the need to destroy young lives by indulging in—'

Unable to continue, Mike wiped an eye with the back of a finger and sniffed. Marianne, seeing the tearful look in his eyes, took his hand and squeezed it affectionately.

'I never realized you felt so strongly about this, sweetheart.'

'It's just that I've never been directly involved before. And seeing those children at that guest house… It's all very well seeing things on TV or reading about them in the papers – well, it becomes sort of sanitized. But when you come up against it this close, it's hard for it not to affect you deeply.'

'It's bound to if you're a normal person.'

'I just wish I could understand why.'

'You're finding it hard to understand because you're a normal person, Mike. You had an ordinary childhood, brought up by parents who loved you…of course you find the idea of child abuse difficult to deal with. Unfortunately, it's not suddenly going to go away – you've got to face that.'

'I know.' He sighed deeply and took another sip of brandy. 'And the reason that psychologist gave about paedophiles fitting a profile of adults who were deprived of love and affection in their childhood….'

'What about it?

'I say bollocks to that. We should all of us be judged by our actions, not from our reasons or motives. If I were to beat you up tonight….'

'Please don't.'

'The end result is the same, whether I was suffering from depression, was drunk, resentful or whatever. You become injured by me. End of story.'

'Isn't that rather a simplistic view?'

'You mean people who are clinically depressed or suffering from schizophrenia sometimes commit violent crimes? Yes, I get all that. But I'm talking about rational, supposedly intelligent human beings who run the country, forming disgusting networks of abuse. And even worse, the people who cover up for them.'

He stared into his brandy glass and frowned. Marianne could see what he was thinking.

'You think the police might be involved in covering these things up?'

'Maybe. I don't know. Or maybe they just turn a blind eye to what's going on. And there are quite a few of them who swap funny handshakes.'

'Freemasons?'

'Yeah, and most of them look after their own.'

'But you were never recruited, were you?'

Mike snorted. 'Well, I was approached once. But can you imagine what would have happened if Dad got wind of me joining that lot? I'd never hear the end of it. Which reminds me: I might pay him a visit in the morning. See how he is.'

'Is he still writing indignant letters to the press about the state of the country?'

'No change there. He's done it all his life.'

'Well, be careful what you tell him about this paedophile ring. He might write a disgusted letter to *The Times* about it.'

Mike giggled, suddenly feeling more relaxed. 'That might not be such a bad thing. Rattle a few cages.'

He reached for the television remote.

'Now let's see if there's anything to cheer ourselves up. There might be some *Father Ted* repeats. Bound to be.'

Chapter 16

Thursday 20 March 2014

Thinking an unexpected visit would be more appreciated than phoning in advance, Mike was surprised to see his father standing at the window, as if he had anticipated his son's visit. Although Mike wasn't superstitious in any way and would happily smash a mirror if he was challenged, he accepted there might be some validity in claims made for belief in telepathy and extra-sensory perception, especially when it came to telepathic communication between families and lovers. It was only a marginal acceptance of something intangible. As far as the supernatural was concerned, Mike's attitude was if it can't be proven, it was a waste of time considering it.

His father gave him a wave as he got out of the car, which Mike returned.

The three-bedroom house in Harrow was built of granite and might have been considered gloomy were it not for the large sash cord windows, a typical feature of this late Victorian building. Tom Halliday and his wife purchased the house in 1992, long after Mike and his brother had grown up and left the family home in south London. His father, at the age of sixty-two, insisted on moving to a house with character, which was close to local shops and pubs, and refused, he said, to end his days on some remote estate, vegetating and watching reality television. Mike's mother argued with his father about his choice of abode. She argued with him about most things, but was never serious, and his father enjoyed being challenged, his mother playing devil's advocate whenever he began a political rant. Then she died of pancreatic cancer in 1998, and Tom Halliday was left to fend for himself. But he was a self-sufficient man, and although he had loved his wife and missed her terribly, he realized he had two choices. Either he could give up or move on. He chose the latter. Having worked as a partner in a firm of chartered accountants in the City for most of his life, since retiring he remained busy, choosing to work part time as a freelance, helping self-employed musicians with their tax accounts. He enjoyed the work, especially meeting and indulging in a few pints with his clients, and it kept him occupied following his wife's death.

By the time Mike had walked the few paces along the short front path his father was already at the front door. A cursory glance at the garden on either side amused Mike and he shook his head and grinned at his father. Following the wet winter, the garden looked drab and colourless, the greyish, muddy earth water-logged and cheerless. It was his mother who had been the keen gardener, and now she was dead, his father let it go untended, then got a local man along to repair the neglect when it got out of hand.

'Garden's looking stylish as usual,' Mike said.

Tom Halliday waved it aside and beamed at his son. 'Hello, Mike. Surprise visit? You're lucky to find me in.'

'Hi, Dad. I would have phoned, only….'

'Doesn't matter. You're here, that's what counts. And all my clients' year end accounts are settled. Come in.'

Mike entered the spacious hallway and then followed his father through to the large kitchen towards the back of the house, noticing the usual abundance of papers scattered everywhere in the living room as he walked through. His father put filtered coffee on, asked after Marianne and Natalie, then gave him news about Ben, his younger brother who worked at an oil refinery in south west Wales.

As soon as the coffee was brewed and poured, and they were sitting opposite each other, Mike knew the small talk, polite family enquiries and news would rapidly end. His father preferred discussions about art, politics, books and music, and his latest political obsessions of who to attack in the letters pages of the broadsheets.

Mike knew he was in for some gentle criticism as he saw his father sit back and observe him through narrowed eyes.

'You still doing the job of a bailiff, Mike, serving writs on poor bastards who are trying to scratch a meagre living in this shit-awful climate?'

'Don't start, Dad!' Mike smiled to show he was ready for anything his father might throw at him. 'Which is worse, wrongly suspecting and convicting Asian men of terror tactics, or handing someone a writ – some poor bastard who's got behind on the payments of his latest Porsche?'

Tom Halliday chuckled. There was nothing more challenging than a friendly discussion or argument, and he could never understand people who took it personally.

'Well,' he began as he sipped his coffee, 'I suppose, on reflection, you were keeping the country safe when you worked in counter terrorism, even though the government likes to control the proletariat by keeping us in a state of fear.'

Mike grinned, refusing to rise to the bait. Instead, he went for a mild attack, knowing how much his father enjoyed a lively debate.

'You've worked as a City accountant for most of your life. You must have represented some fat capitalists in all those years.'

His father laughed. 'Yeah, and we took great pleasure in overcharging them.'

Aware these arguments covered old ground, discussions which had centred around the dinner table when he and his brother were growing up, Mike knew his father clung to them as reminders of his glorious past when they enjoyed lively mealtime debates and discussions. Mike braced himself for another diatribe about UKIP, the coalition or how ineffective Labour was. But his father suddenly surprised him as a faraway, sentimental look came into his eye, and then he leant forward, raised his mug and toasted Mike with his coffee.

'I'm proud of you, Mike. I really am. Whatever you've been involved in, you've always had integrity.'

Mike felt embarrassed and wondered if his father was preparing himself for the unfamiliar territory of his rapidly ageing future.

'Even though I used to work for the corrupt pigs and now I'm a keyhole peeper?' he said, giving his father an awkward, sideways grin.

'Seriously,' his father replied, refusing to be drawn. 'I know you'll always do the right thing.'

Tom Halliday sipped his coffee, leant back in his chair, and contemplated his son with a shrewd and knowing look, a gaze Mike recognized from when he was a small boy whenever his father pressured him to tell the truth.

'What's on your mind, Mike? You look as if you want to talk, to tell me something important.'

'How did you know?'

His father shrugged.

'I'd like to tell you,' Mike explained. 'It's just that—'

'What?'

'What I'm involved in is frighteningly big and dirty, and involves important, almost untouchable people. And if I tell you, I worry you might go and write to the papers.'

'Give me some credit, Mike.'

'Yes, I'm sorry.'

'I give you my word, this will not be a disgusted letter. Promise.'

'That's good enough for me.'

Mike told his father everything, speaking for almost half an hour. His father listened intently, interrupting only twice to ask for clarification where Mike had skimmed over a few details. At the end of the account he frowned thoughtfully, fiddling with his empty coffee mug.

'Well?' Mike prompted.

His father exhaled loudly, displaying his apprehension. 'It seems to me this thing is going to be blown wide open as soon as this mysterious person contacts the publisher, so then there'll be the long overdue investigation into this disgusting affair. But until that happens—' He eyed his son shrewdly. 'You have a good relationship with Marianne. I expect you've talked this over with her.'

Mike nodded.

'And yet you made this visit to north London to talk it over with me. And Harrow's not that far from Barnet. Think it over very carefully before you do anything rash, Mike.'

Mike started to protest. 'What makes you think I'm going to—'

His father stopped him with a raised hand. 'I think you've already made up your mind. I'm only guessing but I assume Marianne's against it. And if you force your way into that house, expecting them to call the police, it might backfire. And I worry for your safety.'

'But why wouldn't they call the police if I force their hand?'

'Maybe you could get them on film and get out of there fast. At least you've got some evidence when the time comes to expose them. You have the photos of whoever runs that house, and the rumours about the house in that document will carry a great deal of weight. But Christ, Mike, be careful. You're dealing with some unsavoury characters. Think about James Gaskell being murdered because of what he knew? No, you need to reconsider. But if you're still determined to smoke out these disgusting perpetrators, who am I to stop you? I know how much seeing those children at that house has affected you. So, I can't blame you for wanting to shake things up at that house. And I really shouldn't be saying this, but I think if it were me, I'd do the same thing in your position. Just be careful, that's all I've got to say. Be very careful.'

He gave his father a sheepish grin. 'Thanks, Dad.'

'It was what you came here for, wasn't it? It was what you wanted to hear.'

Mike nodded again, grateful for his father's understanding and support.

Chapter 17

Mike turned off the main road and drove along the cul-de-sac towards the end of the street. While he was still some 200 yards from the guest house, he saw there was another object erected by the main gate, a tall post which hadn't been there before. As he had already made up his mind to confront the owners of the house, there was no need for caution now, no point in surveillance from a distance, so he intended parking directly outside. But as he got closer, he saw there was a board at the top of the post, and he guessed what it was.

He stopped the car in the street outside the drive, blocking the entrance, and looked up at the board. The house was for sale and in the hands of estate agents. How had this happened? In less than a week, since the start of his investigation, the guest house had been put on the market. It was too much of a coincidence. And he was always sceptical when provoked by obvious coincidences.

He wondered if the occupants of the house were still around, or was this a sinking ship scenario? He suspected it was the latter, but still needed to check. He got out of the car and walked towards the front door. The glass in the door was almost opaque with grime, and all he could see inside the gloomy hallway were unrecognizable shapes in the dark shadows. He pushed the doorbell and listened, hearing nothing. Either it didn't work, or it was in a distant part of the house. There was a large iron knocker on the strip of tarnished wood separating the glass on either side of the door panels, so he banged it loudly several times. It echoed in the gloom, and the sound carried across the street in the stillness of the late morning.

He waited for a few moments, then guessed by the silence that no one would answer. He decided to look around the back. There was no access to the left of the house, as it was shut off by a brick wall and a garage, the metal shutter of the garage secured by a large padlock. To the right was a path leading to a wooden gate. He tried the gate, but it was locked. He pushed it to test the strength needed to force it open, but it seemed too solid to budge. He had no intention of climbing over the gate, since it was well over six feet high, and would probably serve no useful purpose. The house was deserted, the occupants having flown.

Feeling tense as he thought about the house's terrible history, he walked back to his car, his feet crunching on the gravel, accentuating the eerie silence of the grisly building. Before getting into the car, he made a note of the estate agents' name and phone number, got their address from his smart phone before driving away, and shivered as he watched the guest house receding in his rear-view mirror, hoping it was the last he would see of the grim guest house.

***

Estate agents Plunkett and Wilson were less than two miles from the guest house, located in Barnet High Street, next to a charity shop on one side and dry cleaners on the other. It was just ten minutes before noon as he strode into their offices with determination, affecting the confident demeanour of a businessman looking for a suitable investment property. A young auburn-haired woman in her early twenties, sitting at a front desk talking on the telephone, looked up as he entered. She gestured for him to take a seat in front of the desk and began to wind up what was clearly a personal call. She said her goodbyes hurriedly as Mike sat, then smiled.

'Good – morning,' she said, pausing slightly between words to glance at her watch. 'How can I help you?'

Mike didn't return the smile, deciding to play the curt, pushed-for-time prospective buyer. 'I'm interested in purchasing a property you have on the market.'

He saw the panicky fear in her eyes, the tension in her slim neck, and he guessed she was the office junior. He was in luck. She was holding the fort while the estate agents were away and couldn't be expected to conduct any serious decision-making business.

'Well,' she began, recovering slightly and glancing at her watch again, 'Mr Wilson's not here today, but Mr Plunkett should be back just after lunch. Can you tell me which property you're interested in buying?'

'The Gwent Guest House in Erskine Road.'

'Right. I'll just check the details for you.'

She tapped the keyboard of her computer, peered closely at the monitor as she scrolled down and read the details of the property. 'Ah, here it is.' She gave him a puzzled frown and shook her head. 'But no one's viewed this property yet. It only came on the market yesterday. If you'd like to view it, I'm afraid I'm going to have to ask you….'

'I've already seen it,' he interrupted. 'I stayed at the guest house six months ago, so I'm already familiar with it. I'm looking for an investment property in this district – bed and breakfast – that sort of thing. If you could contact the vendor, I'd like to make an offer. What's the asking price?'

'Seven-hundred thousand, but—'

'It clearly needs work doing on it. I could go to six-sixty or thereabouts.'

The office assistant shifted awkwardly in her seat, the faux leather squeaking as she moved. 'Well, like I said, Mr Plunkett will be back….'

He waved it aside brusquely. 'I don't have the time. I've got to catch a train back to Bristol and I'm due in a meeting there at four. Surely you can contact the vendor for me just to make the offer. You have his details, don't you?'

Her frown deepening with insecurity, she stared at the screen again. 'Yes, a Mr Edgar Jessop. But I'm not sure I can let you have—'

He didn't let her finish and stood up, feigning impatience and annoyance. 'Well, I'm sure Mr Plunkett would like to know you may have cost him two- or three-per-cent of a cash deal. If I can't at least contact the vendor in Mr Plunkett's absence to at least let him know I'm very interested in the property—' Mike threw open his arms in a gesture of frustration. 'For God's sake, when I stayed at the Gwent, I got on really well with Edgar.'

Her mouth dropped open. 'You actually know the vendor?'

'Of course, now you've told me who it is. When I stayed at the Gwent I thought Edgar might just be running the place. I had no idea he owned it. And there's no way I can contact him directly, because the phone number I have is for the guest house.'

She hesitated as she looked at the screen, then back at Mike. He glanced pointedly at his watch.

'If I miss my Bristol train—'

She sighed before reluctantly copying Jessop's phone number onto a notepad. She tore the sheet off and handed it to Mike, saying, 'We only have a mobile number for him.'

Mike grabbed it and shoved it into the top pocket of his jacket. 'Thank you. I do appreciate that.' He walked to the door, turned and gave her a smile before leaving. 'I'll give Edgar a ring when I'm on the train to Bristol. And I'm sure Mr Plunkett will be more than pleased with this deal. So well done.'

He saw her starting to reach for the phone as he shut the door, and a pang of guilt about letting her think she had been part of a lucrative sale touched him fleetingly. But treading on a few toes, he felt, was justification for getting information about an evil merchant of misery.

Chapter 18

As soon as Delia Smethurst, Joanna Reeves's PA took the call, she knew this was the important one, the one her boss had told her to expect. Although she had read part of the file that had been mailed to them more than a week ago, and knew the call was probably something to do with it, she wondered why her boss hadn't provided her with more details, almost as if for some reason she was being deliberately kept in the dark about this particular project, one that was blurred by a mysterious secret, and she felt slightly aggrieved she hadn't been included in all the details instead of just a vague knowledge that someone who wished to remain anonymous would be contacting Forum Books to speak with Jo Reeves about the sensational subject she had skimmed when she opened the mail. She appreciated how explosive the subject was, and that it needed to be kept under wraps until the right time, but still felt offended by her boss's secrecy and by not being included in the big mystery.

She wondered if the person contacting them was some sort of whistle-blower like Edward Snowden or Julian Assange. Or someone in the security services, perhaps. But when she picked up the phone and heard Justin Gormen asking to speak to Joanna Reeves, she expected an authoritative, more demanding voice, instead of the youthful stammer of a young man who was clearly nervous and highly strung.

She transferred him to Jo's office, and bit her lip, almost wishing she could listen in on their conversation. But it was far too risky. Besides, she knew that whatever this big secret was, it would eventually reach the ears of everyone in the offices of Forum Books.

***

Mike sat in the car in a residential street in Barnet and made a blocked call on his mobile. When Jessop answered, the voice was guarded, cloaked in suspicion and cracked with age.

'Who is that?'

'I'm a colleague of Sir Geoffrey Scranton.'

A long pause before Jessop replied. 'Who are you? What's your name?'

'I'd sooner talk business and remain anonymous before I give you my name.'

'What do you want?'

'The same thing you've been supplying to Geoffrey.'

'I have no idea what you're talking about.'

'Oh, come on, Mr Jessop, I'm willing to pay – and whatever Geoffrey pays I'll double it.'

The line went quiet and Mike thought Jessop had ended the call. 'Hello? You still there?'

'Yeah, I'm still here. Just thinking.'

'So how about it?' Mike prompted.

'How long is it since you spoke to Geoffrey?'

If he admitted it was recently, Mike knew Scranton could have told him about the guest house being put on the market, so he answered, 'It must be nearly three weeks since I've seen him. I've been busy, but now I feel in need of some recreation.'

He heard Jessop clearing his throat, followed by a revolting phlegmy cough.

'I've encountered a slight problem. We've moved from the location, so we're temporarily without premises. But I hope to be back in business in about six weeks' time.'

Mike feigned acute disappointment. 'Six fucking weeks!' he wailed. 'I can't wait that long.'

'Not a lot I can do about that.'

He sighed loudly for Jessop's benefit. 'No, I suppose not. But maybe you can sell me something to be going on with.'

'Like what for instance?'

'Pictures. Something really…compelling and thought provoking.'

Jessop sniggered. 'Yeah, I've got some hot merchandise. But it'll cost you.'

'How much?'

'Dozen photos could set you back two hundred notes.'

Mike whistled astonishment.

'If you'd sooner risk the internet—' Jessop added.

'No, you're right – that's much too risky these days. I'll pay the asking price. Where and when can I come and collect the merchandise?'

'This evening about seven-thirty.'

'Give me your address.'

Jessop laughed humourlessly. 'Yeah, like I'm some sort of retard. I'll meet you somewhere. I'll bring the photos and you bring the cash.'

Thinking quickly, Mike wondered how he could get the loathsome pervert's address without him suspecting anything. 'I'd sooner not do the exchange anywhere public,' he said. 'Somewhere there might be CCTV cameras.'

'I know just the pub. No cameras. It's a Wetherspoon's in Old Street in the City. The Masque Haunt.'

'How the hell will I find you?'

'I'll have a red and white polka dot hankie in my top pocket, and I'll sit somewhere roughly near the Gents' toilets.'

'OK. I'll see you at the Old Street pub at seven-thirty. Please be there. I don't want a wasted journey.'

'Oh, I'll be there all right. Just make sure you bring the money.'

Mike clicked the phone off. He couldn't believe how stupid Jessop was in arranging to meet him wearing a distinctive hankie in his pocket. He should have arranged the meeting the other way around, so that it was Mike who had to identify himself by wearing something distinctive, giving Jessop a means of escape if he was suspicious. But maybe the man had no reason to be unduly cautious, seeing as Mike was posing as a colleague of Scranton's.

He was about to drive away from the side street in Barnet when his mobile rang, and he recognized the caller as Jo Reeves. He clicked answer.

'Hello, Jo.'

'Hi, Mike. The mysterious person – or people, I should say – who sent me the document extract are coming out of the woodwork. They've made contact and are coming to see me at three o'clock.'

'You said 'them'. How many are involved?'

'I think it's two. And the caller sounded young and naïve, not really what I was expecting.'

'Maybe it's someone who stumbled on the document by accident. And what gender is this person?'

'Male. But I think his partner is female. While he was on the phone, I thought I could hear a female voice whispering and prompting him. And the name he used to identify himself is straight out of a pulp fiction novel. He told me he's called Jake Steel.'

Mike chuckled. 'That's as corny as a seventies sitcom.'

'But little does Mr Jake Steel realize,' Jo Reeves continued, 'that if he wants to sign a book deal – ghosted or not – he's going to have to give me a proper name at some stage.'

'If he's that naïve, maybe he hasn't thought it through.'

'I think that's right. They wanted a down payment of five thousand in cash. I said I'd give them two.'

'Did they agree to that?'

'He argued for a bit, with some prompting from his lady friend, but he eventually agreed without too much of an argument. I heard him hissing at her, telling her to shut up at one stage.'

'Sounds like a strange double-act.'

'A *folie â deux* perhaps. And he doesn't sound that confident, so maybe she wears the trousers in this relationship.'

'I wonder who thought up the stupid pseudonym.'

'I'll soon find out. And I'd still like to know how they got hold of the document.'

'Once we know who he really is, it might lead us to who got the document from John Keneally. And possibly who murdered him.'

'We must catch up on the latest developments as soon as possible, Mike. Maybe some time tomorrow. But now this meeting has been arranged, you need to keep whoever these people are under surveillance and find out where they come from and who they are.'

'I'll park near Forum Books just after three.'

'Don't bother to drive, Mike.'

'Why not?'

'When I told Jake Steel—' She broke into her sentence with a short laugh. 'When I told him parking's difficult round here, he told me he doesn't drive.'

'Good,' Mike said. 'It'll make tailing them easier. I'll call you tomorrow.'

He hung up and checked the time. It was just coming up to 12.30. Time enough to drive home, park the car, grab a quick sandwich and head for Forum Books by public transport.

Chapter 19

Jo Reeves rose as Justin Gormen and his girlfriend entered the office and tried not to let her incredulity show. Surely, she thought, these two characters had to have stumbled on the document by accident. The girl, who said her name was Cyrus, was dressed in retro hippie style: a fringed waistcoat fashioned out of what looked like a brown rug on top of a clashing purple T-shirt with an exploding orange sun design, and olive-green trousers, slightly flared. The young man was more conventional, wearing a khaki parka with a fur collar.

Instead of shaking hands with them, she gestured to two chairs she had placed in front of her desk. Her assistant offered to stay to take notes, but Jo dismissed her briskly, telling her it wouldn't be necessary.

'Now then,' she said, as soon as her PA had left the room, 'let's get down to business.'

'Yeah,' Eva replied. 'We need to talk folding stuff.'

Jo Reeves stared at her, and noticed the assertive statement belied the vacant look in the young woman's eyes.

'First of all, I need to see if you have the complete document. I believe it consists of just over one hundred files.'

As if what would happen in this meeting had been discussed and planned between them both, and this was Justin's cue, he slid a large brown envelope concealed beneath his parka and dropped it onto the desk. As Jo Reeves picked it up, the girl clicked her fingers at it.

'Obviously it ain't complete. We ain't that stupid.'

Jo Reeves sighed and shook her head as she slid twenty A4 pages out of the envelope. Her eyes scanned them quickly as she leafed through the pages.

'Yes, this looks like the genuine article,' she said.

'Why wouldn't it be?' Eva snapped.

'Because whoever owned this copy murdered a respected member of parliament to get it.' Jo Reeves stated, then paused, letting the allegation sink in.

She noticed the deepening frown on the young man's face and the fear in his eyes. 'Where did you get it?' she added.

Eva turned and stared at her boyfriend. 'Over to you, Justin.'

He glared back at her. 'For fuck's sake!'

'I mean Jake,' she corrected herself. 'Go on, tell her, Jake, where you got the document.'

Justin looked at the publisher. 'I found it.'

'Found it?'

'Yeah, it was on a memory stick hidden in our house. Under the floorboards. Probably been there years, since before we moved in.'

'This MP was murdered eight years ago. How long have you lived wherever it is you live?'

Justin hesitated. 'Er – I think we moved in about five or six years ago.'

Jo Reeves could tell he was lying.

'And you just happened to find this flash drive in your flat or house? Do you live by yourself or with your parents?'

Justin froze, unsure of the way the situation was developing, different to the way he imagined it. It was so much easier playing scenes in his head. Seeing himself strutting into the publisher's office and being handed a wad of money. Handing over a completed manuscript. Then more money changing hands. Headlines in the newspapers, his picture on the front page, signing copies of his book from a mile-high stack. But now his mind was besieged by fearful doubts and a terrible suspicion that his father was involved in murder. What he wanted now, more than anything, was to buy time to think, rewind the scene then start over, instead of facing this intolerable silence while the publisher waited for him to answer. He was relieved when Eva came to his rescue.

'What's this got to do with anything?' she said. 'You get a book out of it. The one Jake's going to write. That document's just to prove he ain't making nothing up.'

Jo Reeves stifled a sigh. 'Yes, I get all that, Cyrus. But I need to commission another writer – a ghost writer – to work alongside Jake. A professional who will work quickly and efficiently. Naturally it will be in Jake's name, so he'll get all the credit.'

'And the money,' Eva said.

'Ah, yes. Money. Now I've got one thousand in cash for you, Jake,' Jo Reeves began.

The young woman almost shot out of her chair, and the veins stood out in her neck as she screeched an objection. 'One thousand lousy quid. You having us on? It's gotta be worth a lot more than that.'

'I agree it's worth more than that. And we're willing to pay more. But paying large amounts of cash is a problem. I had difficulty persuading our finance director I needed this money as a down payment for an important project.'

Which was partly true. Jo Reeves had induced Clive Harvey, their finance director, to agree the release of the cash, explaining to him the need for secrecy at this stage, telling him the money was for a down payment on a book they needed to option before it got into the hands of a competitor. It was, she admitted to him, an unusual way of doing business, but this was a one-off, a situation that was unlikely to occur in future. He reluctantly agreed, although she could see he was miffed at not being brought in on the details of the transaction. But she brushed his token objections to the back of her mind when she remembered the conversations she'd had with Malcolm about the dossier. He had urged her, pleaded his case that she should do everything in her power to get her hands on it, whatever the cost. Because once they had the document, then an inquiry could be made official.

'A thousand quid ain't much. It ain't enough,' the young woman bleated.

Deliberately ignoring her, Jo Reeves looked at the young man. 'I have a draft contract made up, giving you an advance of six thousand pounds, and generous royalties for when the book is published. The balance of the advance – five thousand – will be paid by cheque. We're quite happy to publish the book in any pseudonym you care to use, but the contract will have to be in your bank account name, otherwise you won't be able to cash the cheque.'

Justin fidgeted nervously. 'I didn't think...' he began. 'I didn't think it would be that complicated. I want cash. Cheque's no good to me.'

'Sorry, Justin – or is it Jake? – it doesn't work that way. If you don't have a bank account, you'll need to open one.'

'No, I have a bank account. It's just that—'

'That it's in your own name. Well, you could open an account in a pseudonym, but that might prove tricky with most banks. Or you could form a limited company, so that the cheque could be made out to your company.'

'Or,' Eva stated loudly, 'Jake could take the deal to another publisher, who would agree to pay him in cash.'

Shaking her head, Jo Reeves smiled tolerantly. 'I very much doubt any publisher would agree to hand over large amounts of cash to an anonymous person. What explanation would they give to their board members about huge sums of money disappearing?'

'What about this thousand quid?' Justin said. 'I thought it was for what I've already given you. You had the first four files, plus my take on it about those disgusting perverts. And now I've given you another seven files. That's got to be worth much more.'

Jo Reeves sighed as she opened a desk drawer, took out a bulging brown envelope and flicked it open, showing them the notes inside. The young woman leant forward hungrily, and the publisher saw something in her eyes that was more than an avaricious glint. The curtain was raised to reveal a desperation that went beyond a normal reaction to financial stability. It was an impatient craving for something that was now just within reach. She guessed the young woman was a drug addict.

Handing Justin a sheet of paper she asked him to sign for the money.

'What name do I use?'

'You can either use your own name or a pseudonym. As long as it will be the same name that appears on the manuscript.'

'I'll go for Jake Steel then.'

Jo Reeves suppressed a smile and watched as Justin signed the paper. She then handed him the envelope which he stuffed in his pocket.

'Let's go,' Eva said as she stood up.

Jo Reeves raised a hand. 'Just a minute. We haven't discussed the rest of the document. There's another ninety odd files still to come.'

'We'll be in touch about that.'

Jo Reeves watched as Eva edged towards the door. Couldn't wait to get away now her boyfriend had the cash. The next high being her only consideration now.

Justin stood up reluctantly, feeling lost and insecure. He was unsure of how to proceed. Now that he knew whoever had hidden the file may have committed a murder, he feared further involvement with the project and wanted to abandon it. Especially as his father was involved. Throughout his childhood, and in his early teens and formative years, despite his father's long absences from home, he thought of him as a crusader, going out to rescue the planet from human destruction. Now he wasn't so sure of his father's participation with Green issues. And the bitter disappointment in his father grew by the minute. He knew by the very fact that his father had sent him out to get beer and pizzas, then removed the flash drive from its hiding place, meant his old man was involved in the dirty business of child abuse by important people, something that should be publicly condemned.

As he hovered uncertainly, his girlfriend glaring at him from the open doorway, Jo Reeves saw the turmoil in the young man's body language, the way he wrapped his arms protectively across his waist.

'Come on,' Eva ordered impatiently. 'Let's get out of this place.'

The publisher looked Justin in the eye, speaking quietly and passionately. 'It's important to expose these terrible crimes. I know you'll do the right thing, Justin.'

He nodded, then turned away and followed his girlfriend through the PA's office to the exit.

Jo Reeves picked up the phone and dialled Mike's mobile. She relied on him now to find out just who this Justin was, and see if it would link him back to the murder of John Keneally, then perhaps she could still get the book written, even without the rest of the files. As soon as Mike answered, she told him hurriedly that her visitors were just leaving the building, described them briefly, and urged him not to lose them.

***

Mike had no difficulty following them at a reasonable distance into High Street Kensington Underground station. A thirty-pound credit on his Oyster card allowed him to move swiftly through the electronic barriers and keep them in sight always. They caught a Circle line going north and clockwise, and he got into the same carriage, standing at the opposite end from where they sat. He stood close to the doors, so he could jump out and keep them in sight when they got to their destination. He knew following these two would be easy as they had no reason to suspect the publisher of hiring a private investigator. Glancing furtively in their direction occasionally, he saw the young man hardly spoke to his girlfriend. She seemed to be doing all the talking, waving her arms about and jabbering into his ear, while he stared down at his feet, head bowed, pouting and sullen.

They got off at King's Cross and he followed them along the corridors and down the escalator to the Piccadilly Line, where they picked up a train destined for Cockfosters. Again, he got into the same carriage as them and watched as the young man spoke to his girlfriend, nodding occasionally and agreeing with her suggestions, clearly in a better mood now.

When the train was about to leave Wood Green, he almost lost them. They were so busy talking they almost missed their stop and leapt up as the doors were about to close and squeezed through just before they banged shut. Mike did the same, using all his strength to stop the doors closing on him. Bulldozing his way onto the platform in an ungainly fashion, he almost lost his balance. The station exit was behind him, and he found himself facing the young couple as they walked towards him. Caught out, he bowed his head, searching for a button to fasten his jacket. But as they hurried along with the crowds, they barely noticed him. And not once did they look behind as he followed them out of the station and along the busy main street. They walked for about a half a mile, passing rows of small shops, a minicab firm, fish and chip shop, KFC, off-licence, Spar grocer, charity shop, bookmakers, and a bank on the corner by a junction. They turned right at the corner, walked another couple of hundred yards before turning into a side street, walked another few hundred yards and turned left into a small street of terraced houses. When they got to number sixteen, which was on the right-hand side of the road, they began arguing again, and Mike overtook them on the opposite side of the road. When he got to the end of the short street, he looked back and saw the young man had an envelope in his hand. He gave his girlfriend some money, and she gave her boyfriend a wave without looking back as she hurried back towards the main road. The young man went inside number sixteen.

Doubting the young man was the homeowner, Mike thought his best bet would be to research who the house belonged to. He checked the time. It was gone half four. He needed to get over to Old Street for seven, well ahead of that Jessop creep, and knew he would be pushing it if he went home to Ealing first. So, he decided, instead of using his smart phone, he would search for a cybercafé instead, somewhere he could get online information about who owned the young man's house, then return the next day to delve a little deeper.

Chapter 20

Although the pub at Old Street was busy with a good cross-section of customers, including City workers grabbing some alcoholic nourishment before the evening battle with public transport, Mike managed to find a table a long way from the toilets, with the area close to them in his sight. As he wasn't driving, he sipped a large Rioja, and began to relax. It was still only 6: 45 so he phoned Marianne, telling her he planned to eat at the pub and would be home about nine o'clock. Then, after he told her how he had spent the day, she echoed his worries about the guest house.

'Bit of a coincidence, isn't it, Mike?'

'Yeah, that's what I thought. Almost as if they knew I was going to turn up there and cause a scene. I might have a word with Jo Reeves about her PA. She claims she's not been told much about the book and document, and she swears there's no one more loyal in her organisation, but you never know. I can't quite believe she wouldn't have told someone else in the company.'

There was a long pause and he thought Marianne had hung up. 'Hello? You still there?'

'Yes, I was just thinking. Perhaps it is just a coincidence or something to do with that Scranton bloke. Suppose he found the tracker you put under his car—'

'I don't think so.' Mike toyed with his wine glass and added, 'I've been checking his movements at odd intervals. If he's found the tracker, he hasn't removed it. And he's been going into the City where Jo told me he goes regularly, not far from here.'

'Presumably, now the guest house has closed, his filthy perversions have been put on hold. At least, Mike, some of those children will be safe for a while.'

'Yes, but for how long?'

Mike rubbed his stomach, feeling queasy, and wondered if it was the sickening thoughts of child abuse, or whether it was hunger pains. He hadn't eaten anything substantial since breakfast, so he guessed it was probably the latter. Maybe a combination of both.

'So, what about this house where that young bloke lives?' Marianne asked.

'It belongs to a Peter and Pauline Gormen.'

'What did you find out about them?'

'Not much. Like they don't exist. Because the son – if he is the son – is in his late teens, I guessed Peter Gormen might be somewhere in his late forties or early fifties, but I didn't dig up anything. But here's a funny thing. Trolling through Births, Deaths and Marriages at the online Records Office, I came across a Peter Gormen who was born in 1982 and died two years later.'

There was a brief pause while Marianne worked this out. 'You think he stole a dead child's identity?'

'Looks like that's a strong possibility.'

'What sort of people do that sort of thing?'

'Secret service agents or undercover police officers.'

'You're kidding.'

'Didn't you watch the news last year?'

'Yes, but I didn't take that much notice of it at the time. But now…So what do you intend to do about this Jessop character?'

'Follow him, and then…I don't know. I'll just have to play it by ear.'

'Be careful, Mike. Don't take unnecessary risks.'

'Don't worry. This Jessop creep sounds like he might be entitled to a free bus pass.'

'Yes, but you don't know who he has working for him.'

'Try not to worry. I'll be very careful, I promise. I must go, Marianne. I haven't eaten anything all day, so I might just have time to grab a bite before the scumbag turns up.'

'Send me a text afterwards to let me know you're all right and on your way home.'

'Will do. Love you.'

'Love you too.'

He hung up, went to the bar, gave his table number and ordered a chicken Caesar salad. He was served the meal only five minutes later and was halfway through eating it when he spotted Jessop entering. The man was tall and angular, with thinning blond hair like streaks of straw combed over his baldness. He wore a green tweed jacket over a maroon sweatshirt, with a white shirt and dark tie beneath it. He had the red polka dot hankie in his top pocket as arranged, and Mike guessed he was in his early sixties. He hovered at the bar for a moment, his eyes scanning the area by the toilets, then turned to order a drink. Every so often, as he waited to be served, he glanced around, shifty and nervous, waiting to be confronted. He patted his bulging inside pocket, and Mike assumed this contained a package of child porn photographs. Jessop bought himself a pint of lager, then walked over towards the toilets area of the pub. He found a seat and settled down, then quickly knocked back half his beer.

Although he was a long way from his table, Mike avoided looking in his direction, and concentrated on eating, observing Jessop from a corner of his eye. He finished the salad, sipped his wine, then fiddled with his phone. A quick sideways glance and he saw Jessop peering nervously around, searching for his contact. He pushed his plate to one side and checked the time on his phone. It was 7: 40. He wondered how long it would take for Jessop to realize his contact wasn't going to show up. Presumably the man was keen to sell the photographs and pocket two hundred pounds, so Mike guessed he would hang on as long as possible. But he was wrong. Less than a minute later, Jessop looked at his watch, knocked back his beer, then got up from table and crossed the bar towards the exit.

Mike followed him out into the street, determined not to lose him. It was dark now, so tailing him wouldn't be too difficult, especially as there were plenty of people about.

***

There were only three terraced houses on one side of the narrow street in Hoxton, and Jessop's house was sandwiched in the middle. Mike banged loudly on his front door. Jessop, having entered less than a minute ago, opened it almost immediately, staring at Mike with open-mouthed confusion.

'Yeah? What do you want?'

'What I'd like is for all you slimy scumbags to vanish off the face of the earth.'

'Fuck you!'

Jessop started to close the door, but Mike stopped it with his hand, and stepped inside. The hall was gloomy and there was a vinegar smell of fish and chips in the dusty atmosphere. A strip of brightness shone through an open door at the far end beyond the staircase, throwing light onto their two silhouettes in the sombre, narrow hall. Mike's jaw was clamped tight in righteous anger as he glared with hatred at Jessop, who looked like a cornered animal, trapped and scared, his eyes shrinking with fear in his leathery face.

'You…you need a search warrant,' he rasped. 'Get out! You can't come in here without a warrant.'

'I'm not a copper, so I don't need a warrant.' Mike said, and kicked the door closed behind him. He took his smart phone out, clicked the camera image, held it up and photographed Jessop.

'What the fuck you think you're doing?'

'Collecting as much evidence as I can. I've now got a picture of you, along with your guest house, and Geoffrey Scranton's visit last week, with those poor unfortunate children who were abused. But what I'd really like to know is, who funds you? Who's behind it all?'

'I don't know what you're talking about?'

Mike pocketed his mobile, grabbed him around the throat with both hands and squeezed. Jessop's eyes bulged, and he wheezed and whimpered with fear. Mike loosened his grip, and then shoved him hard against the wall, holding him with a hand against his chest.

'You thought you'd try to sell me child porn photos, did you? Were these taken at your guest house by any chance? And I can't believe you work alone, you filthy bastard.'

'I don't know what you're talking about?' There was a distinct tremor in Jessop's voice as he began pleading with Mike. 'Listen, that guest house – OK, I admit I owned it – but I never knew what went on there. I promise you. And that's the truth.'

Mike pushed Jessop harder into the wall. 'Don't give me that shit. I know about you and your past, Edgar Jessop. I know all there is to know about you. You're on a sex offenders' register because of the time you served in prison for your disgusting abuses.'

It was a lie, but Mike knew it was a safe guess. He felt Jessop cringe even further into the wall.

'How did you know about that?'

'I may not be a cop anymore, but I was a detective inspector for many years, so I can get information whenever I want. So, don't lie to me about what went on in that house.'

'Listen, you've got to believe me,' Jessop pleaded. 'People phoned me to make an appointment – important people I'd recognize from the papers and TV. They'd pay me in cash. That's all there was to it.'

'How did they get to hear of what you were doing?'

'Word of mouth soon got around.'

'So, where did the children come from?'

'They were brought in from a home.'

'You disgusting bastard.' Mike shuddered, displaying his revulsion. 'That means you *have* got an accomplice – someone senior at the children's home, and probably other members of staff too.'

Jessop was like a statue carved out of granite, grey and sick-looking, the fear seeping out of him like liquid waste. Mike wanted to hurt him, injure him so badly he would need hospital treatment. Aware of the knife-edge situation, Jessop hardly dared move. Then Mike surprised him dropping his hand and leaning back against the wall opposite.

'OK,' he said. 'I'll give you a chance to make things right and put a stop to this disgusting business once and for all.'

Trying to placate his assailant, Jessop smiled thinly, and spoke in a wheedling tone. 'The Gwent is up for sale now. It's all over, you see. So, there's no need to….'

Mike knew he was lying and smacked him hard across the face with the back of his hand. 'You lying little shit. Had you forgotten what you said to me on the phone when I said I was a colleague of Geoffrey Scranton? You said things would be up and running again in six weeks.'

Jessop gasped and rubbed his cheek, his pasty complexion now emblazoned with a large red mark. Tears burst from his eyes like a tap being turned on and he began to shake as he choked and sobbed. Mike stared at him dispassionately, knowing how abusers and bullies were nothing but cowards, and hated pain when they were the ones on the receiving end.

'When I said I'd give you a chance to put things right, I mean I want names. How involved is Peter Gormen in all this?'

'Who the fuck is that?' Jessop mumbled, sniffed and wiped snot from his nose with the back of his hand. 'I've never heard of him.'

'Don't lie to me, you arsehole. I'll ask you again: where does Peter Gormen fit into this disgusting conspiracy?'

Jessop stared at Mike, shaking his head, fear and genuine confusion in his eyes. 'I don't know…Please! I've never heard of him. I swear.'

As Mike stared at Jessop, he was convinced the man was telling the truth this time. Penetrating a person's mind, the way the eyes revealed what was happening in the brain like a lie detector, was something Mike had learnt in his years as a detective. But he was also aware that paedophiles, more than most criminals, are notoriously adept at lying and manipulation. He stiffened his fingers and poked Jessop in the chest four times.

'If I find out you're lying, I'll come back and kick the shit out of you. You'll never be capable of touching a young kid ever again.'

'It's the truth, I promise.'

Mike stared at Jessop for a few moments, deliberately unnerving the man. He knew there was nothing else he could do for the moment. He had photographic evidence of the guest house, Jessop's involvement and ownership of it, and his home address. Hopefully, once the investigation was complete, Jessop's filthy business might be curtailed. Mike would have enough evidence to give the police and the paedophile would get a hefty jail sentence.

Without saying another word, Mike turned and exited, slamming the door so hard the building shook.

Chapter 21

Friday 21 March 2014

'Blimey!' Mark Simpson said as soon as Mike was connected. 'How you doing, Mike?'

'Hi, Mark. You kept my number in your phone book then.'

'Why would I delete it? I knew you'd be coming to me for help one day.'

Mike smiled. No getting away from the fact that his old detective sergeant was a smart cookie.

'What makes you think I need help, Mark?'

'I had hunch. And why else would you be calling me after all this time?'

'I kept meaning to keep in touch and have that drink we talked about. And now here I am asking you to help with a car registration.'

'Any reason a detective inspector should help a private investigator?'

'Wow!' Mike exclaimed. 'When did the promotion come through?'

'Three months ago.'

'Congratulations! I always knew you'd go far, Mark. And this is just another rung on the ladder.'

He heard Mark Simpson chuckle.

'So now you use flattery to wheedle info out of me. What is it you want, Mike?'

'I need the car make, model and registration for a Peter Gormen,' Mike said, then spelt out the surname

'I hope this isn't anything dodgy I'm involving myself in.'

'Dodgy like you wouldn't believe.'

Simpson laughed again. 'How soon d'you need this?'

'Yesterday would help.'

'I'll see what I can do and call you back.'

Mike ended the call and stared at his laptop. Geoffrey Scranton was at home – at least his car was. If the Gwent Guest House was now closed down and up for sale, presumably Scranton's deviant behaviour was curtailed for a while. And if Jessop was to be believed, for at least the next six weeks. But Mike didn't believe this network of Westminster deviants had only one location to practice their depravity, especially as he had read about the sickening Cyril Smith carrying out abuse at a children's home in Rochdale, and rumours of other MPs visiting children's homes in North Wales. So he decided he would still keep Scranton under surveillance and check up on him from time to time.

When his mobile buzzed, the screen identified the caller as Mark Simpson, and he answered right away.

'That was quick.'

'You got pen and paper?'

'Yes, go ahead.'

Simpson told him Gormen's car was a Citroën Grand C4 Picasso, gave him the registration number, and he copied them onto a notepad.

'Thanks, Mark. I really appreciate that. I owe you a favour. You still in Counter Terrorism Command?'

'No, I'm currently in Vice.'

'Really? Well, I may be able to do you that favour sooner than you think.'

'Just a minute, Mike – before you go. It wasn't much of a favour. You could have got that registration yourself.'

'Eventually. But not as quickly.'

'I know but – there's something else, isn't there?'

Mike grinned, knowing how perceptive Simpson was.

'You're not just a pretty face, Mark.'

'So, what is it?'

'Once I get a picture of this Gormen character, I may need help in identifying him.'

'What makes you think I can identify him? Unless he's a villain or suspected terrorist I once had dealings with.'

'I think he might once have been in the police. Undercover maybe.'

Mike heard Simpson's sharp intake of breath.

'What the hell are you getting into here, Mike? You telling me this might have been one of our undercover men who's gone native?'

'Something like that. I'll be in touch and fill you in on the details. I might be completely wrong about this bloke, but I need to check him out first. I'll be in touch soon. Thanks for your help, Mark.'

***

Surveillance work was monotonous, and Mike hated the thought of sitting in a car waiting for Gormen to show up. He often wished he had someone else to do the donkey work, an assistant he could employ. But that would prove costly. And he was aware that this particular surveillance was problematical. There were too many imponderables for monitoring his suspect. What if Gormen wasn't at home? And what if he didn't live there anymore? Mike had no way of knowing. Once an electronic tracker was in place, no problem. He could relax. But up until that time there was nothing for it but to sit it out, playing a selection of CDs in his car. It could be a complete waste of time.

In spite of having doubts about the surveillance, Mike still drove to Wood Green, arriving there just after 10:30. Parking on the right, about a hundred yards from Gorman's house, he thought of ringing Jo Reeves to bring her up to date on the latest developments, which would also help to kill a little time. He had just got through to her when he spotted what looked like a Citroën sandwiched between a white van and a Range Rover. From where he was sitting, he couldn't see the registration plates so needed to check to see if it was Gormen's vehicle. But he had to move fast.

'Sorry,' he told Jo Reeves as she answered. 'It's Mike, and something urgent has just come up. I'll call you back in a little while.'

He cut the call, got the tracker out of the glove compartment, then headed up the street towards the Citroën. Fortunately, there were not many people around. He could see an old man at the end of the street, talking to a woman on her front step. Apart from these two, there was no one around. Then, as he got close to the Citroën and read the registration, he saw it was Gormen's car. It was only a few yards from the man's house, so he walked into the road on the offside of the parked vehicles and, as soon as he drew level with the back of the Citroen, knowing he was masked by the Range Rover, he clamped the tracker underneath the back of Gormen's car. Then a quick glance around to check that no one had spotted him before he hastened back to his car.

As soon as he was inside his Volvo, he looked in the driving mirror and awarded himself a cheeky grin, knowing he'd been damn lucky. He picked up his phone to call Jo Reeves again when he saw he was about to get lucky for the second time that day. Although he had no idea what his target looked like, he spotted a tall man, wearing black jeans and a navy-blue anorak, about to leave number sixteen. The man turned around before Mike could get a shot of him, and the son appeared on the doorstep. They spoke for a moment, and then the man hugged his son and walked quickly towards the Citroën. Mike had no time to react and get a shot of him, especially as he walked close to the parked vehicles and was now obscured by the white van in front of his Citroën. But at least Mike had seen what he looked like, however briefly, and guessed it must be Gormen.

Ten minutes after the Citroën had departed, Mike followed at a safe distance, heading south towards London city centre.

***

As he drove through Docklands close to the West India Docks and Canary Wharf, Mike saw he was perhaps less than five minutes behind Gormen's car. The signal indicated he was very close now, so he drove slowly in case he caught up with the Citroën. He turned right towards Mudchute and continued along past Crossharbour Docklands Light Railway station on his right until he came to Island Gardens station. A red light stopped him at a pedestrian crossing, and he watched several people hurrying along an alley leading to a riverside park, where he could just about see the dome of the pedestrian tunnel leading to Greenwich on the other side of the Thames. He remembered visiting the area with Marianne and Natalie four years ago, when they walked through the tunnel to spend a day out at Greenwich.

The light turned green and he drove slowly along the main road which ran parallel to the Thames. The road was not that busy, although he saw in his rear view mirror a bus looming up close behind him, the driver clearly irritated by Mike's slow pace. But the tracker showed Gormen had arrived at his destination, so Mike turned right at a road leading to the river. Near the end of the road was a block of flats. He drove by slowly, glancing at the main entrance which looked as if it might lead to a lobby manned by a concierge. The building looked suitably exclusive, and he puzzled as to why Gormen had a family home in a cramped terraced house in Wood Green, and also an apartment not many miles away near Canary Wharf. Unless of course the man was visiting someone. But as Mike drove to the end of the building, he saw there was a short road leading to a steep incline at the side and guessed it must lead to an underground car park. So it looked as if Gormen was a resident at this apartment block. And this, coupled with what he had learnt so far about the man seemed to make sense, suggesting Gormen lived a double life, using a false identity. If Gormen was the resident at this apartment block, Mike wondered whether it was owned or rented in his false name or his real identity, and he made a mental note to check this out at some stage.

He continued along the road for about a hundred yards, then drove around the block, entering Gormen's street from the main road again. He parked some distance from the block of flats on a parking meter. He got out and fed the meter with a couple of pound coins which he kept in the glove compartment for emergencies. Then, making certain he had his camera ready, he sat in the car and waited, hoping Gormen went out for lunch. If that was not the case, after another hour of waiting, he'd have to abort the surveillance, keep an eye on the tracker, then follow Gormen the next time he went out, and try to get a photo of him then. But little did Mike know he was about to get lucky for the third time that morning, as Gormen took a phone call in his spacious apartment.

***

The call Gormen dreaded receiving. Marshall's smooth delivery taking him straight to the point.

'We have to talk right now. How long will it take you to get to get to West India Quay?'

Obviously, Marshall was nearby, and somewhere public because Gormen could hear background chatter, music and distant girlish laughter. Gormen felt nauseous suddenly. If Marshall was already at West India Quay, something urgent must have cropped up, otherwise he would have summoned him to meet somewhere in central in London, giving him advance warning.

'I can walk it in less than fifteen minutes.'

'Good. But take your time. Take half an hour if necessary, because I want you to make sure you're not followed. The crowds at Canary Wharf station will help you to lose a tail.'

Gormen suddenly felt vulnerable. Perhaps he was losing his grip. He had always prided himself on his professionalism, taking few risks, and covering his tracks completely. There hadn't been any major undertakings in recent years, so maybe that was the reason he was getting sloppy and had taken his eye off the ball.

'Who the hell is tailing me?' he asked, his throat suddenly dry.

'I'll tell you when I see you. I'll be at Brown's restaurant and I'll sit outside.'

***

As soon as he saw Gormen leaving the apartment block, Mike raised his camera and managed four photos in quick succession, then lowered the camera quickly as Gormen walked in his direction. He tucked the camera under the passenger seat as the man was only yards away, walking determinedly, now dressed in a dark pin-striped suit, blue shirt and yellow tie, beneath a black Crombie coat. Hurriedly opening the glove compartment, Mike took out two-pound coins, got out of the car and fed them into the meter as Gormen drew near.

The man passed him only a couple of feet away and Mike avoided glancing in his direction, concentrating on feeding the extra coins into the meter. He then went to the passenger door and leaned in, pretending to fetch something to take with him. He glanced through the car's rear window and saw Gormen turning back to see if he was being followed, staring at Mike's car for a moment. But Mike knew Gormen couldn't see him because of the dark interior of the car.

Seeing Gormen reach the end of the street and turn right, Mike shut the car door, locking it remotely as he went after Gormen. But having seen the way Gormen checked to see if he was being followed, Mike guessed that his surveillance might be compromised. At least he had the photos now, so that Terry Baldwin might identify Gormen as the man who set him up to take the rap for the murder of John Keneally. Also, he had enough evidence to expose the man as leading a double life, using a dead child's identity, although Mike had grave misgivings about the sort of people he was dealing with, knowing he was up against some powerful Establishment figures, possibly protected by the security services.

And then, as he hurried along the street, he remembered reading about Cyril Smith in one of his online searches. The Liberal politician was investigated in the seventies by Lancashire police, who had extensive files documenting allegations about him and child abuse. Decades later a senior retired Special Branch officer in Lancashire police went on record as saying MI5 came to Lancashire police headquarters, removed the Cyril Smith files, and took them to London. It was, Mike guessed, the way the power brokers operated, keeping the Establishment free from scandal, and the politicians in their debt.

He turned the corner at the end of the street, and saw Gormen turning left into Marsh Wall, heading towards Canary Wharf. Mike knew he might lose him if they got as far as the teeming station concourse, so he put on a spurt, hoping once they reached the more populated wharf areas, Gormen – even if he looked back – might not be able to identify Mike as the man he passed at the parking meter, and who was so obviously tailing him.

Mike saw him crossing a bridge over West India Dock, and then he entered an office building with a large neon sign which said 'OBICÁ' over the entrance. Mike followed, entered the same building, passing some sort of small restaurant on the ground floor of the office block. When he exited on the opposite side, he discovered he was close to the main concourse and Canary Wharf Underground station. Gormen was difficult to keep in his sights now as so many men in suits swarmed around the piazza in front of the station entrance. Mike thought he'd lost him, and stood still for a moment, focusing on the crowds, trying to single out his quarry. He was in luck. He spotted Gormen stepping onto an escalator leading to the Underground, and tore after him across the concourse, dodging tourists and white-collar employees on their lunch break, and charged on to the escalator. He could see Gormen was almost at the bottom now, so tramped hurriedly down the steps after him. Gormen took a sharp left at the bottom, and then became obscured by an enormous concrete pillar in the cavernous hall. Stepping off the escalator, Mike stopped and looked towards the ticket barriers leading to the station to see if he might see Gormen heading for one of the Underground trains. He was nowhere to be seen. The man had disappeared. Mike rounded the corner by the pillar and happened to look back up the ascending escalator, when he saw Gormen's figure right at the top now, stepping off into the plaza outside. Gasping as he rushed up the escalator, his shirt sticking to him as the sweat of exertion ran from under his arms, it took Mike less than a minute to reach the top. He stepped off the escalator and scanned the concourse, hoping to get lucky once more and catch sight of his quarry. But everything looked the same: entrances and exits looked confusingly similar, with crowds of people either hurrying and scurrying, or loitering and talking, surrounded by skyscraper offices of glass. He glanced in every direction, hoping to spot Gormen, but it was a futile hope. Gormen had lost him.

At least he had the photo, so now he could get it emailed to Tracey, Terry Baldwin's mother. It would save him a trip to Manchester, and it was unlikely the prison authorities would allow him a visit at such short notice. But, as a close relation, it was far more likely Tracey might be allowed to visit her son the next day, and perhaps get the authorities to agree to him seeing the photo. He would suggest to her that she might lie about the photo, tell them it was a picture of Terry's estranged father he needed to see.

Although he regretted losing Gormen, at least he knew without a shadow of doubt that Gormen knew he was being followed. So someone must have told him. Which set Mike wondering who that someone might be.

He returned to his car and made the call at last to Jo Reeves, bringing her up to date on the investigation, and telling her he hoped he might get Baldwin to identify Gormen as Keneally's killer.

***

The waitress came to the table and Gormen ordered a burger and fries with a bottle of beer. Marshall drank coffee and eyed him with what he thought was disapproval as he ordered. Not that he cared about minor details like ordering food. He had to eat, for Christ's sake. His concern was the memory stick, which was still in his possession, hidden in the boot of his car beneath the spare wheel. Unable to think of where else he could hide it, he concealed it somewhere he thought was temporarily safe. His original plan to keep it as an insurance policy might have backfired. But he still didn't know if it was Justin who had found the files and approached the publisher. If it was his son, it would mean his cover was blown after all these years. Perhaps his double life might be exposed. Now he wanted nothing more than to get rid of the memory stick. It had brought him nothing but bad luck. As soon as this meeting was over, he planned to dispose of it. He was only a short distance from the Thames, and he would hurl the fucking thing as far out into the river as he could.

He fiddled nervously with a napkin. Marshall stared at him, his expression deadpan, waiting for him to speak.

'So, you think someone had a tail on me?'

Marshall shrugged. 'If they did, I hope you managed to lose them.'

Gormen smiled, trying to appear relaxed. 'No one could have followed me here after I doubled back in the Canary Wharf Underground. And with all those people around…So what makes you think someone might have been following me?'

'We're not a hundred per cent certain, but we think someone may have identified you. We can't take any chances. So now it's time to take extreme measures.'

Gormen's smile faded. 'But if you're not absolutely certain…' he started to protest.

'I don't give a fuck about whether this man is onto you or not. If he's not, he soon will be. And he's compromised so much that has been built up and protected over the years. The guest house in Barnet has been closed down because of his interference.'

'Is this something to do with that publisher?'

Marshall's eyes narrowed as he stared at Gormen. 'What makes you say that?'

'Because I'm not stupid. That's where all this trouble started. So, have you found out who approached the publisher yet?'

'Not yet. Our source doesn't have that information so far. But we should get it any day now. And once we know whose copy of the documents ended up on the publisher's desk, we can deal with it.'

As Marshall paused tactically, Gormen maintained steady eye contact with him.

'Meanwhile—' Marshall slid an envelope across the table. 'Don't open it here. Take it back to your place, read the instructions and make the arrangements.'

Gormen opened his mouth to object, and Marshall waved it aside with a quick flick of the wrist. 'I know you like working alone, but for this you're going to need some help.'

'I can probably dispose of the problem without anyone else's input,' Gormen objected.

'This one has to be done the way we say it has to be done. Read the instructions.' He got up to leave. 'Oh, and make sure you destroy the orders. We don't want *those* details getting into the wrong hands.'

Marshall turned and walked away across the cobbled stones by the quayside. Gormen watched him go, smarting from his last comment, which he was certain was a cryptic reference to the missing USB file.

Chapter 22

The way Gormen hugged his son as they parted, then changed into his businessman image when he reached Docklands, gave Mike the impression the man would be away from his Wood Green residence for quite some time. So he decided to pay the son a visit and see if he could discover where he got the document from. He guessed it was the father, but he had to be certain.

As Mike neared Gormen's house, a pounding drum and bass beat came from within. No way could neighbours tolerate such a racket, so he guessed most of them must be out at work. He rang the doorbell, keeping his finger on the button for a good thirty seconds. At last Gormen's son must have heard it because the music stopped dead, followed by a pregnant silence. He rang the bell again and listened as heavy footsteps came pounding down the stairs.

'Mr Gormen? Justin Gormen?' Mike enquired, smiling affably as the door opened. 'Or are you using the pseudonym Jake Steel now?'

The young man frowned deeply, almost as if Mike had spoken to him in a foreign language. 'Who are you? What…what you want?'

He bounced against the door frame, then steadied himself. Mike noticed the imbecilic dilation of his pupils and guessed he was high, or at least nearing that state of disorientation.

'Can I talk to you for a minute?'

His girlfriend screeched from the top of the stairs, 'Who is it, Justin?'

'How the fuck do I know?'

Mike watched as she walked clumsily downstairs, clutching the banisters. She came reeling along the hall, threw an arm around her boyfriend, and stared at Mike as if her confrontational stare was enough to prompt him to speak.

'My name's Mike,' he said. 'I'm a friend of the publisher you approached about the book; the one based on the secret document you found.'

'We don't know nothing about that, do we Justin?' the girl said.

Mike inched into the hall slowly, keeping his back against the door to keep them from closing it. He ignored the girl and spoke to Justin.

'Where exactly did you find the memory stick, Justin?'

'What's it gotta do with you?'

'I told you: I'm a friend of Joanna Reeves, and she'd like to know where you got the document from? Was it your father's, Justin?'

The girl hissed in his ear, 'Shh! Tell him to mind his own fucking business.'

Ignoring her, Mike said to Justin, 'I need you to tell me, Justin – this could be important. There might be lives at stake here. Did that file belong to your father?'

'What if it did?'

'Where is it now?'

'I don't fucking know, do I?'

'So, what happened to it?'

'He must've taken it. My old man must've taken it when I went to get the pizzas.'

'When was this?'

'I dunno. Days ago. Weeks. What does it matter?'

'It's of vital importance. So, are you telling me you had the file, and now your father's got it?'

Justin nodded, his head lolling like a puppet. 'I knew it was him had the file cos it was hidden in my bedroom. But he took it when I got the pizzas.' His eyes growing moist, he stared imploringly at Mike. 'Publisher told us someone murdered some MP to get it, is that right?'

'I'm not sure about that,' Mike lied, knowing he had to tread carefully so as not to distress the young man. He couldn't help feeling sorry for Justin, a kid growing up trusting a father who led a double life of shame and corruption. And it was just a question of time when this knowledge would engulf the lad like toxic waste.

'Let me ask you something, Justin. How are you going to get more money out of Forum Books if you no longer have the file?'

'Made a copy, haven't I?'

'I see. So where is this copy you made?'

The girl clamped a hand over her boyfriend's mouth. 'No fucking way, Justin. See what he's trying to do, don't you? Trying to fiddle us out of the money.'

'I assure you….' Mike began.

The girl took her hand away from Justin's mouth, tapped the side of her nose and smirked. 'Justin's old man's got the file. If you want it, ask him for it.'

'But Justin just said you made a copy.'

'He got it fucking wrong, didn't he?' she yelled. 'He don't know what he's saying.'

Justin leant forward, poked his head out of the door and looked towards the main street. 'Shut it, Eva. Mum's due home any minute now.'

His girlfriend laughed and leaned close to Mike. 'He's scared of her is Mummy's boy.'

'No, I'm not.'

Eva pushed Justin out of the way and stepped into the street. 'Oh, fuck this. I've had enough. I'm going home, get changed, then I'll go down the Nelson. You coming, Justin?'

'Yeah. I'll see you down the pub in twenty minutes.'

She gave Justin a withering look, then marched along the street towards the main road. Justin watched her go, a worried look on his face, afraid she might bump into his mother on her way home from work.

'I'd best be off as well.' Mike said. 'I'll see you around, Justin.'

The young man, perplexed and clearly wondering why things seemed to be slipping from his grasp, opened his mouth to say something, but Mike was already striding along the street in the same direction as Eva. He wanted to see where she lived. Once he had that information, he could come back and pick up his Volvo. Then he could get home reasonably early. He'd had enough for one day.

Chapter 23

Saturday 22 March 2014

Drifting in and out of sleep, restless with anticipation, but at the same time scared his hopes might crash as they had in the past, Baldwin stirred in his narrow bed, craving deep sleep. Images bombarded him like scenes in a film: his mother arriving after lunch with the photo; his exoneration; smiles and hugs in the courtroom; apologies; compensation; spending the money; downing pints in a local boozer; walking freely into the bookies.

But more than anything, no more lights out and clang of steel, trapped in a ten-by-six like a caged animal.

He sighed deeply, scratched under his arm, and turned restlessly in his bed once more, knowing how important today might be. Counting the hours till his mother came. It was gone three a.m. Another eleven hours until visiting time, when his mother would arrive armed with the photo. But what if the photo was not of that bastard? He desperately needed to identify the man who framed him, it was the only chest of optimism about to be unlocked after all these years. If it wasn't him, the fucker who'd set him up…Jesus Christ! It didn't bear thinking about. It had to be him. But what if it wasn't? Could he lie about it? Would he get away with it? He had waited so long – too long – with everything now resting on this one glimmer of hope for release. Yes, it had to be the cunt who framed him. It just had to be.

Rattle of keys. Suddenly alert now as he thought he could hear something nearby. Often there were weird sounds in the night when other inmates freaked out in their nightmare-disturbed sleep. But this was different. From the deep dark night of silence came a squeak of steel moving on hinges, followed by a slight draught as cool air entered the cell. He was facing the wall, so he turned to see what was happening. Had someone entered the cell? What was going on? The only time a screw would enter a con's cell in the early hours was if there was some sort of disturbance, or a security breach which would involve a major search of every cell. But there hadn't been anything like that for a long while, everything ticking along tolerably.

He turned in time to see the shadows moving towards him as he struggled to raise himself from the bed. A hand covered his mouth as he let out a muffled cry. He felt his legs being pinned down by a bony, heavy weight. Hands grasping his neck, fingers curling around, blocking off his breath. He wanted to scream, cry for help through the hand gagging his mouth, but fingers squeezed tightly against his nose, and he had no air. And all he could hear was his own muffled panic as he tried to move sideways, away from the terrible weights holding him down, but he was trapped, unable to move an inch. His chest heaved painfully as he searched for breath. The hands pressed tighter. His head swimming now as the terrible pain and pressure in his lungs tightened like a giant fist. His brain spinning faster and faster, sucking him into a black whirlpool. No more thoughts. No more breath. Nothing.

Chapter 24

Relieved to be spending a normal family Saturday at home, Mike almost welcomed the supermarket shopping trip, even though he got tetchy towards the end when they faced long queues at the checkout. But at least that was normal.

Back home, as he helped Marianne unpack the shopping, his mobile rang. He didn't recognize the number, and he answered it with a degree of caution, thinking it might be a sales call.

'Hello?'

There was a pause, and then he heard a loud, strangled sobbing. 'He's dead,' the woman wept. 'Terry's dead.'

It was Tracey Baldwin, Terry's mother.

'What happened, Tracey?'

Marianne shut the fridge door and stood very still, staring at her husband. She knew the call was bad news, could see it in his face, and was curious to know what had happened.

Feeling tension tightening like a steel clamp around his head, Mike pressed the phone hard against his ear while Tracey Baldwin sobbed. 'Tracey,' he said. 'Tell me what happened?'

'They found him in his cell this morning. Hung himself they said.'

'Oh my God, Tracey. That's terrible. I'm sorry.'

'I can't believe this has happened. I was going to see him this afternoon. But now—' Her voice trailed off and she wept quietly.

Mike caught Marianne's eye, and saw a mixture of concern and curiosity in her expression. He cleared his throat quietly before resuming his conversation with Baldwin's mother.

'Tracey, I'm sorry. I really am. I thought we had a good chance of finding the man who killed the MP and getting Terry released.'

'That was why,' Tracey yelled in anger now, 'I was taking the photo in for Terry. And he goes and tops himself before I get there. It don't make an ounce of fucking sense.'

'No, that does seem—'

'Stupid!' Tracey hissed.

'When did they tell you about it, Tracey?'

'Less than an hour ago.'

'Did they say if he'd left a note?'

'No, there was no note. But they said prisoners who do that sort of thing do it from desperation and don't usually leave a note.'

'So, if he hanged himself, did they tell you how he managed to do it?'

'No, they didn't say. But I was told the coroner had already been before they called me. And he said it looked like suicide. Nothing more. But they said there'll be an enquiry.'

Mike guessed the conclusion following the enquiry would be a verdict of suicide. But it was no coincidence that Baldwin's death happened just before his mother had arranged a visit so that he might identify Gormen as the MP's killer. And who, Mike wondered, knew of this visit? The only one he could think of was Jo Reeves – and why would she pass on this information to someone suspected of using any means to suppress the evidence? There was her husband, of course, who might have mentioned it to other colleagues working in his constituency or someone in the House of Commons. And there was also the publisher's PA. Jo Reeves had mentioned how trustworthy she was, so may well have confided in her.

Mike heard Tracey sniffing. 'Hello, Mike. You still there?'

'Yes, I'm sorry, Tracey. I know this is of very little comfort following so close to Terry's death, but I'm still investigating this strange murder of John Keneally, and I intend getting to the bottom of it. I know it's not a great consolation, but perhaps it might help to clear your son's name.'

There was a slight pause before Tracey spoke. 'And then maybe—'

She stopped speaking and Mike asked her what was wrong.

'I feel guilty for even thinking of it. I'd sooner have Terry back. But—'

'But what, Tracey?' Mike prompted.

'If Terry spent eight years for a murder he never did, shouldn't there be some sort of compensation?'

Glad Tracey was unable to see his cynical smile, Mike replied, 'I'm not sure about that. After all, the authorities may well say he was guilty of breaking and entering, so it would be an uphill struggle to get any financial benefit from his death. It's not easy at the best of times.'

'Oh, I don't want to benefit from his death,' Tracey protested. 'I just want them to know how much me and me brother have suffered all these years. Terry got on OK wiv me brother, he did. And the only thing them fuckers in charge understand is by hitting them where it hurts. Make them pay.'

'Yeah, I can understand how you feel, Tracey. But first let's wait for the results of the enquiry, see if I can find out who really killed Keneally, and then see if we can clear Terry's name. The compensation might prove trickier.'

Tracey began sobbing again, and Mike suspected it wasn't just for the loss of her son, but also for a doubt about receiving a pill-sweetening compensation pay-out. He made a few more utterances of sympathy, told her he would be in touch about the murder investigation, then ended the call.

Marianne turned away from switching on the electric kettle and looked at her husband questioningly. 'Strange that Terry Baldwin commits suicide just as he's about to identify Gormen as the man who may have murdered Keneally. Who else knew you had Gormen's photo, and Terry Baldwin was about to identify it?'

'Jo Reeves. Her husband, obviously. Then maybe her PA at Forum Books. And if she's blabbed to others in the company—'

'You're forgetting someone,' Marianne broke in. 'What about that banker we had dinner with?'

'Dennis Lorcan? Yes, I had thought about him but—'

'But what?'

Mike shrugged. 'I don't know. I suppose it's to do with the fact that he gives a great deal of money to a child abuse charity. And he supports and runs it. Why the hell would he do that if…'

Marianne interrupted him again. 'Oh, come on, Mike. Aren't you being naïve? Who was the most successful serial child abuser and raised millions of pounds for charity?'

'Jimmy Savile.'

'Exactly.'

'Yes, the most brilliant smokescreen in history.'

'And you don't think this Lorcan might be doing the same thing?'

Mike bit his bottom lip thoughtfully.

'Well?' Marianne prompted impatiently after a pause.

'When I was a DC, I worked in the Vice Squad for many years…'

'And that makes you an expert on paedophiles?'

'Let me finish. Marianne. I was about to say we profiled hundreds of paedophiles and child abusers, and no way does Lorcan fit any profile.'

Marianne shook her head vehemently. 'But you don't know anything about his personal life.'

'In the car on the way back from dinner at Wimbledon last week, remember I told you I researched details about the banker? What I neglected to tell you at the time, because I didn't think it was relevant, was about some of the gossip I unearthed about him. Details about his private life. Quite the playboy is Dennis. His first marriage ended in divorce because his wife discovered he was having an affair with a French model. And there have been others as well.'

Marianne leant back against the kitchen sink, folded her arms, and gave Mike the expression of scepticism that he knew so well, her eyes mocking him, and a corner of her mouth lopsided.

'So how does being a playboy absolve him from child abuse?'

'It doesn't. But paedophiles usually suffer from feelings of inadequacy – feelings of inferiority when participating in proper grown-up sex. They tend to target children purely for their own pleasure, which also gives them a feeling of power. They don't have to make the effort of satisfying another person and dealing with the complexities of a proper relationship.'

'And you think Dennis Lorcan, by being a high-flying playboy, has no interest in sex with children?'

Mike sighed deeply. 'OK. I admit having affairs with loads of attractive models and actresses doesn't make him immune from that disease, all I'm saying is that he doesn't fit the usual pattern of paedophilia.' He saw Marianne was about to object, and added hastily, 'I'm aware his playboy behaviour could just as easily be a smokescreen for something darker, but all I'm saying is that it seems less likely. That's all.'

'But this still brings us back to someone murdering Terry Baldwin to stop him from confirming Gormen's identity.'

'There is another possibility of course.' Mike smiled and waited for Marianne to cue him.

'Which is?'

'That Baldwin may have taken his own life.'

'Yes, and I'm next in line for the throne in this country.'

Mike laughed, then went and kissed Marianne on the lips. She responded briefly before looking deep into his eyes.

'Seriously. What are you going to do, sweetheart?'

'Well, obviously what I told Jo Reeves was passed on by her to someone else – someone who has the power to inflict damage on anything to do with this investigation, whether it was the closing down of that guest house or disposing of Baldwin. I need to talk to her and find out who she or her husband have confided in.'

Mike glanced at his watch. 'I might pop up to the office and call her now. Then after that I'm going to relax, enjoy the weekend, and forget all about this case.'

Marianne giggled. 'Yeah, like I said: I'm next in line for the throne.'

***

After Mike had given Jo Reeves the news of Baldwin's death there was a long silence which he didn't attempt to fill, knowing she was working out for herself the fact that the information about identifying Gormen's photograph would have had to come from her.

'It has to be someone at Forum Books,' she said after a lengthy pause. 'But Delia's the only one who knows. Unless…'

Mike completed her sentence. 'She told someone else in your firm.'

'I find that hard to believe. But I will ask her. If she did pass on the information, I know she wouldn't have done it deliberately.'

'Have you any new employees, who started working for you recently?'

'No, I don't think so.'

'And what about your husband?'

'I can't think it would be Malcolm. Although he knows what's going on, he couldn't have told anyone because he's been in Berlin since Monday. In fact, he flew out there on Sunday night.'

'When did he get back?'

'Late yesterday.'

'Could he have spoken to anyone when he got home?'

'He went straight from the airport to the Commons.'

'Maybe it's someone he speaks to regularly at the Commons. Could I speak with Malcolm and ask him?'

'I'm afraid he's taking a surgery at Lewisham. And he usually switches his mobile off. He'll be back later, but we must leave almost immediately. We're going to the Cotswolds for the rest of the weekend. But I'll talk to Malcolm on the journey, and I'll text you with anything I find out. And keep a close eye on Geoffrey Scranton.'

'But I thought with the guest house closing down…' Mike began, but Jo Reeves interrupted him.

'This has come from Dennis Lorcan who has been involved with some of the victims of abuse. Apparently, several of the victims have told him there's another house or home – I'm not sure which – near Maidstone in Kent, and Scranton also went there regularly over the years.'

'I'll watch Scranton carefully,' he mumbled. 'Have a good weekend. What's left of it.'

'I'll try to. And if I get any joy from what Malcolm tells me, I'll text you.'

'Thanks.'

They hung up. Mike sat at his desk without moving, staring into space. He could feel his mood falling fast into the darkest part of his soul. Another house of despair. How many more were there dotted around the country so that sexually inadequate but powerful people could vent their frustrations on helpless children? This time, if he followed Scranton to such a place, he wouldn't hold back. He would cause havoc and bring it to the attention of the police and press. And he would batter Scranton into the ground and make the bastard suffer.

Chapter 25

Sunday 23 March 2014

Sitting opposite one another in a quiet corner of the Anglesey Arms in South Kensington, Marshall watched as Clifton sipped his large Bombay gin and tonic. Then Clifton watched as Marshall fastidiously sipped a small cognac, as he waited for him to make the first move. Both watching and waiting.

Careful not to reveal his true feelings, Marshall's impassive expression concealed the utter contempt he felt for the man, with his round, bloated face and piggy eyes, a florid drinker's complexion and an inadequate comb-over. There was nothing Clifton wouldn't do for money. And the expression in Clifton's eyes said it all. He knew he was onto a winner. He had the upper hand because his special services were desperately needed, and he felt relaxed and confident.

Wiping his lips with the back of his finger, Marshall then placed the brandy glass carefully on a beer mat, holding it with both hands, almost as if it was a fragile ornament.

Clifton watched the prissy, almost effeminate behaviour of the man who was about to employ him on a freelance basis, and he found it difficult to disguise how much he despised Marshall. Nevertheless, he always managed to keep his true feelings in check. No sense in biting the hand…

'I expect you're wondering why this emergency meeting on a Sunday afternoon,' Marshall said.

Clifton said nothing; merely raised his eyebrows in anticipation of the explanation.

'Without going into too much detail, one of my undercover operatives has turned sour. I've just discovered that he kept a USB flash drive he should have destroyed many years ago.'

'Presumably this flash drive contains sensitive information.'

Marshall clicked his tongue in irritation. 'Of course it does. Do you think I had orders to destroy it if all it contained were family snaps?'

Resenting Marshall's sarcasm, just for an instant Clifton's piggy eyes narrowed. But as the luring image of money flashed through his brain, he forced a foolish laugh and nodded acceptance of his own stupidity.

'Sorry. I guess it's important. Why else would you want it returned?'

Marshall leant forward in his seat; his eyes intense as he glared at Clifton. 'I don't want it returned. I want it destroyed. The last agent was supposed to have done that eight years ago. But he kept it.'

'Why would he do that?'

Marshall shrugged. 'Perhaps he thought he could make more money.'

'Blackmail, you mean?'

'Maybe. Either that or he kept it to secure his own safety.'

Clifton chuckled. 'Didn't work, did it? So how do I get this flash drive?'

'We have it on good authority that it's in a house in north London. Part of what's on the drive has already been leaked and we can't allow any further disclosures.'

'And you want me to—' Clifton broke off and looked around, knowing he needed to choose his words more carefully. 'You want me to locate the item, and then dispose of it?'

Marshall's lips tightened as he shook his head. 'No, this calls for extreme measures. And it must be done in the early hours of tonight – Monday morning.'

'Extreme measures,' Clifton echoed with a smile. 'Presumably this will be a rewarding assignment.'

Much as he distrusted and disliked Clifton, Marshall knew he was the right man for the job. No qualms about what he had to do so long as it was lucrative.

'You won't be discouraged by our generosity,' he said.

Chapter 26

After a quiet, relaxing Sunday afternoon, Mike left Marianne and Natalie watching early evening television while he caught up on some of his administration. There had also been several more mundane enquiries for his investigation services which he needed to sort out, thinking that maybe he could fit a couple of easy ones into his schedule.

Just before seven-thirty, he checked the tracker on Scranton's BMW and saw the ex-MP was heading south across London Bridge. Remembering what Jo Reeves told him about the children's home near Maidstone, Mike was immediately alert. He followed the tracker on his laptop for fifteen more minutes and noticed the ex-MP's car had passed New Cross Gate Tube station and seemed to be heading for Lewisham. Mike opened his desk drawer and took out a road atlas and checked the route. It looked as if Scranton was heading towards the A211 which would take him to Swanley, and from there it wouldn't be far to Maidstone.

Mike dashed downstairs and told Marianne and Natalie he had to go out because something urgent had come up.

Marianne looked up from where she was lounging on the sofa, a worried expression on her face. 'It's late on a Sunday night, darling...'

Without letting her finish, he waved it aside. 'I haven't got time to argue or explain, Marianne. I need to get going.'

She struggled to get up from the sofa and followed him out into the hall, where he grabbed his leather coat, patting his pockets to make certain he had everything he needed.

Marianne put her arms around his waist, reached up and kissed him.

'Please, Mike, if this is something to do with Scranton, promise me you'll be very careful. I still can't get it out of my head that there are some very dangerous people involved in all this.'

He hugged her briskly. 'It's only surveillance and collecting further evidence,' he said. 'Hopefully for when an official investigation to these horrendous crimes takes off.'

She stood and watched as he left, a pattern of worry lines etched on her forehead.

***

Crossing the river at Putney Bridge, Mike then made for Beckenham and Bromley, which would eventually take him towards Sidcup and Swanley. He was an hour behind Scranton, if not longer, since the ex-MP had already joined the M20 just as Mike was setting off. But as Mike tracked him, he noticed Scranton seemed to be slowing up. As he joined the A20 at Swanley, Mike saw the BMW was only just coming off the M20 at Junction 4. He wondered if the man might be lost or, having taken a wrong turning, he might have had to stop and consult a map. After all, the closing of the Gwent Guest House had probably necessitated a visit to another home he hadn't visited for several years.

As he joined the M20, Mike realized he would be only half an hour behind Scranton, which was unusual, considering how late he began tailing him. So why was Scranton driving so slowly? Perhaps the man was lost and stopped to use his mobile phone, probably to get directions. But why not use a satnav? Being over cautious, maybe, reluctant to leave electronic traces to his destination. Mike saw his car was now stationary somewhere just off the M20, near a place called West Malling. Not an area Mike was familiar with. But now the gap between their two cars had lessened considerably. Then the tracker showed Scranton's car was on the move again, heading along the A228 in the direction of Tonbridge.

Moving slowly again. Perhaps lost and looking for directions.

Instead of heading straight on for Tonbridge at the next roundabout, Scranton took the first exit left. Only five minutes behind him now, Mike slowed down, going at a steady pace up a steep incline. As soon as he reached another roundabout, a road sign gave the direction as Paddock Wood and Tunbridge Wells. It was a dual carriageway, and Mike eased up his speed in the inside lane because he was almost on top of the BMW now and thought he could see the taillights in the distance as Scranton reached another roundabout. Apart from the ex-MP's car there was very little traffic about. He had seen only one other vehicle going in the opposite direction on the other side of the carriageway. Up ahead he saw a sign saying, 'River Medway', and he guessed the carriageway crossed the river, even though he couldn't see a bridge.

He couldn't have been more than a hundred and fifty yards from where he would cross the river, having reduced his speed to thirty, when the bright beam of a vehicle dazzled him in his rear-view mirror. It was driving dangerously close behind, so he pressed hard on the accelerator to ease the distance between them. Suddenly the headlights disappeared. He felt the pull on his Volvo as the vehicle behind him overtook on the outside lane. Out of the corner of his eye he could see it was a large lorry, heavy, solid-looking – perhaps a vehicle used for transporting skips. There was something about the reckless way it zoomed out from behind his Volvo and was now dangerously close on his offside that told Mike this was a set-up. He eased his foot off the accelerator, hoping the lorry might overtake him; instead, there was an almighty battering crash. The Volvo shuddered and shook like a boat in a stormy sea, and a monstrous tearing of metal jarred as the lorry barged into the side of him. He lost control of the steering wheel as it spun in his hands, and he guessed the lorry was trying to force him into the crash barrier and the River Medway. He banged his foot hard on the accelerator to get ahead of the lorry. The car shot forward, uncontrollably zigzagging, a damaged wheel bouncing hard on the tarmac. The lorry also accelerated and swerved out to the right before turning back sharply and colliding with his Volvo, so forcefully it hit the crash barrier. Squeal of rubber. Grating metal splintering savagely as the car plunged and bounced, upside down and sideways. Something slammed into his head. His wrist twisted painfully, and the seat belt bit into his chest as the car veered over the embankment and plunged into a field, the impetus rolling it over and over, the sheer force squeezing the metal, bending it and compressing it like cardboard. A cracking sound, which could have been inside his head. Was he upside down or upright? Was he injured? It was hard to tell. He had lost his bearings and he struggled to remember what had happened. His brain penetrated by groaning and creaking noises as the car caved in. Harsh discordant sounds as protesting metal reverberated. Gradually the grating noises subsided, followed by watery sounds, dripping and leaking. His head was hazy, and he was disorientated. But then his memory returned, everything becoming clearer now.

Someone tried to kill me. Someone wants me dead.

And he was stuck inside a car, squeezed tight in a compressed coffin. If they discovered the crash hadn't worked, would they hang around to make certain?

He searched for the door handle, but the pain in his wrist discharged an ice-cold burning in his bones like an electric shock. He fumbled for the seat belt with his right hand and managed to unclip it. Then felt for the door handle on his right and pushed. It was jammed. But suddenly it creaked, and there was a splintering of metal, then a blast of cold air hit the chamber as the door was pulled open. Fear and panic as banshee screams inside his head warned him of his powerless situation. There was nothing he could do to help himself if they decided to finish him off. It was the end. It was useless trying to resist. And then he heard several non-threatening voices of concern.

'You all right, in there?'

'Is he OK?'

'Have you called an ambulance?'
'I've done it. They're on their way.'
'Is he injured?'
'Better not move him.'
'I wasn't going to.'
'You'll be all right, mate. The ambulance is on its way.'
Such relief. Welcoming voices, like a vision swimming into his brain. He held an arm out.
'He wants you to pull him out.'
'I thought you said don't move him.'
'Best to get well clear of the car. In case it goes up.'
Relief as friendly arms pull him free of the wreck. Standing up, arms supporting him. Faces shimmering out of focus. The pain in his head like a pounding rock. Smiling at his rescuers. Yes, such relief.
And then everything went black as he passed out.

Chapter 27

Monday 24 March 2014

Cursing as he drove along the street and finding nowhere to park, Clifton wondered if he could risk double parking. It was three a.m., so it was unlikely anyone would leave for work this time in the morning. Even someone working shifts. Another hour or so at least before any shift workers would be up and about. And if he double-parked near the target's house, he could probably do the job in less than five minutes. Easy money, really, for what he had to do. Although, when he thought about it, two grand down payment and two grand on completion hardly merited hoisting the flag and celebrating, especially as he was taking all the risks. Face it, if it all went horribly wrong, he was the mug facing a long, long stretch. And it was no use crying after the event or trying to get those powerful bastards to get him off the hook. Blokes like Marshall would just disappear, posted somewhere safe and distant with a new identity.

He had to admit though, every precaution had been taken. The risks were minimal, as they usually were. So slight, in fact, that he always felt recklessly secure working for this well-oiled, highly efficient machine. They were pros. Highly methodical and organised. And he had to hand it to Marshall – even though he couldn't stand him – the man left nothing to chance, usually taking every precaution. It was all in the details. Towards the end of their meeting earlier in the day, he'd been given another false ID and handed a driving licence in that name just for this one assignment. Presumably, even the unobtrusive little Ford Ka he was driving was clean and registered in that name.

Reaching the end of the street, and finding no available parking spaces, he drove around the block and returned to the target's house, double parking less than twenty yards beyond their front door. He cut the engine and switched the lights off.

A quick check to see there was no one around before he got out of the car, leaving the door slightly open. Hurrying to the back of the car and opening the boot, he took out the plastic five litre petrol can, placed it at his feet, then fumbled beneath loaves of bread and other random items of shopping in a Sainsbury's bag for the two plastic washing-up liquid containers which he had filled with petrol.

He smiled, mentally applauding himself for this extra detail, concealing the washing-up liquid containers beneath what looked like weekend shopping, so that if he were stopped by an over-zealous copper and asked to open the boot, all the arsehole would find would be a spare can of petrol and a bag of shopping.

He moved quickly and stealthily towards the front door. Pushing the letter box open, he knelt, took one of the washing-up liquid containers, poked it through the gap and squeezed a stream of petrol as far into the hall as possible. As soon as the container was empty, he repeated the same action with the other one. Then he unscrewed the top of the petrol can, attached the hose to it, and tilted the petrol into the hall. Once the can was empty, he moved it to one side next to the wheelie bin, along with the washing-up liquid containers. There was no use pretending this was anything but arson, and as the petrol containers were wiped free of his prints, what did it matter if he left them at the scene of the crime?

Carefully slipping his gloves off, he took a box of Swan Vestas out of his pocket, struck a match and dropped it through the letter box. He waited, listening for a crackle and seeing if anything flared up. Nothing. He cursed, held three matches against one another, struck them, held them close together until they were blazing brilliantly, then dropped them through the letter box. This time it worked. He saw the flare and heard the whoosh as the flames swept along the hall. He stared through the letter box for a moment, enjoying the rush of power from his mind-blowing act as he watched the flames overwhelming the hall.

He shut the letter box, turned and went back to the car, then remembered to close the boot before getting into the driver's seat. He sat watching the house for a moment, seeing how quickly the flames took hold. Already he could see the flickering, dancing flames through the downstairs windows, and knew it wouldn't be long before the whole house was an inferno.

He switched the ignition on and drove away, a self-satisfied look on his face. A job well done. And another two grand would be coming his way.

Chapter 28

Marianne took the day off work and went to pick Mike up at the hospital. He was about to be discharged when she arrived at ten. The concussion he suffered was temporary, nothing serious, and he'd recovered soon after the ambulance arrived at the hospital. He considered himself lucky. Even his wrist, although painful, was nothing more than a bad sprain. He had wanted to discharge himself on the Sunday night, and get a cab home, but because of the blow on the head they insisted on keeping him in for observation. He didn't object too much, because he needed to give a statement to the police, and he needed this as a reference for the insurance claim on his car.

As Marianne drove out of the hospital car park, he could see she was wound up. 'I hope you're satisfied,' she said.

'What are you talking about?'

'Last night I asked you not to follow this Scranton creature. But you wouldn't listen. I knew – I just knew – there was something wrong the way things were going with this investigation of yours.'

'I wish I had your telepathic skills.'

She flashed him an agonised expression.

'Look,' he began, 'how was I supposed to know I was set-up? Someone knows I put a tracker on Scranton's car, which was how he managed to lead me into that trap.'

'Someone tried to kill you, Mike. Can't you get that through your thick skull? Apparently, you just missed ending up in the river.'

'I admit it was a narrow escape.'

'How can you be so blasé about it?'

A twinge of pain in his wrist and he suddenly felt ratty, raising his voice to her. 'What the hell d'you expect me to do?'

'Well, clearly whatever I say won't make much difference one way or the other.'

Realizing her unsympathetic mood was because of her deep concern for his safety, and feeling guilty for snapping at her, he softened his voice. 'Sweetheart, you know that's not true. I always value your opinion. It's just that I feel someone has to do something about this horrendous abuse of children.'

'Yes!' she pounced. 'The law. The police. Not a private citizen working from home.'

He was silent for a moment. Then he said, 'I'm not sure I trust the police anymore.'

'How come you've suddenly changed your tune?'

'I'm not talking about the rank of detective inspectors or sergeants – I'm talking about the higher echelons who seem to take their orders from Westminster and the secret services. They crack a whip and the Chief Constables and Assistant Chief Constables jump. Know what else I discovered online? A high-ranking officer in the Lancashire police came forward after his retirement to say they had a thick file on Cyril Smith and his abuse of young boys. This was back in the late sixties. Then an MI5 officer came and took the files away to London. That was the last they ever heard about it, allowing Smith to carry on abusing young children for decades more.'

'That's terrible. And it shouldn't have been allowed to happen. But it's history, and it's out in the open now.'

'But it's still going on. And it must stop. And someone must do something to stop it.

Marianne turned to look at him and spoke through gritted teeth. 'Why are you on a one-man crusade? You against the Establishment.'

'Watch the road!'

Marianne veered towards the centre of the road and swerved back to the left again.

'You need to take the next right for the M20,' Mike informed her.

Marianne was silent for a few minutes while she concentrated on driving down the slip road and on to the motorway. They travelled a good five miles before she spoke again.

'So why did this officer in Lancashire wait until his retirement to come forward with this story?'

'They make things hard for whistle-blowers. It could mean a loss of pension.'

'And what did you tell the police about the accident last night?'

Her sudden change of tack almost threw him.

'I told them some nutter in a lorry – someone who was either pissed or angry – ran me off the road.'

'Why the hell didn't you tell them the truth about how you were set-up by Geoffrey Scranton, and someone deliberately tried to murder you?'

'I think that might have complicated the issue.'

‘Oh! The truth complicates issues now.’

Mike sighed and rubbed his wrist. ‘In this instance, it would. Can you imagine what the young DC who interviewed me would have made of my long and involved story about a murdered MP and a missing file, leading to my tracking an ex-MP who was part of a Westminster paedophile ring? He’d have thought the copper who tested me for being over the limit might have got the reading wrong.’

Marianne was silent for a bit as she thought about the implications of his explanation. When she spoke, her voice was quiet and subdued, and Mike guessed she was worried and resolved to set her mind at ease.

‘What happens now, Mike? Where do you go from here?’

‘I think I need to speak to Malcolm Reeves to find out who he’s in contact with over this affair.’

‘God!’ sighed Marianne. ‘I just wish…I just wish this whole thing could be resolved as quickly as possible.’

‘I’m sure it will be, just as soon as Justin Gormen and his girlfriend give the rest of the document to Forum Books. Hopefully it will all come out in the open then and my investigation will have ended.’

Mike went to glance at his watch, realized he wasn’t wearing it because of his sprained wrist, and looked at the time on the dashboard clock. It was a few seconds after eleven, so he clicked the radio to BBC 4 to catch the news bulletin. The first story was about a Chinese plane spotting what might be wreckage in the south Indian Ocean, possibly from the missing Malaysian aeroplane. But it was the second story that made them both sit up. A report of a fire in Wood Green in which a family was believed to have died, the item gave no further details, and Mike and Marianne could only speculate that it might be Gormen’s house. Soon after they arrived home, Marianne, having already taken the morning off work to go and fetch her husband, decided she would at least do a half day, and asked Mike to promise to let her know if there was further news about the house fire.

Mike sat glued to the television news at one o'clock and saw the Wood Green house fire had now become the main item, and it was already known that the occupants were the Gormen family, and the two bodies found were believed to be the mother and son, although it was too soon to tell conclusively. If that was the case, they would be looking for the whereabouts of the husband. His photograph, which looked like a passport picture, was flashed onto the screen.

Mike had a brief conversation with Marianne at her workplace and gave her the news, telling her he would be contacting his old sergeant at the Met to bring him in on the case, and to see if he might be able to discover Peter Gormen's true identity. He thought he heard Marianne muttering, 'Thank, God!' and knew she was relieved he had chosen to contact the police.

After ending the call to his wife, Mike knew it was time to confront Malcolm Reeves, to see if he could discover who he might be providing information to about the investigation. He had his suspicions, but he wanted it confirmed.

Chapter 29

Gormen sat in his spacious Docklands flat staring at the television screen, willing himself to cry. But all he felt was a sort of dazed numbness, a terrible emptiness, as though someone had lobotomised part of his brain.

Deep down he knew he was to blame for disobeying orders and keeping the document. But for Marshall to take such extreme measures was something he couldn't come to terms with. He didn't stop to rationalise and face the unpalatable truth about himself, that he had murdered others for money, to protect the rich and powerful. All he could think about was his wife and son, the part of him that was more precious than his real identity.

Looking back on it, to the very beginning of their lives together, it had been a delicious game. Pretending.

Inhabiting an alter ego, giving him the best of both worlds. The trouble was, now came the sudden realization that the phoney Peter Gormen was his true self, the person he had become and wanted to be, a role he had played so convincingly that he had even begun to fool himself. He juggled with both his lives, using his real identity as an indulgence, and that gave him carte blanche as a paid assassin, enjoying a life of luxury, and also living his family life as a lie, but one which he truly thought of as the unattainable one he desired.

Pauline and Justin! Now they had vanished from his life, ceased to exist as if they might never have been born. But they were still with him in memory. The only family life he had cherished and known.

Brought up in a Dr Barnardo's home hadn't been so bad when he thought about it. He had never known his parents, and never would. He was tucked up in his baby seat in the back of the car when it crashed. Eighteen months old when it happened, so there was no memory of his parents. He discovered when he was in his early teens that both his parents were only children, so they had no siblings who might take on the parenting responsibility after their sudden death. Not a single doting uncle or aunt. Things might have been different had one of them had a brother or sister. But that was storybook stuff. That Charles Dickens nonsense where everything turns out all right in the end and the orphan finds he belongs to a loving relative and is blessed by a wealthy inheritance.

Gormen knew life wasn't like that, and he often spent hours fantasizing about how his life might have turned out if his parents hadn't perished in that car crash. He often indulged in playful daydreams about being brought up by his perfect parents. After all, he had no reason to think his mother and father would have been anything other than loving. He wasn't like other kids in the home. Most of them had been abandoned by a single parent. This gave him feelings of superiority, knowing his life might have gone in a different direction had it not been for that fateful accident. That was why he knew it was up to him, and him alone, to make something of his life. And he could choose who he wanted to be. He soon developed a talent for pretending. And this talent helped shape his development in undercover work.

But now it had reached a crisis point. It was different when you had the upper hand, and you are the one to choose who lives and who dies. But who was he trying to kid? He had never made that decision. It was others who gave the orders. He always had to serve somebody, and it was like any large conglomerate – you had no contact with the top dog. You didn't even know who that was. However dirty the business, it was run along the same lines as any other organisation, Marshall being his line manager. But who gave Marshall the orders? Whoever it was had ordered Marshall to carry out the murder of his wife and son. And now, as far as Gormen was concerned, they had crossed the line.

Following the one o'clock news, he switched off the television, and sat drinking neat whisky, staring into the distance, seeing troubling images of death in his head. Now he could see clearly all the suffering he had caused, not only from the heinous crimes he had committed, but also from his involvement in the child abuse cover-up. But still his eyes were as dry as parched earth.

It took him until six o'clock to drink the entire bottle of whisky. He should have been drunk, and although his head buzzed with strange sounds, and images writhed like snakes uncoiling, reminding him of death and loss, he remained comparatively sober.

He clicked the remote and watched *BBC News*. More was added to the story of the fire at his house. Identifying the bodies as those of a young man and a middle-aged woman, they assumed that it was the mother and son but would have to wait on forensics for confirmation. Then they flashed up his passport photograph again, asking him – or anyone who knew him – to come forward. Perhaps they thought he might have done it, set fire to his own house. They had an interview with one of the fire chiefs who said it was undoubtedly arson as the fire had been started by an accelerant, and they found empty petrol containers abandoned near the front door.

How long would it take them, he wondered, to discover his identity? They still named him as Peter Gormen, and the house and all his documents were in that name, so it might take them some time yet. But it would happen eventually. All it needed was someone from his past to recognize his picture. Unless, of course, Marshall and his controllers wiped out the traces and persuaded the right people to bury the information.

As he thought about his family and the false past they had now destroyed, and all because they needed to cover up for some powerful paedophiles, he began to outline a plan in his muddled head. The lines had been crossed and there was no going back. And however fuzzy his head was from consuming too much whisky, he was clear about what he had to do.

He got up from the leather sofa, took a couple of steps across the living room and was relieved to note how steadily he walked. He went into the bedroom and opened one of the drawers under his double bed. Concealed beneath a bundle of spare bedding was the snub nose .460 Smith and Wesson Magnum which had never been fired. He spun the barrel of the revolver, seeing there was a round in every chamber, made sure the safety was on, then placed it next to his alarm clock on the bedside cabinet.

He set the alarm for four a.m. As every copper knew, dawn was the optimum time to catch someone unawares.

Chapter 30

A splitting headache shot Mike's mood into a dangerously high level of outrage, especially when he thought of the way he'd been set up by Scranton. When he telephoned Jo Reeves, she told him her husband was in the House of Commons and was unreachable. Frustrated at being unable to speak with Reeves to get to the bottom of who was getting the information about his progress in the investigation, Mike made it clear to her that it was now a matter of urgency that they speak. She told him her husband would probably be free around six or seven that evening, and asked him what the problem was, probing him for information, almost as if she filtered knowledge of the intelligence before passing it on to her husband. Mike didn't construe anything suspicious into her way of handling the situation. He knew that as a committed MP her husband's time was probably valuable and taken up with high-level meetings and consultations. Not only that, but as CEO of Forum Books, it was her company who was his client, the ones paying him for the investigation. But now, knowing there was an obvious leak, possibly in her company, he became circumspect about giving her too much information, especially about the attempt on his life, because he had no way of knowing if the perpetrators knew he had survived the crash and suffered nothing more than a severe bruising and sprained wrist. But if she went and told someone that she had spoken to him, he guessed the information of his survival would soon be known. Unless, of course, the information was leaking via her husband, who was for the moment unreachable, and therefore it would be a safe bet that the road accident resulting in failure was not yet known.

After the phone call, Mike made himself coffee and a sandwich, and took some more pain killers. Then he did a quick check on his laptop to see if the tracker was still in place on Scranton's BMW. As he suspected, it had been removed. Clearly Scranton, having been informed of the tracker under his car, and then colluding in the attempt to murder Mike, had destroyed it.

Now that Gormen's photograph had been shown on the news, then having promised Marianne he would bring the police into the equation, he tried telephoning Mark Simpson, to see if he could get a positive identification of the suspected killer's real identity. But when he got Simpson's voice mail asking him to leave a message, Mike slammed the phone down, grabbed his coat and left the house.

***

As he sat on the Northern Line train heading for Archway, Mike knew what he was doing was foolhardy, if not downright stupid, but he needed a channel for his fury. And having forgotten to ring the insurance company to see if he could arrange a courtesy car, it contributed to his growing anger and frustration. But the head-aching pressure of the rage building inside him had almost dissipated by the time he reached his destination.

Unable to find a cruising taxi at Archway, he began the long walk up Highgate Hill. Halfway up, near St Joseph's Catholic church, he stopped to get his breath back. There was a pub on a corner, opposite the church, and he was tempted to stop for a beer. He decided against it and summoned up the strength to carry on up the hill to the village. His head ached, and he felt uncomfortably hot from the steep walk, although he shivered occasionally whenever his wrist pained him. But the journey and the walk gave him time to cool down, to start thinking rationally. What if Scranton wasn't home? He had no way of knowing where Scranton was now the tracker was gone. Was this a completely wasted journey? Was it simply an impulsive act of vengeance? And what if he confronted Scranton's wife instead? What would he say to her? I have evidence your husband has been abusing young children and conspired to murder me last night. She would think him mad, slam the door in his face and call the police. And he couldn't blame her. Like many wives and partners of offenders, she would be the last to suspect her husband of any wrongdoing.

Knowing from his years as a Met detective how difficult it often was to suppress emotion; Mike was self-knowing enough to appreciate that it was something that had to be done if he needed to remain in control. Decisions had to be arrived at calmly and rationally, the heat removed. It was the only way to arrive at a satisfactory conclusion.

Breathless after the long walk, he arrived near the top of the hill leading to Scranton's home, and found himself outside a pub called the Flask. Having grave doubts now about pursuing someone who might soon be brought to justice, Mike's thirst for beer overcame his thirst for revenge, so he went inside and bought a pint of lager. As it was a reasonably warm day, and he needed to cool off after his walk, he sat outside on one of the benches. He downed half the pint thirstily, shivered as he thought about evil monsters like Scranton and Jessop, then swept them out of his head, deciding to abandon what he knew was a pointless act of revenge. The best justice for the victims of abuse was public humiliation and a custodial sentence for the likes of Scranton.

But now Justin Gormen had been murdered, the house gutted by fire, there was slim chance of resurrecting the formal investigation of the Westminster paedophiles. So now Mike knew the only chance of arriving at any sort of justice was to try to discover who was behind it all.

He took out his smart phone and decided he would give Malcolm Reeves another call on his mobile, in case he switched his phone on between meetings. And if he got his voice mail, he would text to impress on him how urgent it was for them to meet. He had just tapped on to his list of contacts when his attention was diverted to an overweight man coming around the corner and into the pub grounds. It was Scranton. Taken completely by surprise, Mike lowered his head and stared into his glass, but Scranton walked past without glancing at him. Of course, the man had never seen him before. Why would he recognize him?

He watched as Scranton entered the pub, then waited to see if he came back out again. But after five minutes had gone by, and there being no sign of Scranton coming to sit outside, Mike picked up his pint and entered the pub.

There were six customers in the bar, two standing at the bar, and another three at a table. In a far corner sat Scranton, sliding his stubby fingers across a small tablet, in between taking large gulps from a pint of bitter. Mike stood watching him for a moment, hating the sight of him – his double chins, and his bloated, overfed face.

The barman looked at Mike questioningly, saw the pint in his hand, and thought he had come in because it was too cold to sit outside. Ignoring him, Mike walked over to Scranton's table, pulled a chair out, and sat down. Scranton looked up frowning, then became agitated and annoyed. He waved a finger at other empty tables.

'That seat is free, and so is that seat, and that seat. What gives you the right to sit here?'

Mike fixed him in his sights, hoping the man could see the venom in his eyes.

'I'll tell you what gives me the right to sit here, Scranton, because I want to sit opposite the man who tried to have me killed last night in a car crash.'

He watched as the colour drained from Scranton's face.

'Let me introduce myself. My name is Mike Halliday. I expect you've heard of me, even though we've never met.'

Nothing moved in Scranton's face. He could have been carved out of stone. He was so frozen with shock, even his eyes looked like glass marbles.

'But I expect you've got a perfect alibi for last night,' Mike continued. 'However, you're forgetting I used to be a cop and we have things like CCTV. It's how we catch a lot of criminals. Unless you can prove someone else was driving your BMW last night—'

Like a dog shaking off water, Scranton trembled, pocketed his tablet and began to rise. Mike used his right hand to grab Scranton by the wrist.

'Sit down, Scranton, and listen to what I've got to say. Or I'll cause such a scene the police might have to be called. And you wouldn't want that, would you?'

Scranton slumped heavily into his seat, his shoulders sagging with defeat. 'W-what do you want?' he stammered.

Mike half-grinned, but his eyes were cold and unsmiling. 'I'll tell you what I want. I want to see you suffer, for all the suffering you've caused others.'

'If it's money you're after—'

'You think you can just buy your way out of your guilt? Wave money at someone and everything will be washed away? Not this time, Scranton. Not this time.'

Scranton's chins wobbled as he shook his head. 'I don't think you realize what you're up against if you think you can come in here and threaten me—'

Mike banged the table with a clenched fist, then pointed a finger in Scranton's face. 'Don't think you can call on your friends in high places to back you up, you smarmy git. Once the police and CPS have all the evidence, you'll be publicly humiliated before they lock you up. And you know what happens to nonces in prison, don't you? You'll never be able to touch the food without feeling sick, knowing someone has spat or pissed in it. Or worse. That's what you've got to look forward to, you evil bastard.'

Scranton licked his lips, and tried to raise his beer glass, but his hand shook too much. 'I…I'm sorry. I wasn't threatening you. If there's anything I can do to sort out this mess—'

Mike laughed harshly. 'It's too late for that, Scranton.'

'Can't we please come to some sort of arrangement?'

'I have another copy of that file – the one that Lord Albion conveniently lost,' Mike lied. 'Your murdering friend Peter Gormen kept it when he should have destroyed it – but of course you know that, don't you? But did you know his son made another copy of the document which he gave me before he died in that fire. And soon it'll be in the hands of the police? No, you couldn't possibly know that, could you?'

'Please…please. Can't we do something – anything – to sort this mess out?'

'It's a mess of your own doing, Scranton.'

'How much do you want?' Scranton snivelled. 'I'll give you whatever you ask. Only…please…I beg you….'

'Did any of those children beg you to stop when you abused them?' Mike shouted.

Scranton, fear in his eyes, looked towards the bar, noticing how the barman was now staring at them.

'Please,' he begged. 'This is my local. They all know me in here.'

'They won't just know you when the story hits the media, they'll know what you've done as well. How will that feel, eh?'

'You've no idea, have you? No idea what it was like.'

'What are you talking about?'

Scranton fought back tears now, his voice croaking. 'When I was a child. I was overweight. And not a good-looking child. They used to bully me. So much so, I wanted to....' He broke off.

Mike pushed his chair back and stood up. 'Are you trying to tell me this is all about taking revenge on children? You're an adult for Christ's sake. It doesn't excuse anything.'

'Please,' Scranton pleaded. 'I'll do anything to make it right.'

'It's too late for that. You've destroyed too many lives. How many of those kids d'you think might never recover from what you did to them? I hope you rot in hell for it.'

Mike turned and walked hurriedly from the pub without looking back. As he walked towards the village high street, trembling with pent up rage, he became aware of people stepping out of his way and giving him a wide berth. He realized it was probably a mixture of his dark mood and the enormous bruise on one side of his face that scared them. He needed to calm down, so he went into another pub, bought a double whisky, and sat in a corner, waiting for the anger to subside.

His phone bleeped, alerting him to a text message. It was from Malcolm Reeves.

'Mike, Jo told me we need to meet urgently. Appreciate delay not good but I can't make tonight. Can we meet early tomorrow morning, to sort this thing out? Nine a.m. at Fortnum and Mason's Fountain Restaurant, Piccadilly? Use the Jermyn Street entrance. Let me know if not convenient. Malcolm.'

At first Mike was irritated, and his anger began to rise again. Then he focused on his whisky, took another sip, and tried to calm himself. It was now just gone four p.m. The meeting was only another seventeen hours away. He decided he could wait that long. Apart from which, he felt physically sick after his ordeal, and needed the time to relax and recover before encountering any more obstacles.

***

Arriving home about five minutes before Marianne was due back from work, Mike found Natalie engrossed in watching *The Simpsons* on television. She glanced at her father, and her mouth dropped open in alarm.

'Dad! You all right? You look terrible.'

He smiled, flattered she cared enough to tear herself away from the TV. He leaned over the sofa, kissed the top of her head, then said, 'I'll live. I just feel exhausted, like something a dog's been chewing. Other than that, right as rain.'

'I would've come to the hospital with Mum this morning. Only she said you were all right. She's like making out school's more life-and-death than your accident.'

Mike laughed. 'She's probably right.' He touched the side of his head. 'It's only a bruise. But it was no accident, Natalie.'

'Have they found the wankers who ran you off the road yet?'

He caught himself tutting at her use of bad language, then followed it with a smile to show it didn't matter.

'No, and I don't think they will,' he said. 'But your TV programme has just reminded me. I need to phone my old detective sergeant, who's now an inspector.'

Natalie frowned. 'Yeah, like how come it reminded you to phone a detective?'

'His name's Simpson. Mark Simpson.' He glanced at his watch. 'Your Mum's a bit late.'

'She rang to say she'd be back about half six and could you order a takeaway?'

'How about Chinese?'

Natalie's attention was drawn back to the television. 'Yeah. Whatever.'

Mike went into the kitchen, unpinned a folding menu from the notice board and used his mobile to phone an order for a set meal for two people with a couple of extra dishes. Then he tried calling Mark Simpson again. He expected the voice mail again and was surprised when Mark answered after two rings.

'It's Mike Halliday, Mark.'

'Hi there, Mike. What can I do for you?'

Mike could hear much background noise, talking and music, and assumed Mark was in a pub.

'You know I asked you for the car registration for a Peter Gormen. Well, I have his photograph now—'

'And you want me to see if I can ID it. If you email it to me, I'll see what I can do.'

'There's no need. It's been on all the television news. He's wanted in connection with a fire at his house in Wood Green. And he seems to have disappeared.'

'Christ! I thought the name rang a bell. What's your involvement with this man?'

'I've been tailing him for a client – a publisher who's been sent details of a sensitive government document. And I think Gormen may once have been an undercover cop.'

A long silence, apart from the background music.

'Hello, Mark. You still there?'

'Yeah, I'm still here. And I can't let you have the details of his true identity, Mike. I'm sorry.'

'Why's that?'

'I've no idea. But if the media get hold of it because of your involvement, and they know I've been speaking to you, it could have serious repercussions.'

'On your career, you mean?'

'I'm sorry, Mike. I'm going to have to go. Let's speak soon and have that drink. See you around.'

The call ended, and Mike stared at the mobile interface for a moment, wondering why the police wanted to keep Gormen's true identity a secret. Was it because he was an ex-undercover cop who had become a hired killer? And was it because he was hired by some powerful forces in the country? Mike had never been one to support or believe conspiracy theorists, but because of recent events, he was starting to feel differently about the dominance of the state and the way it protected the rich and powerful.

He heard the key in the front door latch, followed by Marianne's cheery call that she was home, and he dismissed his cynical thoughts and went to greet her.

Chapter 31

Tuesday 25 March 2014

The weird images floating around in his head were not alarming, and he became aware that this was nothing more than a dream as his brain surfaced into consciousness. The dream had not disturbed him, and he felt relaxed, as he often did after a long and peaceful sleep. But the horror of his situation as he blinked open his eyes and saw Gormen standing over him launched palpitations of alarm throughout his body. He tried to move, but his arms just above the wrists were bound tightly to the wooden arms of one of his chairs. A sickening smell of plastic under his nose, and he wanted to gag. He wanted to speak, to reason with his captor, but his speech would be muffled by the strip of gaffer tape covering his mouth.

How the fuck had Gormen broken into his house? He remembered going to bed just after midnight, as he usually did. So somehow Gormen must have managed to break in and…

And then what? He didn't remember being disturbed in the night. So somehow or other Gormen must have used something to keep him from waking. Chloroform, maybe?

He made eye contact with Gormen, and a coldness in his chest, as if he might have swallowed a block of ice, paralysed him with a terrible fear. Light streamed through the French windows, and he could see the Thames at the end of his long garden, shimmering and glinting as the sun shone on the water. He had no idea what time it was and guessed it must be early morning.

He blinked several times, and his eyes watered as he became more able to focus on his familiar surroundings.

He knew it was useless to try to speak, otherwise why would Gormen have gagged him?

And then the horror of his frail situation increased as his eyes were drawn to the occasional table Gormen must have moved from in front of the built-in alcove bookcase. On it stood objects which sent razor sharp slices of fear through his nerve ends. A pair of pliers, a corkscrew, and disposable cigarette lighter. He knew what Gormen had in mind and he made a muffled and unintelligible plea, shaking his head helplessly. It was wasted on Gormen, who stared at him with a hatred so deep it was unnerving. It was a cold and calculating abomination, and he saw not the slightest sadistic satisfaction in Gormen's face for what the man was about to do.

Marshall cursed himself for being so stupid as to underestimate the man's feelings for his family. He thought Gormen used them as a cover for respectability and his false identity; he had no idea the man had become a loving husband, even if it was only on a part-time basis. It was ironic, when you thought about it. But even worse, it meant Gormen was out for revenge. If only he would remove the gag, Marshall was certain he could talk him round. There would be offers of other lucrative jobs, perhaps a new identity and a bonus for his inconvenience. Because, when all was said and done, that's all it was – an inconvenience. And Gormen was equally attached to his bachelor lifestyle, his young women and trips abroad. Surely, he wouldn't want to jeopardise all that for some stupid act of vengeance.

After staring at him dispassionately for a long while, Gormen picked up the pliers, and Marshall cringed back in the chair.

'It's not you I'm after,' Gormen said. 'I realize you are only another cog in the operation – quite high up, admittedly – but I want the top man, the one who gives the orders. I want whoever ordered you to have my family murdered. Oh, I realize you can't say much as I've covered your mouth. But that's so that no one can hear you scream. Because, you see, I'm going to inflict such terrible pain on you, you'll gladly give me his name. And that's the only way it'll work. How else will I believe what you tell me? The pain is going to be so intense, the only way it will stop is when I have his name. And just to make certain you haven't given me a false name, you will need to be at the end of your pain threshold, begging me to reveal the truth.

'Admittedly, pulling out a person's fingernails systematically is not very inventive – a bit old-fashioned, I suppose. But I don't have time to spare for psychological torture or anything as sophisticated as water boarding, which could take weeks – months even, depending on a person's stamina. So, I will resort to good old physical pain.'

Marshall shrank back, his spine pressed tight against the wooden slats in the chair, as Gormen held the pliers menacingly close to his face.

'You made a terrible mistake thinking my son still had the memory stick containing the document,' Gormen went on. 'And he may have sent a part of the dossier to the publisher, but it was only an extract. I got the flash drive back. And guess where it is now?' He suddenly raised his voice as he thought about the futility of the recent events. 'It's at the bottom of the Thames in Docklands. I got rid of it there after I met you on Friday. Killing my family was unnecessary. Pointless.'

Marshall tried to communicate through muffled speech, tried telling Gormen it was a mistake. Surely the man in his line of business must understand how easy it is to make mistakes. Collateral damage. And wasn't the biggest mistake of all Gormen's fault, by not getting rid of the USB file when he was told?

'Let me guess what you're trying to say. You're trying to tell me it was all a mistake, yes? And maybe it's my fault for not destroying the file in the first place. Well, maybe you're right. But to burn my wife and son to death like that – the only family I've ever known. You think I was just going to lie down and let that happen? Just shrug my shoulders and carry on as normal? No, you and your controller have made a grave error and I want to know who is responsible. I'm not going to give up till I find out. Now – I think it's time to get on with it.'

As Gormen moved around to Marshall's right side, Marshall screamed through his gag, his eyes wide with terror. Gormen raised the thumb of Marshall's right hand, slid the edges of the pliers between the nail and the skin, and began to peel back the nail slowly, inflicting the maximum amount of pain on his helpless captive. Marshall's screams through the gag got louder and more frantic, and already his throat felt red raw. He tried to raise himself from the chair, following the direction of the pliers as it pulled the nail upwards away from his thumb. Tears sprang into his eyes and rolled down his face as the excruciating pain blinded him and numbed his brain. The torture was horrific, and he knew it was just a start, there was a lot more to come.

As Gormen prised the thumbnail away, the screams got louder. Then the excruciating pain subsided, and he was left shivering and hot, his body convulsed and trembling with shock.

Gormen stood up straight, held the pliers up, showing him the bloodied thumbnail. 'Another nine to go,' he said. 'Think you can stand the pace?'

Marshall's head fell forward as he sobbed, his body shaking uncontrollably. For a moment Gormen wondered if he might suffer a heart attack. If that happened, he'd never find out who was responsible for the death of his family. He cupped a hand under Marshall's chin and raised the man's head. Marshall's tearful eyes blinked as he tried to focus through the tears.

Gormen smiled grimly as he spoke. 'Don't want you having a heart attack and escaping your punishment. Yes, punishment. I want you to suffer. And I don't think you're a brave man. You've never really done any field work, have you? What were you? Just a crafty little disinformation spreader. Little more than a cowardly civil servant. And they promoted you, didn't they? Gave you more responsibility, allowing you to make life and death decisions from a distance – like your gentleman's club in St James's. I know more about you than you think. I never liked or trusted you, Marshall. Years ago, I kept a watch on you, and you led me to this nice house in Sunbury. I was looking to the future, you see. Which was why I kept the USB file. How was I to know my son would find it, and things turn out the way they did? But he didn't deserve to die for it, Marshall.'

Gormen's rage suddenly erupted and he dropped the pliers on to the table before smacking Marshall in the face.

'So now you're going to tell me who was responsible.'

Marshall, making muffled noises as he tried to speak, blood pouring from his nose, indicated with nods of the head that he was compliant, ready to talk.

Gormen studied him carefully, taking his time, waiting for the groans to dwindle, before continuing. 'You think you can fob me off by agreeing to talk so easily? You must think I'm a simpleton, Marshall. I realize you're probably a physical coward, but you could still feed me lies. The only way I can get at the truth is for you to experience so much pain you'll be desperate to tell me. The only way I will stop is when I get the truth. And guess what, Marshall? I will know when you're lying, and the pain will start over again.'

Gormen turned and looked out of the French windows, seeing a launch pass by on the river. 'Get much trouble with flooding earlier in the year, did you?' he taunted his captive. 'Still, that's the least of your worries now, isn't it?'

He picked up the pliers again and moved this time to Marshall's left side. 'Another thumbnail? Good to have a routine I always think.'

He attached the pliers to the thumbnail of Marshall's left hand and bent it slowly. Marshall's chair almost left the floor as he rattled and shook with pain and wounded-animal noises burst through the gag as the agony of the torture reduced him to a shivering wreck. Sweat and tears poured from his face like rivulets of rain.

Still worried the man might suffer a heart attack, Gormen ripped off the gag, as Marshall shuddered and moaned. 'You had enough, Marshall? Ready to talk now?'

'Listen to me,' Marshall gasped. 'These people, if you find out who they are and expose them, it won't do you any good. You'll be a dead man.'

'Right now, I'm not sure I care about that.'

'I can get you a huge pay-out. Compensation for your loss. Don't throw everything away because of what's happened. I can arrange for you to receive an enormous sum of money. Enough to give you a good living without having to work for it.'

Gormen, unmoved by the offer, picked up the strip of black gaffer tape and shoved it back over Marshall's mouth.

'You just don't get it, do you? It's not about money. My compensation will be total annihilation – yours and whoever controls you.'

Chapter 32

Malcolm Reeves sat at a table in Fortnum's Fountain Restaurant, a desk diary in front of him with his mobile phone on top of it. He glanced at his watch, and saw it was a little after ten past nine. The restaurant, which had been open for over an hour, was already doing a brisk trade, which quite surprised the MP, although he could see the customers seemed to be mainly foreign visitors, no doubt making an early start, so they might cram in as many sights as they could in one day.

He ordered coffee and a scone, and a few minutes later Mike arrived breathlessly, having walked hurriedly up the escalators at Piccadilly Tube station.

'What happened to your face?' Reeves asked, staring at Mike's bruise, which was now a palette of purple and yellowish-brown.

'Just an accident,' Mike replied as he sat. 'Nothing to worry about.'

Reeves glanced at his watch pointedly which annoyed Mike, who was not about to apologize because he suspected that everything that happened with the case – the guest house closing, Baldwin's death, the arson murders of the Gormen family, and the attempt on his life, were all down to Malcolm Reeves and someone he had unwittingly and naïvely passed information to.

'Glad you could eventually see me,' he told the MP, letting his insincerity show.

A waitress appeared at the table almost immediately. He asked for a black coffee and, having eaten no breakfast, ordered a croissant.

'Jo told me of your concerns,' Reeves kicked off.

Mike looked incredulous. 'Concerns? They're more than concerns, Malcolm. Three people dead in less than two weeks, and the only way the information about the investigation could have been leaked is either from someone Jo's been speaking to or it came from you. Personally, I would plump for the latter.'

Flustered, the MP opened and closed his mouth several times before finding a voice. 'When Jo mentioned it, I racked my brains for who it could possibly be, and I couldn't come up with anyone. I haven't told my assistant, colleagues in the House, or anyone I can think of. It's a mystery.'

Mike sat back, pausing for dramatic emphasis. 'So that leaves only one person. Dennis Lorcan?'

Reeves screwed up his face. 'Dennis? He's actively involved in funding his charity for victims of abuse. Why would....?'

'A smokescreen!' Mike cut in. 'Think how Jimmy Savile operated, fooling everyone from the Royal Family to the prime minister with his fund raising for charity. They ended up giving him a knighthood, an effective camouflage for his crimes.'

'Even so, I've seen nothing to suggest Dennis has any interest in children. Just between you and me, he's a bit of a womaniser. He's attracted to grown-up women, not children.'

'That's what I told my wife.'

'And what did she say?'

'She wasn't buying it. She thinks it could be Dennis Lorcan.' Mike pointed at the MP's desk diary. 'Why don't we go through the events from when I first took on the case, and you can work out when and what you said about the case to Lorcan?'

Reeves donned a pair of reading glasses and rifled through the pages until he reached mid-March. It was a page a day diary, and Mike saw by the handwritten scrawl on each page how full it was. Reeves used a pen to scroll down as he searched for relevant information on each page.

'There's nothing about the case until the date when you and your wife came to dinner and met Dennis and Jennifer.'

The waitress appeared, and they both stopped speaking and waited for her to place their order on the table.

'That night,' Mike said after she had left, 'when we came to dinner was when Dennis Lorcan discovered I'd been to that guest house and had every intention of returning. Don't you remember how he tried to talk me out of it?'

'I seem to think I did that as well.'

'But maybe, seeing how upset I was by a visit to that house, he thought I might ignore the advice. So, he gave orders to shut it down and put it on the market. All it would take would be a phone call.'

Reeves shook his head doubtfully. 'But look how upset Dennis was when you told him about the children. He almost broke down.'

Mike produced a cynical smile for the MP's benefit. 'Malcolm, from my years in the Met, I've seen criminals break down convincingly to protest their innocence. It's easy to do. They convince themselves that what they are saying is the truth, and when they think about the stretch behind bars, that's what brings on the convincing waterworks. Now, let's look at what you told Dennis following dinner that night.'

'Nothing. I couldn't have told him anything. I flew to Berlin on Sunday night.'

'And nothing else happened the week you were away. I collected evidence – evidence which I passed on to Jo. When did she bring you up to date on the case?'

'I think that was Friday afternoon, before I was due to fly back from Berlin.'

Reeves suddenly gasped, his mouth opening in shock. 'Oh, shit!'

'What's wrong?'

'That was when I bumped into Dennis. He was staying at the same hotel as me. Apparently, he was in Berlin for a conference.'

'And you can bet your life that was no coincidence, was it?' Mike concluded.

***

Wondering if his captive could survive long enough to give him the information he needed, Gormen stood back, dispassionately observing Marshall's drooping head. He reflected on his actions, wondering if it might have been better if he hadn't rushed things. Three more fingernails and still Marshall hadn't told him what he wanted to know. Which was when he resorted to the cigarette lighter. Marshall screwing his eyes tight shut as the lighter flame came nearer. So Gormen grabbed an eyelid, forcing it open, and let the flame burn into the socket. The scream Marshall let out was blood-chillingly grotesque. And now the man was nearing the end. There was only so much he could take.

Still holding the lighter, Gormen flicked it on and off, letting Marshall know he could soon suffer more of the same.

'That was horrifyingly painful, wasn't it?' He spoke in a soothing voice, mirroring the way his captive talked. 'You'll be blind in that eye. So now I'll give you an option. Tell me what I want to know, and if I believe you, I'll leave your good eye alone. The alternative is total blindness. So, if you don't tell me the truth…well, I'll let you work that one out. You'll be in darkness for the rest of your life. You ready to talk now? Just give me a nod if you are.'

Gormen stared at him, waiting. Presently, with great effort, Marshall gave two small nods. Gormen ripped the gag off and bent down, his ear close to Marshall's mouth.

That was the moment Gormen believed what Marshall told him.

***

Mike was deep in thought as he watched Malcolm Reeves hungrily devouring the scone, as if the knowledge of the betrayal had boosted the MP's appetite. His own appetite had shrunk, and the thought of eating repelled him.

'So now what?' Reeves mumbled through a mouthful of scone.

'I think we ought to confront Lorcan right away.'

'We?'

'Yes, he knows you and trusts you – even though he's been using you.'

'There's a preliminary bill in the House that's being debated this afternoon. Besides which, I think we ought to put this in the hands of the police. Go through the proper channels. You have enough evidence now. And your evidence along with the information I was giving Dennis, and the way…' He broke off as he saw Mike shaking his head. 'What's wrong?'

'Peter Gormen took a dead child's identity, and that's the name in which he married and in which his son was registered. I think when he started out, he may have been an undercover cop for the Special Demonstration Squad. Since then he may have been recruited by Christ knows who. But in my researches, I discovered one of the mourners at Jimmy Savile's funeral was a Freemason and I recognized him from when I worked in counter terrorism. He was a secret service man. Either MI5 or MI6.'

'And you think he might be involved with Dennis Lorcan?'

'I can't be sure. And I've got no evidence to back it up. All I'm saying is it's hard to know who to trust.'

'But we can't fight this alone. When Jo engaged you, all she wanted you to do was spy on some suspected paedophiles like Geoffrey Scranton and find out who had the USB file.'

Reeves's phone rang. He looked at the interface and said, 'It's Jo. I'd better get it.'

Mike tugged at a few more strands of croissant, dunked them in cold coffee, swallowed and winced as he forced the food down. He listened as Reeves paid attention to what he was told, and Mike guessed some vital information was about to be relayed but hadn't a clue what it was.

'No, I didn't hear the nine o'clock news,' Reeves said. 'I'm in Fortnum's with Mike.' Pause. His eyes widened. 'When did this happen?' Another pause as he listened to his wife's message. 'Oh, I see. Well maybe there'll be more details later. Thanks for letting me know. I've got to go, darling. I'll call you later and let you know what's happening.'

He ended the call and stared at Mike. 'Just before Jo called, we were talking of the devil. Well, now the devil is no longer with us.'

Irritated by Reeves's dramatic indulgence, Mike snapped, 'That's a bit cryptic, Malcolm. Just tell me what's happened.'

'Sorry. Yes. Geoffrey Scranton is dead. He had a heart attack last night on his way home from the pub. That's all I know, and that's all Jo knows at this stage.'

Mike froze, his expression inscrutable.

'So that's another one who escapes justice,' Reeves added.

Saying nothing, Mike thought the way he hounded Scranton in the pub probably contributed to the man's death. Now he regretted his actions, not because he felt any guilt towards the despicable ex-MP but because of the way the victims were again cheated from any judicial procedures.

'What are you thinking, Mike?'

'Same as you. Bastard's gone and cheated his victims from justice. He should have been publicly humiliated and jailed for his crimes.'

As he said it, Mike felt responsible. But there was no way he was going to unburden himself to Reeves about the meeting with Scranton, mainly because he felt it was time to move on and ensnare the big game.

'What's the bill being debated in the house?' Mike asked.

'It's about free school dinners.'

'Which is more important, that or the enquiry into the Westminster ring of paedophiles to try to expose them?'

Reeves shifted uncomfortably in his seat, wondering where Mike was going with this. 'Well, the latter, I suppose,' he admitted reluctantly.

'Well, here's what I suggest. You call Lorcan up and tell him I've provided you with new evidence; and a copy has been made of the document and we think we know who has it. He'll have no reason to think you no longer trust him. And you can also tell him you're with me, and we need to give him this evidence as soon as possible because we may need his financial input to take this a step further.'

'But what's the point? We know the calculating shit's responsible for everything that's happened, so what do we hope to gain by meeting him?'

'Confrontation. Put him on the spot, tell him we know what he's done, and we can prove it.'

'Won't he just deny it?'

'He might, but I suspect he's smart enough to realize we've sussed what's been going on.'

'But I don't understand what we hope to gain by this confrontation.'

'Lorcan strikes me as a classic psychopath. Once he realizes we're onto him, my guess is he'll enjoy boasting about his misdeeds. And my intention will be to let him think we can't prove anything, and afterwards leave with our tail between our legs.'

Frowning, Reeves stared at Mike questioningly. Mike grinned and tapped his chest.

'I'll be wired up, of course. Everything that's said will be recorded. So, make the call, Malcolm. And let's see if we can nail the arsehole.'

***

Taking his time now – no need to rush – Gormen smiles mercilessly, wallowing in the supreme feeling of power. Thumbs up or down, it is his decision who lives or dies, just as it was in the past. Only now it's different. These are not orders. His decision and his alone. Total control. And total power over life or death. And confident he now has the information; he can finish it. Only one way the coin will land. Heads or tails, either way you lose, Marshall.

He walks behind Marshall's chair, leans over the coffee table and picks up the Magnum from where he'd left it. Clicks off the safety. He hears Marshall stirring, feeling unnerved by something happening behind his back.

Holding the gun at his side, Gormen walks and stands in front of him, waits for him to feel his presence. In a moment, he blinks open his one good eye and focuses on his torturer. He seems to have lost the ability to comprehend what is happening to him. Then his eye follows the line of Gormen's arm down to the gun. Now he knows there is not a shred of hope. But at least the pain will soon be gone, even though he doesn't want to die.

Gormen raises the gun. Staring into the black hole of the barrel, waiting for the blast, Marshall realizes why shooting squads blindfold their victims and closes his eye. He waits. Nothing happens. He waits and waits, hardly daring to breathe. All he can hear is his own shallow breathing, and somewhere in the distance the lapping of water and the song of birds. Perhaps Gormen has changed his mind. Maybe he'll let him off the hook.

After what seems like an immeasurable interval, he dares to open his eye.

'Goodbye, you spineless cunt,' Gormen says, and pulls the trigger.

All it takes is the one bullet and Marshall ceases to exist in a bloody microsecond.

Chapter 33

After driving to Ealing so that Mike could get wired up, Malcolm Reeves felt nervous and twitchy as they set off in his Saab for Lorcan's house in Virginia Water.

'I'm still not sure we're doing the right thing,' he said. 'Lorcan's not a fool. He might guess you've come wired up. Isn't this quite common in your line of work?'

'I guess it is. But don't forget, he doesn't know we're on to him. I was impressed by your phone call. It would've fooled me, that's for sure. And he has no reason to suspect you no longer trust him.'

'No, but the fact that I'm bringing you with me might look like a set-up. I've never suggested you meet with us before.'

'Except for dinner at your house two weeks ago. Whose idea was that?'

Reeves was silent as he thought about it.

'Well?' Mike prompted.

'I think it was Jo who wanted to invite you to dinner. But now I think about it, I'm not so sure. It might have come from Lorcan. I seem to remember he made light of it, saying he'd be interested in meeting a real-life private eye. And then, yes, I remember he became quite serious. You know – joking apart, it would be good for us all to put our heads together.'

'So, there's no reason for him to be suspicious.'

'No, but if he's told us nothing but lies – and his charity for abused children really is a smokescreen – what makes you think he'll admit to anything incriminating which you can get on tape?'

Not wanting to worry the MP with his intentions, Mike changed the subject, leaning forward in his seat to check the signposts as they drove towards Brentford.

'Do you know this part of the world, Malcolm?'

'Not really. I did study the map while you got wired up.'

Mike chuckled, mainly to put Reeves at ease. 'Still using maps, Malcolm? Bit old-fashioned, isn't it? So which route are you thinking of taking?'

'Over Kew Bridge and through Richmond.'

'No, I'd go right at Brentford, through Isleworth, Twickenham and Kingston, then pick up the M3 and we're practically there. Incidentally, when you phoned Lorcan from Fortnum's, and you told him you were with me, how did he react?'

A pause as Reeves thought about it. 'He was quiet at first. Almost as if I'd dropped a brick. There was a deathly silence, and I was about to ask him what was wrong, but then he recovered and said it would be good for the three of us to meet. Why d'you ask?'

Mike hesitated, then said, 'Because I think Lorcan paid to have me killed. The bruise on the side of my head is from my car crashing when a lorry forced me off the road. I was lucky to survive. So, when you spoke to him earlier on, he probably hadn't expected me to be in one piece. Strapped up in traction in a Kent hospital at the very least. When he passed on the message about the children's home in Maidstone which Scranton might be visiting, it was a way to get rid of me.'

'So, Scranton was in on it as well.'

'He probably had no option but to agree to what they told him to do.'

'For Christ's sake, Mike, why didn't you tell me this earlier on?'

'Because I was worried about what you or Jo might say to him. I didn't want him to be warned about my surviving the accident with nothing more than a bruise and sprained wrist.'

Petrified of the meeting with Lorcan now, Reeves turned to say something to Mike and almost went over a red light. He slammed on the brakes and screeched to a halt, stopping slightly beyond the white line.

'I don't think I can go through with this meeting,' he said, blowing out his breath.

'It'll be fine. Didn't he say his wife's in their house in Tuscany? And he'll give his staff the day off? So, there'll just be the three of us. Nothing to worry about then.'

'Except,' Reeves said, as the lights turned green and he pulled away.

'Except?' Mike questioned.

'He never goes anywhere without Jimmy, his bodyguard. The man's more a minder than he is a chauffeur, which is why he's always with Dennis. And Jimmy's an ex-SAS and mercenary soldier. They don't come tougher than Jimmy.'

'Shit!' Mike exclaimed. 'Now you tell me.'

Chapter 34

After a recent shower of light rain, followed by a burst of sunshine, glass glistened attractively on the towering buildings at Canary Wharf, so that even detractors of modern architecture and high-rise buildings may have been awed by the sight. But not Gormen. Not now. He had too much on his mind, and barely noticed the familiar skyline as he drove by. He was more concerned about his carelessness in forgetting to grab a few more rounds for the Magnum. One bullet was all it took to dispatch Marshall, but he had no way of knowing how many more he might need before the day was over. He could have kicked himself for this unprofessional error. It may have had something to do with his recent bereavement, but he still cursed himself for lack of foresight.

He only hoped the police might not know his real identity yet, in which case he could return to his apartment and stock up on more ammunition. But if the police knew his identity, then they would know his Docklands address. And if that was the case, there was no way he could get any more cartridges.

Cautiously sticking to the speed limit now, he turned right from Marsh Wall, heading towards the Thames and his flat. Once past Island Gardens, he slowed and became even more vigilant, his eyes scouring the streets for any sign of a suspicious-looking vehicle with two men inside. As he neared the end of his street, and seeing little traffic about, he indicated and pulled over to the right, stopping just short of his street. Then, when the main road was clear of traffic, he eased the Citroën forward a few yards, blocking off entrance to the street, and looked towards his flat. He didn't want to drive along the street, which would be blocked off by the river, except for a narrow street at the end which would take him into a parallel road to his own.

He squinted, adjusting his focus to see if there were any suspicious looking cars parked outside his apartment building. But anyone living in his block would no doubt park underground, unless they wanted to dash in for something they might have forgotten.

And then he saw them, about two-hundred yards away, sitting in a silver Renault, the car facing towards him and the main road. They couldn't fail to notice him. And then the car moved forwards, coming towards him at a rapid pace.

No more than fifty yards away, a bus was coming along the main road towards him, and there was a UPS delivery van behind him, driving on the left. Hoping the bus might delay his pursuers from pulling out into the main road for a moment, he slammed his foot on the accelerator and pulled out into the left-hand side of the road, missing the bus by a few yards, but causing the delivery van to slam on its brakes. Swerving in front of the van, his Citroën fishtailed, and he heard the van's squeal of brakes and an angry blast on the horn. He took his foot off the accelerator and managed to control the swerve, then as the car righted itself, he accelerated again. Just after the church on the right, he swerved left into Marsh Wall, tyres burning and squealing on the tarmac. Before taking the corner, a glance in the mirror showed the Renault pulling out into the main road from behind the bus.

He put his foot down hard, and hurtled along the road, reaching sixty now in the speed restricted area. A small hatchback in front, doing less than thirty, blocked his access to a clear run, and there was a large delivery lorry coming towards him on the opposite side of the road. He increased his speed, squeezing his car through the narrowest of gaps. The lorry tooted aggressively as he narrowly missed colliding with it but clipped the offside front of the hatchback. There was an almighty crunch of tearing metal, but he ignored it and accelerated, raising his speed to seventy.

In his mirror he saw the Renault overtaking the hatchback, which had pulled to one side, and they were hurtling towards him, closing the gap. He knew he had little chance of losing them now – unless it was on foot.

As he sped toward South Quay station and the pedestrian crossing, he unclipped his seatbelt. The lights turned red, and he spotted at least half a dozen pedestrians starting to cross. He kept his hand on the horn, alerting them to his urgency to escape the pursing car. The blast of his horn and the roar of his engine warned them of his suicidal approach, but two pedestrians already halfway across, rather than get off the road, froze with fear, their mouths wide with horror as his car hurtled towards them. He swerved around them, almost hitting the barrier on the opposite side of the road. No other vehicles were coming towards him, so he took the next right turn into Admirals Way, which he knew led to the West India Dock walkway and Canary Wharf. Approaching a small private car park by the dock at speed, with a barrier blocking the entrance, he braked, slowing the car but not stopping it, opened the door and leapt clear as his Citroën ploughed into the barrier with a crash of metal.

People approaching the dock turned in alarm and saw the abandoned vehicle crashing through the barrier and hitting parked cars in the private car park. Mesmerized by the incident, frozen with shock, most people didn't notice him running along the dockside towards the metal bridge leading to Canary Wharf. Pedestrians crossing the bridge, and hearing his trainers pounding insistently on the metal of the bridge, moved out of his way. He glanced back and saw his pursuers running along the quayside towards the bridge. One of them he noticed was heavy and overweight, and he thought he could easily outrun him. But the other man was slim and fitter looking.

He ran into the building opposite the bridge, crossed the foyer to the exit on the opposite side, and ran towards the Underground station. The only way he thought he could lose them now would be the way he had done the same thing only three days ago, when Marshall warned him of a possible tail and instructed him to take precautions.

At the top of the escalator, a quick glance back before stepping on to it, and he saw the slim man bursting through the doors. Gormen knew he'd been spotted, because he saw the man pounding across the concourse, in a direct line for the Underground entrance.

He stepped quickly on to the escalator and ran down the steps. He counted the time it took him to reach the bottom. He counted to fifteen as he reached the last few steps, and a glance back told him his pursuer had just stepped onto the escalator. He needed to time his escape perfectly. He disappeared behind the enormous grey pillar so that he could no longer be seen by his pursuer and began to count, giving his pursuer time to almost reach the bottom. Then he emerged from behind the pillar and followed some Japanese tourists on to the ascending escalator, bent down and pretended to be doing up his shoelace.

Glancing back over his shoulder, he saw his pursuer standing in the vast hall with his back to the ascending escalator, clearly trying to see if his quarry had run for the Tube trains. But as the escalator was about halfway up, he heard an urgent shout from the descending escalator nearby.

'Hey! There he is! There he is!'

He'd been spotted by the overweight man who was now almost level as he descended. As they were nearly opposite one another, the man launched himself onto the middle separating the two escalators, intending to lunge and grab Gormen. But Gormen was quicker and fitter, and as the man was in a more precarious position balanced on the steep sloping parapet between the escalators, Gormen clenched his fist tight and hit him in the jaw. The man cried out as he lost his balance and fell back on to the descending escalator. Ignoring the loud thumps of the man's body bouncing down the escalator steps, followed by screams and cries of alarm, Gormen continued running up the escalator, and made it to the top without bothering to look back to see if the athletic man was after him. He swung right and ran quickly for the steps leading towards One Canada Square, then turned sharp left for Cabot Place. He tore through swing doors and dashed towards Canary Wharf DLR station. He saw the indicator at the top of the short flight of steps leading to the platform showed there was a train heading for Bank in one minute. As he ran up the steps, he heard the train rattling into the station. He made it to the top, just as the doors opened and passengers emerged. Breathless and wheezing, he hauled himself into the carriage and clutched a commuter pole for support. A couple of passengers stared at him. He glared back at them and they looked away in embarrassment.

The doors closed, and the train left Canary Wharf. It was only a few hundred yards to the next station, West India Quay. He hoped the more energetic one of his two pursuers hadn't seen him get on the train. He could almost sprint to the West India Quay station in the time it took the train to reach it. But someone who hadn't lived for many years in Docklands as he had, wouldn't know that.

The doors opened at West India Quay, and he was relieved to see only one passenger getting into his carriage, an elderly black man. The carriage doors closed, and the train continued its journey to Bank, although he had no intention of going the whole way. If his pursuers guessed he might be on a DLR train heading for Bank station, all it would take would be a quick phone call, and there'd be an unwelcome welcoming party waiting for him. There was no way that was going to happen. So, just to make certain, he would get off at Westferry and head for West Ham and change on to a Tube train.

He smiled grimly as he thought about his mission now, and where it might end. The death of his wife and son may have left him squirming and feeble, as if his life was slowly draining away, but his recent actions gave him a renewed energy, and he intended to use it to create havoc. Death and destruction.

Chapter 35

As they searched for Lorcan's house in the exclusively wide road in Virginia Water, peering for names or numbers of houses, Mike sighed impatiently.

'I thought you said you'd been here before.'

'I have. But even though these mansions are classy houses for the stinking rich, they still manage to make the area look uninvitingly similar. An upmarket anywhere place. I mean look at them. High walls and hedges masking mock Palladian mansions.'

'So, what name or number are we looking for?'

'That's just it. I have no idea. Most of Dennis's visitors will be invited and will know where to come.'

'Or they'll have satnav.'

'OK. No need to rub it in. But most of these houses lack names or numbers. How is anyone supposed to find them?'

'So how did you find it when you came here before?'

'I was brought here for a meeting with the executive officer of the charity. It was during the day, and I was sure I would remember where it was.'

There were no other cars about, and none parked in the road. As they drove along the wide, tree-lined road, which seemed never ending, Reeves peered through his window at the wrought iron gates as they passed each house. The grounds of the houses were so big, and the distance between each gate and driveway so long, that Reeves drove quickly between each. He had just overshot one house when he pulled up sharply.

'I think it was that entrance back there. I distinctly remember the semi-circular brick wall was set back from the road like an alcove in front of the gates. Yes, I'm sure it was that one. I'll just reverse back.'

Mike placed a hand on Reeves's. 'No, better still, let's leave it parked here.'

Reeves turned to look at Mike, frowning. 'What on earth for? He's got a huge driveway going through extensive gardens, with enough parking space in front of the house for dozens of cars.'

'Malcolm,' Mike began to explain patiently, 'I wish I knew why I suggested walking up to the house. It's just…just that during my time in the police, I learnt that criminals get found out because they're too lazy to walk short distances, so they often get clobbered because of CCTV picking up their registration numbers, which are easier to identify than faces.'

'No need to worry about CCTV.'

'What d'you mean?'

'Our man has never installed cameras in his house. Or the grounds.'

Mike shook his head disbelievingly. 'And he's got no dogs either because he's allergic. A billionaire with hardly any security in a luxury palace. Are you kidding?'

'He did take great pains to explain to me when I came here, that he has such important visitors attending high-powered meetings, and they all value their privacy and anonymity.'

Mike snorted. 'In other words, secrecy. Members of the Bilderberg Group, maybe?'

'So, you know about that.'

'I guess the man thinks he's invincible. Laws don't apply to people like him.'

Mike shifted in his seat and thrust a hand into his back pocket.

'What the hell are you doing?'

'Why we came here, Malcolm. Switching the battery on for our talk with Lorcan. Come on, let's take a walk.'

As they walked away from the Saab, Reeves clicked the remote to lock it. Mike chuckled.

'I wouldn't have thought there'd be many car thieves in this district, Malcolm.'

Reeves smiled weakly and they walked back towards the gates of Lorcan's house. 'I still don't see why we can't drive up to his house,' he said.

'If we tell him we came by public transport, and caught a taxi from the station, he'll think there was a witness to our coming here.'

Reeves halted, his fingers twitching nervously. 'What the hell do you think might happen in there?'

'Nothing, Malcolm. He's probably responsible for ordering those murders, but he daren't shit on his own doorstep. Especially as there is a witness to our arrival.'

'But that's just it. There isn't. This taxi driver is a fiction.'

'Yes, but he doesn't know that. Calm yourself, Malcolm. We are entering the lion's den, but the lion's had his teeth pulled.'

'Yes, but he can still use his claws.'

Mike laughed. 'You sure this is his gaff?'

'Ninety-nine per cent. I remember the wood in front of the house, masking it from the road, giving it total privacy from any camera wielding paparazzi. Although Dennis usually manages to avoid press intrusion, other than from his sexual peccadilloes with minor celebrities and models.'

There was a push button intercom attached to the driver's side of a wall, and Mike gave the MP a nod, indicating he should be the one to announce their arrival.

'Who is it?' the intercom voice spoke, clearly and with no preliminary crackle from the electronic device, almost as if the person answering was close by.

'It's Malcolm Reeves and Mike Halliday to see Dennis Lorcan,' Reeves announced.

'Come up the drive and park in front of the house.'

The gates swung open smoothly and they both stepped into the driveway. The gates closed behind them as they walked along the drive through the wood on either side. The wood was dense with mainly well-established rhododendron bushes, grown to enormous heights.

The woods triggered in Mike an uneasy feeling of supernatural tension harking back to childhood memories of evil witches and ogres, and he thought he might have been mistaken in telling Malcolm to leave the car in the road. He was suddenly reminded of a decades old case when a villain stabbed a detective. The villain's name was Kenneth Noye, who had been involved in the Brink's-MAT gold bullion robbery, and a Scotland Yard undercover detective keeping Noye under surveillance at the villain's Kent property was stabbed by him and died. Noye's defence claimed that as it happened on his property, he acted in self-defence and was acquitted of murder and manslaughter.

Mike dismissed the idea of a similar thing happening to him and Malcolm, and tried to convince himself that his apprehension came from the strange atmosphere created by the silence of the district, broken only by the crunch of their shoes on gravel, and the twisted and entangled density of the thicket on either side.

As if echoing Mike's uneasiness, Reeves said, 'I've never felt so nervous in my life. I think it's these woods. I'd have felt better if we'd driven through them.'

To set the MP's mind at ease, Mike made light of the situation. 'You know, I was impressed by the way you handled the phone call to Lorcan. You lied so convincingly. But I expect as a politician you've had a lot of practice.'

Reeves was about to reply, but as they rounded a curve in the drive, they came in sight of the house, an imposing reproduction of a Georgian mansion, a faux stately home, with a large circular car park at the front, a fountain in the middle, and steps leading up on either side to a massive door. Through one of the front-facing high windows they could see a chandelier glinting.

'Impressive,' Mike admitted as they approached the fountain. 'Even though it's mock Georgian.'

Parked in front of the steps was a black four-by-four Shogun.

As they got nearer the steps, the door opened, and a man appeared. He stared at them open-mouthed, looked towards the woods through which they had just walked, and frowned deeply. He wore light blue chinos and a charcoal sports jacket.

'Hello, Mr Reeves,' he said. 'Where's your car?'

'Hello, Jimmy,' Reeves replied. 'We came by train and caught a cab from the station.'

'The cab would've brought you up to the front door.'

'Oh,' Reeves said lightly, 'we fancied the exercise after the train journey.'

Lorcan's chauffeur and bodyguard, Mike noted, was unexpectedly short. Perhaps no more than five feet six or seven, wiry and dark haired, and probably in his mid to late thirties. But Mike knew it would be foolish to underestimate someone from their appearance, and experience had taught him that some of the toughest gangsters and terrorists were small.

'You must be the first people ever to walk up from the road,' the bodyguard observed. 'But Dennis is expecting you. So, you'd better come on in.'

As Mike and Reeves walked up the steps towards him, he gestured to the doorway and smiled.

'After you, gentlemen. After you.'

As they entered, Mike glimpsed the fearful tension in the MP's face, and began to doubt the sanity of his mission. And as Lorcan's bodyguard shut the door behind them, he realized they were trapped in a web of power and Machiavellian depravity and there was no turning back now.

Chapter 36

Greeting them with wide open arms and a disarming smile, Dennis Lorcan then shook hands with them, saying, 'Hi, Malcolm. Thanks for coming over. And good to meet you again, Mike. Can I get you a drink? I think the sun is over the yardarm. What about a twenty-five-year-old malt whisky? A good drink for a special occasion.'

'Special occasion?' Mike questioned.

'Isn't that why you're here? Because you know where there's a copy of the missing dossier, and with my help you might be able to purchase it.' He looked Reeves in the eye. 'Isn't that right, Malcolm?'

Mike noticed way the banker questioned the MP like a barrister in a courtroom, challenging him to contradict himself. But Reeves handled it well and was unfazed by the subtle provocation.

'That's perfectly correct, Dennis.'

As the bodyguard crossed the spacious living room to fetch drinks from a large drinks' cabinet, Mike took in the enormous living room at a glance. Bookcases in alcoves with finely bound books, a marble mantelpiece with a fireplace the width of most people's bathrooms, chintzy curtains and furnishings, two of the most enormous sofas he had ever clapped eyes on, all dominated by a glittering chandelier, and an enormous flat screen television at the far end of the massive room. And he guessed the oil paintings hanging on the walls, which appeared to be impressionist, were worth a small fortune, although he couldn't identify any of the artists.

But then, he wasn't there to admire the man's taste in art.

Smiling, Lorcan gestured to one of the sofas. 'Why don't you make yourselves comfortable?'

As they sank into one of the enormous sofas, sitting a few feet apart from one another, Mike and Reeves waited while Lorcan's bodyguard came over and handed them both sparkling cut glasses of malt whisky. They thanked him as Lorcan was handed a glass, with which he toasted them.

'How was your journey? Traffic not too bad I hope.'

'They came by train,' the bodyguard said, 'and caught a cab from the station.'

Lorcan feigned puzzlement. 'I wondered why I couldn't see your car out front. Come to think of it, I don't recall hearing a taxi.'

'He dropped us at the gate, and we walked up the drive,' Mike said.

Rubbing his chin thoughtfully, Lorcan said, 'How very strange. I don't think I've ever known anyone walk up from the road.'

'Just what I said,' Lorcan's minder commented, then moved to the fireplace and stood in front of it with his legs apart, and hands behind his back, like a Praetorian guard defending his master. Mike thought the demeanour looked ridiculous on such a short man standing dwarfed by such a huge fireplace. But he didn't doubt the man's hawkish tendencies.

'Before we get down to business,' Lorcan said. 'Tell me what you think of the malt.'

They both held it to their nose in unison before taking a small sip.

'Exquisite!' Reeves remarked.

Staring at Mike with a false smile, Lorcan raised his eyebrows questioningly. 'Mike?'

'Quite pleasant. Though I'm not really a whisky drinker.'

'You should have said, and I would have offered you something else.'

Mike raised his glass. 'This is fine.'

Lorcan leant over and placed his own glass on a massive coffee table. 'Would you both excuse me for just one minute? I need Jimmy to run an errand for me.'

Lorcan waved his fingers at his minder, and they both left the room, closing the living room door behind them.

Tense and anxious, Mike and Reeves tried to hear what was being said, but the conversation between master and servant was muffled.

'What d'you think that was about?' Reeves whispered.

'I have no idea, Malcolm. You told me Jimmy's the bodyguard, so with him out of the way, clearly Dennis trusts us enough to talk to us alone. Or maybe he doesn't want Jimmy to know what's being discussed.'

'I'm not so sure.'

'Relax, Malcolm. Everything'll be fine.'

'I wish I had your confidence.'

'You're doing fine.'

They heard the front door slam as the bodyguard left the house on whatever errand he'd been sent on. Lorcan came back into the room, virtually parodying a genial host as his welcoming smile broadened. He picked up his whisky glass and sat on the other sofa at a right angle to his guests, took a sip, held the glass up to study its colour, and sighed contentment.

'Now then,' he began, 'you mentioned a copy of the dossier. Tell me more.'

Reeves looked towards Mike, waiting for him to take the lead.

'It's a bit tricky to go into details about who has the copy,' Mike said. 'Because I agreed to honour this person's anonymity. For their own protection.'

Lorcan looked from Mike to Malcolm and back to Mike again, his eyebrows raised in a calculated expression of bemusement. 'I'm not sure I understand.'

From outside came the sound of a car starting up, followed by the crunch of tyres on gravel.

'That'll be Jimmy going on a fact-finding mission for me,' Lorcan explained, then said to Mike, 'You were saying about this person who has a copy of the file. How did they come by it?'

'We think it came from Peter Gormen, who presumably double-crossed whoever he was working for.'

'But I thought it was Gormen's son who had the copy, some of which he took to Forum Books.'

'That was the original USB drive – the one taken from John Keneally eight years ago. Gormen made another copy, which he passed on to someone else to guarantee his safety. Now this person wants a million for it.'

Lorcan whistled through his teeth and shook his head.

'Small price to pay,' Mike added, 'to protect Westminster's finest.'

'But how do we know it ends there? They could make another copy and so on and so forth.'

Mike shook his head. 'I guarantee that won't happen.'

Lorcan's eyes became frosty as he tried to control his anger.

'You see,' Mike continued, 'this person knows just how information in this case has leaked, and everyone involved has wound up dead. Or in my case, an attempted murder. You haven't asked me, Dennis, how I came by this whopping great bruise on the side of my head. But maybe you already knew.'

Reeves turned his head sharply towards Mike, wondering where this was leading. It wasn't what they had agreed in the car. The plan was to tell Lorcan that Mike had obtained the memory stick from Gormen, had concealed it in a safe place, and had now been corrupted by the lure of easy money.

'I haven't a clue what you're talking about,' Lorcan said. 'So, you've got a bump on the head. How the hell would I know how you got it?'

Reeves felt his stomach churning inside, and let his breath out slowly, praying Mike would stick to their original plan. It had been agreed that Mike would eventually admit to possession of the extant document, coaxing the banker into arranging another killing, only this time the police would be waiting, reinforcing the evidence against Lorcan and producing a watertight case against him. But now Mike seemed to be deviating from what they had agreed, and if Lorcan was dangerous and psychopathic, he was risking both their lives. Was Mike simply relying on a recording of this conversation to convict Lorcan? The lump in Reeves's throat felt like a stone, and he wished he hadn't listened to Mike.

'I think you know bloody well how I got it,' Mike replied. 'Because you arranged for me to be killed in a motor accident.'

Reeves closed his eyes in despair, wondering if Mike had become unhinged by his desire for a reckoning. They shot open again as he heard Lorcan's false, barking laugh.

'I think you've been watching too many movies. Whatever happened to you had absolutely nothing to do with me.'

'No? All the information I gave Jo, who is my client, found its way back to you via Malcolm. And you just happen to turn up at Berlin and bump into him, and then three people die when he passes on that information.'

'All right, let's just suppose what you say is true – and I don't for one minute admit that it is – there isn't a shred of concrete evidence linking me to the death of anyone connected with the dossier.'

'You're forgetting something, Dennis. You've gone to extreme lengths to destroy the evidence contained in that document. And you've failed. Because I know who has a copy.'

Lorcan smiled humourlessly. 'Seeing as you accuse me of having everyone murdered who might have had the document, presumably you're not about to tell me who it is.'

'On the contrary.' Mike returned the smile and paused dramatically.

'Well?' Lorcan snapped, irritation rising.

'I do. I have the copy.'

Lorcan stared at Mike, peering at him through narrowed eyes. 'I don't believe you. How the hell did you get a copy of the file? Not from Gormen, that was for sure.'

'I got it from his son. Got him to run me off a copy. You see, Justin was a junkie who'd do anything for a fix, so it wasn't difficult.'

'If, as you say, you have a copy of the file, and you think I tried to rescue it to have it destroyed, and was responsible for the deaths of all those people, why did you come here?'

'I'm not getting any younger, Dennis. And work in the private sector's not worked out, so half a million will do me nicely, thanks.'

'You mentioned a million. Who gets the other half?'

'Malcolm does.'

Lorcan stared at the MP, a sceptical downward turn of his mouth forming into a sneer. 'So, convince me, Malcolm – and explain to me why the sudden change of heart. Surely the shining knight hasn't sold out for a mere half a million. Your wife must gross that in a good two or three years.'

A swishing and crunching noise of tyres on gravel, and the roar of an engine being driven with urgency, signalled the return of Lorcan's minder.

'Ah!' Lorcan exclaimed. 'Here's Jimmy back so soon. Excuse me while I let him in.'

Lorcan hurried to the door, closing it behind him, and they heard him talking to his minder in the hall, but couldn't hear what was being said.

Mike lowered his voice almost to a whisper as he spoke to Reeves. 'Malcolm, it's up to you now. You've got to convince Lorcan you can be bought. Christ Almighty! It can't be that difficult. We've had so many corrupt MPs in the past, fiddling their expenses. Everything hinges on you making him believe you're prepared to sell out for money.'

Reeves wiped the flat of his hand down over his face, like a child wanting a scene to disappear. When he opened his eyes again, Mike saw him staring regretfully at some distant location, wistful and dreamy, and wondered if it was fear shrugging off responsibility and waving a white flag.

'You've got to do this,' Mike urged. 'Malcolm! Pull yourself together.'

Reeves turned to Mike and spoke in a monotone. 'He's not going to believe me. Nothing I say will convince him.'

'You've got to try. Don't give up now, for Christ's sake.'

'There's no fucking point – no fucking point in lying to him about being corrupted by money. He'll know I'm lying. Don't you see, Dennis Lorcan is highly intelligent. Just because he's corrupt doesn't mean he thinks everyone else acts in the same way. He's intelligent enough to know there are incorruptible people on the planet. He'll see through it, Mike. He knows we're trying to lead him into a trap. It won't work. I should never have fucking listened to you. We should have gone to the police like I said.'

'For Christ's sake calm yourself,' Mike hissed. 'There's nothing he can do to us here. And if I can get him to admit—'

The door swung open and Lorcan marched into the centre of the room, followed by his bodyguard. He stood with clenched fists on hips and wore a reptilian smile at odds with the cold clinical emptiness in his eyes.

'Jimmy's little errand proved interesting,' he said. 'It seems no taxi driver exists to witness your arrival here. I believe that is your Saab, Malcolm, parked a hundred yards up the road from my gate. So, you both lied about the train journey. Why did you do that, I wonder? Was it because you expected me to believe there are many witnesses who saw you getting off the train at Virginia Water, including a cabbie who ran you from the station?'

Sunk so low on the sofa, Mike felt insecure and struggled to get to his feet.

'So, what if we did come here in Malcolm's car? What difference does that make?'

'The difference between someone knowing you came here, and nobody knowing where you are.' Mike started to speak but Lorcan stopped him with a raised hand. 'What I find so irritating in all this is how you treat me like some sort of cretin.

'Did you think, Malcolm, I would believe you could be so easily bought for half a million quid? You're an idealist, on a mission to rid the world of bad men. But it's a losing battle, Malcolm. Soon as you get rid of one, there'll be another to take his place. You think the world turns on its axis? Wrong, my friend. The world turns on money and power. Has done since cities were built and money was invented.'

Glaring at Lorcan, Mike gave him a slow handclap. 'Congratulations. Like all psychopathic megalomaniacs, you can't resist the empty speech signifying nothing. And I've met a few like you in my time. You fool people into mistaking guile and cunning for intelligence.'

'But intelligent enough to see through your little plot to make me think you have a copy of the dossier. And did you expect me to fall for the wiretap? No doubt you're recording everything we say.' Lorcan chuckled. 'Not that it makes any difference now.'

'You can't keep us here,' Mike said, preparing to slug it out with Lorcan's bodyguard if necessary. 'I think it's time we left, Malcolm.'

As Reeves shifted on the sofa, preparing to rise, Lorcan nodded to his minder.

'Jimmy!'

With a neat and skilful movement, Lorcan's minder opened his jacket, whipped a pistol out from a shoulder holster, clicked the safety off, and aimed it at Mike.

'Take a pew, Mike. And you can remain seated, Malcolm.'

Mike stood his ground defiantly, staring at Lorcan with disgust.

'I said, sit down!' Lorcan barked.

His minder brought his left hand up to steady the gun aimed at Mike's head.

Looking down the barrel of the gun, which Mike recognized as a Browning Semi-Automatic Hi-Power pistol, with up to thirteen rounds of nine-millimetre cartridges, capable of killing a man at fifty metres, he knew he had no option but to obey. He sat down, perched on the edge of the sofa.

'Now then,' Lorcan said, 'just to be certain about the dossier – it's a lie, isn't it, Malcolm? There is no copy, is there? It was a trick to set me up, wasn't it?

Numbed by their nightmare predicament, Reeves shrank back into the fabric of the sofa, staring with horror at the black hole at the end of the Browning's barrel.

'Well?' Lorcan snapped.

'No, there is a copy of the dossier. Mike has it.'

'You see,' Mike said, 'I told you there was.'

Lorcan smiled grimly. 'Not a very convincing liar, are you, Malcolm? I expect you know how the Provisional IRA got results. Kneecapping it was called. A bullet through the knee ensures the person will probably be in a wheelchair for the rest of their days. Not a pleasant prospect, is it? And quite painful I shouldn't wonder.' He turned to his minder. 'So, Jimmy, if you would do the honours and put a bullet through one of Malcolm's knees.'

Lorcan's minder took a pace forward and aimed his gun at the MP's knee.

Reeves, eyes bulging in his colourless face, emitted a short whimpering sound which caught in his throat.

'Wait!' Mike shouted. 'I don't have a copy of the file. It was a lie.'

'I thought as much,' Lorcan smiled triumphantly, then turned to his minder. 'No need for the knee-capping, but keep them covered, Jimmy.' He locked eyes with Mike. 'I take exception to being called a psychopath. I'm no sadist, and don't wish to cause unnecessary suffering. I only do what is required to ensure my survival, and the survival of the fittest – my friends in high places.'

'So now what?' Mike demanded.

Lorcan pursed his lips and shrugged. 'I'm thinking. You both seem to have driven down a cul-de-sac, and it's hard to know where you go from here.'

Mike looked towards Lorcan's bodyguard. 'Mind if I ask you something, Jimmy? Has your boss told you how all this is to do with children being sexually abused, which he has taken great pains to cover up?'

The bodyguard looked at Mike expressionlessly and remained silent.

Lorcan clapped his hands delightedly, and laughed, as if he had just learnt they were all going on a pleasant outing.

'Jimmy knows most of my business, and he's loyal and trustworthy. And why wouldn't he be? I'm in my early sixties. Jimmy's only thirty-six. By the time I slow down and retire in another ten years, Jimmy'll be in his forties, and I've guaranteed he'll be a millionaire by then.'

'So, in the end it all boils down to money and power. And what about all those vulnerable underprivileged children? How many young lives have you ruined just to satisfy your perversions?'

Lorcan coloured, angered by the accusation. 'I'm not a paedophile – believe me. There is no way I could…not with children…the thought disgusts me.'

'And yet you're the instigator – the one covering for this paedophile ring in Westminster.'

'The wheels of democracy must continue to turn. Arms have to be sold, wars must be fought, deals have to be brokered, and puppet governments have to know who really owns and feeds them.'

'You – the money men. And that's how you remain rich and powerful. Those politicians owe everything to you and your kind – members of your exclusive club.'

'Exactly. And it's been going on since the birth of time and will continue long after you and I have shuffled off this mortal coil. There are big people and there are small people; some who do the eating and some who get eaten. That's just the way it is. A fact of life.'

Mike, his throat dry and hoarse, asked, 'So where do we go from here?'

Lorcan ignored him, walked over to an occasional table and picked up a cordless phone. He tapped in one digit and waited. Mike stared down the dark barrel of the Browning, then caught the bodyguard's eye. He knew he hadn't a hope in hell of overpowering the ex-soldier, and his mind became fuzzy and confused, clutching at bizarre fantasies of crazy escapes.

He and Reeves heard in the deathly silence of the room, the ringing of the telephone from Lorcan's handset. It stopped with a click as someone answered.

'Hello,' Lorcan said. 'Lorcan here. Requesting an extreme verdict.'

They watched as Lorcan answered someone's probing questions with cryptic coded answers.

'Yes, the paradox is parallel and demands immediate action. That's correct. Location? Here in Virginia Water. My place. An extreme verdict and clean-up campaign beginning in an hour if possible. Yes, thank you. We'll be waiting for you.'

Lorcan hung up, replacing the phone in its recharging cradle. Mike made one desperate attempt to talk his way out of their terrible predicament.

'You can't expect to get away with this, Lorcan. I've rarely known a criminal to escape justice.'

'Rarely is the keyword,' Lorcan replied. 'In this instance I think I have every angle covered.'

'With one exception.'

'What's that?'

'You'll find it hard to explain what happened to Malcolm's car. Wherever you dump it….'

'That's where you're wrong,' Lorcan interrupted impatiently, wanting to get this over with quickly now. 'Jimmy here will drive the car two or three hundred miles to another city, where it will eventually be discovered as having been abandoned. It will be a mystery the media will cherish for months on end. Why did a private detective and Member of Parliament drive to Birmingham or Leeds or Bristol, and vanish without a trace? My God, the media will just love it. It'll run for months. The circulation of every newspaper will go through the roof.'

Malcolm Reeves, his voice quivering, made a desperate attempt to change the course of his dark destiny.

'Listen to me, Dennis, Jo's not stupid. She knows I've always been in touch with you. She'll be able to work out who was behind it all.'

'Like I give a fuck. There'll be speculation, rumours, but no proof. And if she accuses me publicly, I'll sue. I'll turn her into one of the paupers you're so keen on saving.'

He turned to his bodyguard and gave him a small nod. Mike looked at Reeves, searching his mind for any sort of emotion, but all he could find was an empty, hollow darkness enveloping him. But he knew he had to make it right between them.

'I'm sorry, Malcolm,' he started to say. 'I should never have….'

Like lightning striking, or a plane crashing through the roof, the crash was so loud and startling that Mike thought at first this was how it ends. A whining, roaring engine noise, glass shattering, and then the cracking, splintering racket froze everyone in the room for a moment. A spluttering engine protest, and more glass falling and cracking like shards of ice falling from buildings in winter.

'It's the conservatory!' Lorcan yelled.

His bodyguard was already out of the door. Mike and Reeves stood up, ready to make a break for it, but stopped as they heard a gunshot. Lorcan, his face tormented by images of suffering, knowing his supremacy may have reached the furthermost point of his destiny, clutched his chin as if he was choking. Another two shots followed in quick succession.

'Jimmy!' Lorcan rasped. 'You OK, Jimmy?'

He stood stock still, staring at the open door, waiting for his bodyguard to appear. The time slowed to a crawl. Mike and Reeves, their breath held tight in their lungs, listened for every sound following the almighty crash and gunshots. And then they heard it. A wheezing scuffling noise, like someone in pain. Shuffling and dragging of feet along the hallway. Then a cough.

'Jimmy!' Lorcan begged, pleading for his protector to save him.

'Jimmy's as dead as your fucking soul,' Gormen said as he entered, his gun aimed at Lorcan's head. 'I guess you must be Dennis Lorcan. Back away. I don't want scum like you standing so close.'

As Lorcan shuffled backwards away from Gormen, they all noticed the dark red patch on the gunman's left shoulder, the torn hole in his anorak, and the colour spreading rapidly outwards like an overflowing pool. Soon the man would pass out, and Mike wanted to get to his gun before Lorcan did. He moved sideways slightly and took a couple of paces forward towards the door and Gormen's left. But the adrenaline pumping through the gunman gave him a keen sharpness and he turned the gun on Mike.

'Stop right there. Who the fuck are you?'

'Mike Halliday. I'm a private investigator.'

Gormen aimed the gun at Lorcan's head again. Despite looking as if he might pass out at any moment, his eyes flared with hatred. 'We've never met,' he told Lorcan. 'But you know who I am. Name's Peter Gormen. I'm the one who did all your dirty work.'

'I don't know what you're talking about,' Lorcan said, his voice quivering with dread. 'I think you've got it wrong. I've never heard of you.'

'According to Marshall, you're the man at the top of this disgusting heap of shite. Marshall took orders from you, and so did others in the service. But it was Marshall who told me what to do. And you were the one who told him to burn my house, with my wife and son in it—'

'That must have been Marshall's idea,' Lorcan stammered. 'It had nothing to do with me.'

'That's not what Marshall told me.'

'He must've been lying.'

'I don't think so because—' Gormen began, then gritted his teeth as the pain got to him. 'Because I believed what he told me. No one – especially a fucking worm like Marshall – could take that much pain. He talked near the end. Then I killed him. Put him out of his misery with one bullet in the brain. And now—'

He thumbed the hammer back on the revolver. Lorcan cringed, raising his hands in front of himself for protection.

'No, listen to me. Your wife and son weren't supposed to die. It was a mistake. I told Marshall to torch the house, not with anyone in it.'

'You're lying, you fucking arsehole.'

'What do you want?'

Gormen looked momentarily confused. 'Want?'

'Name your price. I can give you as much as you need to live in luxury for the rest of your life. Think about that for a moment. Think how much you could be worth.'

Gormen stared at him with dead eyes. Lorcan mistakenly thought he was weighing up the prospect of receiving a huge pay-out.

'Three million in an offshore account. I can pick up the phone and make it happen right away.'

'You don't get it, do you? It's not about money. But you wouldn't understand, would you, Lorcan? You just can't understand how important my wife and son were to me. And there's no getting them back, is there, Lorcan? With all your money and power, you can't make that happen, can you?'

'But Marshall told me – about your other life – the women and the trips abroad. He told me your wife and son were a cover.'

'Originally, yes. When I was an undercover cop. But they were my home. The only real thing that mattered to me. And now you've taken that away from me.'

Lorcan's rubbery face, wet with sweat, implored, pleaded, begged like a whimpering dog. 'Please, Peter – please. I'll up it to five million. Five million. Think about that. Just put the gun down and I'll make a call and you'll be rich. Rich. You'd like that, Peter – only please put the gun down.'

Mike watched Gormen intently, wondering if he might be tempted to take Lorcan up on his offer. But then, almost as if the stab of pain in the gunman's wounded shoulder reminded him of his precarious mortality, he turned down Lorcan's offer by pulling the trigger. Even in such a vast room the blast was like a thunderbolt, and the banker would have been dead before he heard it. His life over in a flash, the bullet hit him bang in the centre of his forehead, passing clean through his head. Mike and Reeves stared aghast and unmoving, mesmerized by the horror of what they were witnessing as a stream of blood sprayed the finely bound books on the shelves behind, but the banker's body, as if unaware of its final exit, remained upright for a fraction of a second before collapsing in a bloody heap.

As Gormen looked down at Lorcan's body, it was hard to tell whether it was with regret or satisfaction. All emotion seemed to have been wrung out of the man, leaving little more than the husk of a lifeless human. An acrid smell hung in the air, and from another part of the house came the residual sounds of machinery creaking and simmering following Gormen's destructive entry.

As if unaware of the presence of the two men, Gormen continued to stare at Lorcan's corpse, an expression of loathing spreading across the lower part of his face, which looked like nothing more than the demonstration of a distasteful experience. It seemed to Mike and Reeves that time stretched unbearably as they listened to their own shallow breathing. But the suspension of time was an illusion, and soon they knew they had to confront Lorcan's killer.

On hearing Mike clearing his throat gently, Gormen came out of his trance and turned to look at them both, the gun now pointing at Mike's midriff.

'And who's this other guy?' Gormen asked Mike.

'This is Malcolm Reeves, an MP. He's investigating the allegations of a ring of paedophiles in Westminster.'

Gormen pointed the gun at Reeves.

'So, without your interference, maybe my wife and son would still be alive.'

'I doubt that,' Mike said. He knew he had to talk quickly and persuasively to talk the deranged gunman from putting a bullet into one of them.

'Listen to me, Peter: the man behind all this is dead. You've got the justice you came here for. And, if I'm not mistaken, the gun you're holding – a Smith and Wesson snub nosed Magnum has only five rounds. Marshall took one of them, didn't he? And I'm only guessing but – maybe your second bullet disarmed Jimmy in the other room back there, and you killed him with the third. Lorcan took the fourth cartridge, so that only leaves one round. And there's two of us.'

Mike saw Gormen's eyes shifting rapidly to the door and guessed what he was thinking.

'Yes, you should have picked up Jimmy's Browning before you came storming in here. That wasn't very professional, was it? And I know you're a pro, Peter. You were probably a good undercover officer once. So, where did it all go wrong? Was it the lure of easy money and the attraction of living two lives? There's no such person as Peter Gormen, is there? He doesn't exist. What about your other life? Your real identity. Who are you really? Who is the man behind the mask? I'd like to know, Peter.'

Gormen stared at Mike, a wild look in his eyes, and then he said, 'What the hell does it matter now?'

In an instant, Gormen turned the gun around, held it to his temple and pulled the trigger. The sound this time was more like a whiplash crack, and Gormen's head was thrown backwards on impact and he fell to the floor with a crash.

Malcolm Reeves, shocked and traumatised by yet another senseless death, was paralysed for an instant, and then the nightmare ordeal of the crises erupted, and his entire body began shaking and trembling. He tried to control himself, tried to get a grip of the situation, needing a diversionary tactic to keep himself from going to pieces. He struggled to slip his trembling hand into his pocket and took out his mobile. He had just tapped in the first nine when Mike went over and stopped him.

'What are you doing?'

'Don't make that call, Malcolm.'

'We need to call the police.'

'No, we don't. We were never here.'

'What are you talking about?'

Mike gripped Reeves by the shoulders and faced him. 'Listen to me, Malcolm. You heard Lorcan calling for a clean-up. You know what that was about, don't you? When whoever it is gets here, they'll find the wrong people have been eliminated. Then they'll do one of two things. They'll either go away again and leave someone else to discover the corpses, or they'll clean up the mess, and that'll be the last anyone hears of it. Either way, I don't give a shit.'

'But it's not right. It's just not right,' Reeves burbled. 'The police could be here in minutes. We need to call them. And we can't escape from the fact that we are involved. We were here, for fuck's sake. We were here. We are witnesses.'

'But what will this do for your career as an MP?' Mike stressed. 'Think about it, Malcolm. Whatever happens now, we can't change anything. We can walk out of here as if nothing has happened. If this crime scene becomes a major police investigation, it's clear what happened here. Two men murdered by Gormen, followed by his suicide. It so cut and dried, it doesn't need us as witnesses for Christ's sake.'

Reeves pondered the implications, then began a tentative objection. 'I still think...'

'No, you don't,' Mike cut in, let go of Reeves, bent over the coffee table and picked up their whisky glasses. 'We need to get out of here quickly.'

Mike stepped over Gormen's corpse, careful not to tread in any blood, walked to the door, and looked back at Reeves. 'Careful where you walk, Malcolm. Don't get traces of blood on your shoes.'

Reeves followed, stepping gingerly over Gormen's body. 'Where are you going?' he asked Mike.

'To wash the glasses.'

As Mike hurried along the hallway, in front of a sweeping circular staircase towards what looked like the kitchen, his curiosity got the better of him and he stepped into the enormous dining room. Jimmy's body lay at the head of a dining table large enough to accommodate at least fifty people, with another grand chandelier hanging over it. At the end of the dining room was a sliding glass door leading into a massive conservatory which looked out onto a garden of spacious lawns, flower beds and a lake beneath overhanging willow trees. At the end of the conservatory, broken jagged glass everywhere, slashed like scenery in a Salvador Dali dream sequence – PVC pillars and frames bent and broken, and part of the roof had collapsed. The conservatory looked like it had taken a missile hit, and in the centre of the area a large garden tractor, its bodywork still smouldering, had crashed through the glass doors and wrecked garden furniture and smashed and crushed ceramic plant pots.

'Way to make an entrance,' Mike commented.

He put the glasses on the floor, then knelt over the Jimmy's body, and frisked him, careful to avoid getting blood on his hands.

Shocked, Reeves asked him what he was doing.

'I don't know about you, Malcolm, but I don't want to walk down to the main gates and find I have to climb over them. I reckon Jimmy here has a remote on his key ring.' He stood up and jangled the keys in front of Reeves. 'Yes, here we are.' Then he picked up the glasses, brushed past the MP, and went in search of the kitchen.

The entrance to the state-of-the-art kitchen was on the other side of the circular staircase. Mike, determined and hurrying, ignored its functional splendour and made straight for the sink, where he washed the glasses and dried them carefully with a tea towel. Reeves hovered, thinking about the implications of leaving the crime scene, but gradually came around to Mike's way of thinking.

'If we were never here, we need to get out fast. Now. In case someone comes to the house. Parcel delivery or something.'

Mike used the towel to pick up the glasses by their rims. 'I think these glasses are the only objects that had our prints on them. I'll return them to the drink's cupboard. Do you remember touching anything else?'

'No, I don't think I did.'

'Neither did I. I'll wipe the edge of the coffee table, just to make sure.'

The MP suddenly pointed at Mike's chest.

'What?' Mike questioned, looking down at his shirt and jacket, wondering if he'd caught a tiny blood splatter.

'The recording,' Reeves explained. 'You've been recording everything that's happened here.'

'Soon rectify that, Malcolm. I'll wipe it clean. Now come on, let's get these glasses back into the drinks cupboard.'

Mike dashed back to the living room, careful not to step in any blood particles, and replaced the glasses in the drink's cupboard. Reeves, standing in the doorway, watched him, and avoided looking at the two corpses. Mike wiped the edges of the coffee table, stepped over Gormen's body again, and stood by Reeves in the doorway.

'Did you touch the door handle?' he asked.

'No, I think the only ones who did that were Dennis and his bodyguard.'

'Good. Saves me wiping it. A door handle wiped clean of any prints would get a forensics manager wondering who cleaned up after the crime. I'll bring the tea towel with me, use it to open the front door, then get rid of it when we're miles away from here. Come on. Let's go.'

As Mike walked towards the front door, he turned back and saw Reeves hesitate.

'What's wrong?'

'I'm having second thoughts about this.'

'Well don't!'

'If anything goes wrong, how do we explain what we did in these few hours?'

'Listen, if this crime becomes public, we can come forward and give our evidence – everything we know up until our meeting at Fortnum and Mason. And after that meeting you spent two hours at my home in Ealing. I showed you the photographs I took of the guest house in Barnet, and any other evidence I've collected, and we discussed the case in depth. So now we both have a perfect alibi. Each other. Right. Let's get out of this mausoleum.'

Reeves remained rooted to the spot, unable to move his feet, and Mike wondered if this was shock from witnessing such carnage.

'What's wrong with you?' Mike demanded.

'Do you confide in your wife, openly and honestly?'

'Yes, I do, Malcolm. But this shocking event must be kept under wraps. Like soldiers returning after the Great War, we'll never tell them. How can we possibly describe what went on here today? I don't like doing it, but that's the way it has to be.'

Reeves thought about Mike's reasoning for a moment, then nodded and said, 'I'm sure you're right. But what happens if one of us suffers from delayed shock and talks in his sleep?'

Mike shrugged. 'Dreams are never logical. I wouldn't worry about it.'

But after they left the building, marching towards the gate, Mike did worry about it, thinking about his relationship with Marianne, how he always told her everything, creating a deep trust over the years which had never been broken. And he thought about how flimsy that trust would become once he stopped confiding in her, having to lie about his involvement in the killings at Lorcan's mansion should it become public.

As he walked along, he caught himself subconsciously tapping the pocket which contained the warrant card, knowing the promise he made her had been broken.

A life and death situation. Maybe it was justified.

But that was in the past now, and he had yet to use the warrant card.

Chapter 37

After being dropped off by Malcolm in central London, Mike caught the Piccadilly Line to Wood Green. It was just gone half-two when he got there, and it didn't take him long to find Justin's girlfriend's house, having followed her there less than a week ago.

The house was like the Gormen house, but this one was run-down, the paintwork peeling, a thick layer of grime on the windows, and the wheelie bin overflowing with garbage.

He listened and thought he could hear voices from inside the house, one of them a child's. He rang the doorbell and waited. Presently a woman, white and slim but with enormous, top-heavy breasts, flung open the door. A young, mixed-race boy of about eight or nine sidled up beside her. Mike could see by the red rims around his mother's eyes that she'd been crying.

Showing her his old warrant card, he said, 'Detective Inspector Halliday. Do you think I could have a word with your daughter Eva?'

She looked scared and clutched her son for comfort. 'She ain't here. What you want with her?'

'It's about her boyfriend – Justin Gormen. He was killed in that fire, and I'd like to speak to her about it.'

She looked defeated and desperate, and a tear trickled out of an eye. She quickly brushed it away, ashamed to be seen weakening and crying. Her large breasts heaved as she tried to control her emotions.

'I know Eva done it cos of what happened.'

Mike suddenly felt his last remaining hope collapsing like a house of cards.

'What's Eva done?' he asked.

'She overdosed on drugs. They found her in the park. I went to the hospital, to the Accident and Emergency, and they managed to save her. Only—'

She stifled her sobs and wiped the tears away with the flat of her hand.

'What's happened to her?'

'By the time we got there, they'd transferred her in an ambulance to a mental health place. We never even got to see her. And I can't get to the other hospital cos I can't leave Timmy on his own. I had to get him out of school before we went to the A & E.'

The boy looked up at her, striving to appear mature and caring. 'You go, Mum. I'll be all right.'

She squeezed his shoulder affectionately. 'We'll phone up, Timmy. See how she is. Then we'll try and see her tomorrow if we can.' She looked defensively at Mike. 'My hubby's away. At sea. He's in the merchant navy.'

'So where is Eva now?'

'A hospital in Enfield. Mental Health Trust they said. Christ, I can't remember the name of it now. I've got the phone number if you want it.'

'Yes, please, 'Mike said. 'That'd be a great help.'

She turned and disappeared into the darkness of the hall, while the boy stared at Mike, guarding his domain. Eva's mother returned and handed him a scrap of paper with two phone numbers on it.

'That's the mental health place,' she said pointing to the top number. 'And that one's my mobile. If you speak to her, would you give me a quick ring to let me know how she is?'

'Sure,' Mike agreed. 'I only know her as Eva. What's your surname?'

'Williams.'

'Thanks Mrs Williams. I'll ring you as soon as I've spoken to her.'

'Thanks. I'd appreciate that.'

She shut the door and he hurried along the street towards the main road, tapping in the hospital number as he went, hoping it wouldn't be too far away.

***

He caught a taxi from Wood Green to Enfield and asked the driver to wait in the car park for him, making certain the cab couldn't be seen from the Mental Health Trust reception. Then he dashed breathlessly into the building, pretending it was in response to an emergency. The female receptionist frowned questioningly at him from behind the counter. He held up his warrant card and announced himself.

'How can I help?' she asked.

'This really is an urgent matter, and a sensitive issue,' he said persuasively, showing her the warrant card. 'You had a Ms Eva Williams brought in, following a drugs OD. Is she OK?'

'She'll survive. I think she's with one of the psychiatric nurses right now. What's the problem?'

'Her belongings. Did she have a handbag or anything when she was brought in?'

'She had a small backpack. Why?

'I need to know if there's a USB flash drive, a memory stick, inside it.'

The receptionist hesitated, and Mike hoped the urgent atmosphere he generated wouldn't deteriorate into a job's worth situation. 'I'm with counter terrorism at Scotland Yard, and this is a matter of state security,' he lied. 'Could you please look inside the backpack and see if it's there?'

She nodded. 'I think the bag's under her trolley still. I'll go and get it.'

'Thank you.'

He waited while she went through swing doors leading to the wards. She returned moments later with the small leather backpack, and rather than hand it to him, went back behind the counter, keeping the backpack low on her desk, and unzipped it. She took items out of the bag slowly – a purse, brush, a half-drunk bottle of mineral water, packet of Polo mints, a small cosmetic set and packet of tissues.

'There doesn't appear to be anything else,' she said, moving a hand around inside the empty bag.

Mike felt a sharp stab of pain in his bad wrist as he became aware of the futility of his hunch. He'd been hoping Eva might have kept the USB copy which her boyfriend admitted making. But if it was Justin Gormen who had hidden it at his house, then it would have perished in the fire.

And then he noticed the small zip compartment at the same time as the receptionist. He waited as she unzipped it and slid her hand inside.

'Ah! This feels more like it,' she announced as she tugged her fingers out of the small opening.

He felt a surge of excitement as he stared at the small blue plastic USB flash drive, she showed him in the palm of her hand.

'That must be the one we're looking for,' he said. 'Thanks for that. Now if you could just let me have it, and I'll head back to....'

The receptionist interrupted, shaking her head. 'I can't just hand over a patient's belongings without getting permission from the Caldicott guardian.'

'How long will that take?' Mike looked over his shoulder. 'Only my sergeant's waiting in the car, the motor revving. We need to get back to the Yard urgently.'

'It shouldn't take long,' she said. 'I'll see what I can do.'

As she exited through the swing doors again, Mike was relieved to see she had left the flash drive, along with the rest of the girl's belonging behind the counter. He reached over, grabbed it, left the building hurriedly, then ran as fast as he could to the waiting taxi.

***

He was home just after the time Natalie usually got back from school, and then he remembered she would be back later today as she was attending a rehearsal for a school theatre production. Relieved he could conclude what had been a traumatic investigation, especially during the last five hours, he went into his study and shut the door.

After changing his shirt, and wiping the recording, he booted up his computer, slotted the flash drive into the USB port and checked it was a copy of the original dossier of the investigation conducted by James Gaskell. He read the first couple of pages and saw it was the same as the extracts Jo Reeves had given him. He was tempted to read the dossier from start to finish, but the sense of urgency gripped him by the throat now and he couldn't wait to see the powerful network of perverts obliterated, and all the culprits jailed and humiliated before it was too late.

Only one way to do it now.

Searching the internet for the editorial email addresses of every newspaper, radio and television company he could think of, he made a note of at least three dozen of them. Then he opened his email account, clicked on Compose, and in the Subject line typed 'Copy of Lord Albion's Missing Dossier'. He began to type in the email addresses, and as he wrote some of the addresses, he imagined the blinding headlines.

He included every national and regional newspaper in the UK, and followed this with European journals like *Le Monde, Der Spiegel* and *la Republica.* and at least a dozen others. Next, he typed in some of the US dailies like the *New York Times, Washington Post* and *Wall Street Journal.* Then he included television and radio media: *Channel 4 News, BBC News* (TV and Radio), *ITV News* and *Channel 5 News.* Finally, he added the dossier as an attachment.

He sat staring at the monitor for a moment, wondering how Jo Reeves would react. After all, she was his client, paying him to get the information for her book.

But this was more important, bringing the details out into the open. He was the one who had seen the guest house, and the children leaving it, and it made him angry. Angry because most of the child abuse crimes went back so many decades and had been allowed to continue long after Gaskell first started his investigation, all because Lord Albion had conveniently lost the file, claiming he didn't remember it as being a document of much importance at the time.

Ironically, he thought, had it not been for a murderer like Gormen disobeying his orders, perhaps Malcolm Reeves would have had little ammunition with which to proceed with an official enquiry. Now it would be hard to ignore the dossier.

But what of the book? Would Jo Reeves accuse him of having broken their agreement, since the story reaching the public domain would destroy its exclusivity? Too bad. It was time to bring the abusers to justice, so they wouldn't escape public humiliation and degradation like so many of them had, dying of natural causes. No matter how old or infirm, they deserved to pay the price. And it had to be soon, before they were too far gone to escape justice for their heinous crimes.

He sat and thought for a moment about what to put in the main body of the email, wondering whether to include his name and phone number. He decided against it; the dozens of emails that would hit his Inbox tomorrow morning would be enough to cope with for a long while. He kept the message simple:

'Attached is a genuine copy of the missing dossier handed to Lord Albion by James Gaskell in the 1980s concerning a scandal about a ring of paedophiles in Westminster, an official enquiry begun by Malcolm Reeves MP.'

It was done and ready to send. He waited a moment, imagining the email fluttering through the ether like a winged messenger. He hoped it would eventually damage the people who thought they were too big and powerful, untouchable and protected and could do whatever they liked.

As an afterthought he added Jo Reeves's address to the list, so she would know he had gone public, and it wouldn't come as a nasty surprise the next day. He could send her a separate email after it was gone to explain his reasons, and maybe offer his story of the investigation as part of a book package. Leaving out, of course, the details of the carnage at Lorcan's mansion in Virginia Water.

His hand poised over the Send button, he felt a nervous ripple in his stomach as he anticipated the fuss and clamour in the newsrooms when they discovered the dossier was the genuine article. He stared at the screen for a good half minute, took a deep breath, then clicked it.

Message Sent.

He smiled, sat back and relaxed.

Now let the investigation begin.